Eclipse

Other Books by Rae D. Magdon and Michelle Magly

All the Pretty Things

Dark Horizons Series
Dark Horizons – Book 1
Starless Night – Book 2

Rae D. Magdon

Amendyr Series
The Second Sister - Book 1
Wolf's Eyes - Book 2
The Witch's Daughter - Book 3
Wolf Eyes – Book 4

Devil Wears Yellow Garters

Fur and Fangs

Lucky 7

Tengoku

Michelle Magly

Chronicles of Osota - Warrior

Eclipse

Rae D. Magdon
&
Michelle Magly

Desert Palm Press

Eclipse
(Dark Horizons – Book 3)

By Rae D. Magdon and Michelle Magly

©2020 Rae D. Magdon and Michelle Magly

ISBN (book): 9781948327916
ISBN (epub): 9781948327923
ISBN (pdf): 978194837930

Desert Palm Press
1961 Main Street, Suite 220
Watsonville, California 95076
www.desertpalmpress.com

Editor: Cal Faolan, Kellie Doherty
Cover Design: Rachel George

Printed in the United States of America
First Edition December 2020

Dedications

Michelle Magly

For Bethany. You are the partner I always dreamed of being with, but never dared hope that I'd find. Thank you.

Rae D. Magdon

To Kellie and Cal, who worked so hard to edit this book. Thank you for helping me finish Taylor and Maia's adventure at last.

Chapter One

MAIA WOKE IN DARKNESS, surrounded by dry heat and struggling to breathe. She reached for the other side of her cot but found no one there. *Taylor is gone,* she thought, as she had every single morning for the past two months.

The scratch of claws on metal beyond her door had awoken her. Distant voices, speaking languages she wouldn't understand but for the translator implanted in her ear. The cot's thin sheets had twisted around her legs like a tangled fishing net, and she kicked her feet free.

Sitting up, she studied her room's only features—a vertical series of shelves built into the wall, a humidifier spouting steam, a metal sink, and a rectangular mirror. Worlds away from the luxury she'd grown up with. It was even smaller than the suite she'd been imprisoned in back on Earth.

Not all naledai accommodations were so spartan. Most rebels on Nakonum decorated their bunks with colorful pictures and tokens, but Maia hadn't done the same, even though she was fortunate enough to have been assigned a room of her own. She couldn't comprehend how naledai lived in such close quarters without going insane. Her people valued social connections, but naledai warrens were something else.

Maia rubbed the stiffness from one of her shoulders, wincing as her webbed fingers met chafed, flaking skin. The lack of humidity on Nakonum was another problem. It was one of the main reasons her people hadn't dug all the rebels out from underground yet; that, and sheer naledai determination.

Fighting exhaustion, Maia dragged herself out of bed and over to her shelves. She had few possessions. Two basic ikthian robes to wear on alternating days, which had been provided to her by the rebel commissary. A water bottle. Soap, lotion, and a scrub-brush for her scales. A pistol of her own (although armor and most weapons had to be signed out). Lastly, a datapad.

Maia reached for the water bottle first. She took a long drink, then refilled it from the sink, ignoring her reflection in the mirror. The cosmetic surgery she'd undergone to become less recognizable to the Dominion still unsettled her. Her nose, brow, and jawline had only been subtly altered, but it was enough.

Turning up the humidifier, Maia then reached for the datapad. She flopped back onto the cot, activated it, and began recording.

***

Journal of Dr. Maia Kalanis
Jor'al, Nakonum. 07.252.307 PTC

My Taylor is gone.

Whenever I wake, it takes me several seconds to remember that she is not beside me. I turn to look for her but see no mess of black hair. No sloping shoulders. No dark, bleary eyes coming into focus as she shakes off sleep and smiles at me.

We did not share a bed for long, but I often find myself reaching, searching for a body that is no longer there. I try not to think about where Taylor is now, or the suffering she has endured on my account, but such thoughts beat like waves, relentless and unceasing.

Growing up, my elders told me journaling was essential for chronicling the many great achievements of the ikthian species, but keeping this journal feels as useless as it is painful. To be imprisoned in the echo chamber of my own mind is agony. Taylor's imprisonment in Daashu, the notorious prison near my homeworld of Korithia, is surely worse.

I do my best to remain busy. Every day, I train with Akton, a brave naledai soldier and my dear friend, on the shooting range. There may come a time when my natural toxins cannot protect me. They failed to protect Taylor the day she gave herself to the seekers for my sake, after all. I spend the rest of my time in the medical bay. When we find Taylor, I must be able to handle any emergency. I could never forgive myself if I did not have the knowledge and skill necessary to save her yet again.

On further reflection, perhaps I do know why I have resumed journaling after abandoning the pursuit for so many cycles. Taylor is important to me. My impulses may be sentimental, but I long to preserve something of her. I will save her, even if it means leaving the relative safety of Nakonum, the naledai homeworld, where the rebels have hidden me despite the atrocities my species has committed against theirs. Should I fail, however, it comforts me to know that some part of Taylor will remain, even if it is only her name on a datapad.

My knowledge of human religious beliefs is limited. According to Taylor, many humans believe their soul changes form, moves to a different plane of existence, or reincarnates into a new host. That last possibility is similar to most of the naledai belief systems I have encountered. The naledai are a communal species, so it follows that they fear the idea of losing their loved ones forever. I empathize deeply.

I have never been religious myself. Unlike many ikthians, I do not believe we are being watched by the Ancients so our species' worthiness as their successors may be judged. My research into the genetic history of the Milky Way has made it clear to me that our creators were as mortal as any ikthian, naledai, or human. The Ancients may have guided all our species' evolution, and they possessed technology beyond our current levels of understanding, but they are not supernatural.

I must find what comfort I can in other ways. The atoms and elements of which our bodies are composed were forged in the hearts of stars. When their cores collapse, their matter spreads throughout the galaxy to form nebulae. Eventually, new stars are born from the ashes of the old.

No matter what happens, Taylor and I will never truly be gone. We will only change form. Perhaps someday, millions of years from now, our atoms will find each other again. But I have not given up. I will do everything possible to save Taylor in this lifetime, and not even the fear of death will stop me.

***

Taylor stared at the spigot in the middle of the ceiling, licking her lips despite splitting pain. Would water come today? Would it be enough to soothe the sandpaper ache in her throat, or merely dampen her tongue? She knew waiting would only drive her crazy, but she couldn't help herself. Her cell provided no other distractions.

This time, her patience was rewarded. The pipes hissed, and water dribbled from the spigot, spattering her face. Nothing had ever tasted as sweet. Taylor drank so fast she nearly choked. When the water stopped, she licked the floor for the rest, ignoring the taste of cold, dirty metal.

Wiping her mouth, Taylor sat with her back against the wall, wincing at the stab in her ribs. A recent beating had broken at least one of them, and it hadn't healed right. Sitting hurt but moving was worse.

Not that there was anywhere to go. Her cell was fifteen paces, heel to toe, in either direction. Twenty-one paces diagonally. Taylor knew because she paced whenever she had the energy.

The food, though. That was almost worse than being kept in a box. A prison guard threw slop into her cell at random, with little care for where it landed. The goo stank of rotten fish, but Taylor ate it anyway. She didn't want to die without seeing Maia again.

She knew Maia and her friends would save her. Some of them must have escaped Tarkoht Station alive. Maia must have survived. That was the thought Taylor clung to in the darkness, when she felt herself losing hope. Somewhere out there, Maia was looking for her, coming up with a way to rescue her.

The hiss of an outer door broke through Taylor's haze. She flinched. It was a sound that often interrupted her restless sleep, both real and imagined. Real this time, though. The electromagnetic restraints around her wrists activated, pulling her hands behind her back. Taylor cursed. One of her shoulders was still burnt from where an interrogator had gripped it to deliver toxins—not enough for a lethal dose, but enough to cause unimaginable pain.

The circular door to Taylor's cell spun open, retracting into the wall one segment at a time. A guard entered, dressed in light black protective gear. Possibly male, from the width of his shoulders, but Taylor wasn't sure. The lower half of his face was concealed behind a protective filtration mask, but his palms were bare. The flash of silver made Taylor curl against the wall. Bare ikthian skin meant pain.

"Stand." The guard's voice burbled and popped like fetid water, completely different than the soothing river of Maia's voice.

Taylor stood, though it was a struggle, restrained and weak as she was. She'd learned early on to pick her battles. A second ikthian waited outside her cell, wearing an identical uniform, and carrying a lightweight rifle. That was one thing Taylor had noticed during her stay at Daashu. Guards always travelled in pairs.

Both of them took her bare arms in their webbed hands, directing her down the barren tube of the hallway. Only the circular outlines of other cell doors interrupted its dull grey surface. It was like walking through cave tunnels, chilly and monotonous, the air so dry it hurt to breathe.

After two turns, they arrived at another door. It looked similar to the others, but Taylor's pulse spiked. She had memorized how many steps and turns it took to get there. She knew what lay beyond. Every time she saw this door, the same dark thought whispered in her mind–*Will I leave the room alive?*

The guards led her into a barren cube, twice as big as her cell, with a metal chair in the middle. Its armrests had restraints and its legs were bolted to the floor. Taylor didn't resist as the guards strapped her in, knowing she'd need all her strength to deal with the coming pain.

Then the questions began.

"Where is Maia Kalanis?" the first guard asked.

Taylor swallowed around her cracked tongue and focused on her breath. *In. Out. In. Out.* Resistance training had taught her to calm her body's reactions while fear and pain passed through her. *This is temporary. Everything is temporary.*

The second guard smacked Taylor with an open palm. She grunted. Her cheek burned with a thousand icy needles, and her eyes and nose streamed. Ikthian poison was one of the most potent toxins in the galaxy. The guard had only added enough to burn her face, but even that was agony.

"Where is Maia Kalanis?" the first guard asked again.

Taylor couldn't answer. Too much pain. Burning, boiling pain. Only when her interrogator raised his hand for another strike did she overcome her dizziness.

"Tarkoht," she rasped.

It had been weeks, perhaps even months since her capture. Tarkoht Station had exploded, and Maia was hopefully long gone, but an answer—any answer—would buy her a few precious seconds to manage the pain. Another interrogation resistance technique–offer outdated information.

"Where is Odelle Lastra?" the guard asked.

"Tarkoht."

The second, silent guard seized Taylor by the throat, cutting off her air. His bare palm blazed, eating at Taylor's flesh like scalding oil. She screamed. Her still-healing ribs were knives in her side. *That's their goal. To make me lose hope. To fool me into thinking it'll never end. But it will because Maia will save me.*

After what felt like an eternity, the guard released her throat. "Where is the rebel base on Nakonum?"

Taylor took several panting breaths. "I was never there. I was on Tarkoht."

"Is the traitor Sorra their leader?"

"No."

Her interrogator whispered something to his partner, who left without a word.

Taylor slumped in the chair, struggling to ignore the stabbing ache in her side. This was different. None of her interrogators had ever left in the middle of questioning before.

This is it, a despairing voice said inside her head. *I don't know any current information. They've figured out I'm useless, and they're going to kill me.*

Another woosh of the door, and the second guard returned. With him was a new prisoner, the first Taylor had seen since her capture–an ikthian woman wearing the ragged remains of a chin-high yellow dress. Despite her flaking scales and hollowed eyes, her face was startlingly familiar.

Taylor gasped. She knew that face. Those eyes. The faintly spotted pattern on the crest. In her pain-drunk, sleep-deprived state, a spark of joy! "Maia?"

Shock crossed the ikthian prisoner's face. Her mouth fell open. "You know my daughter?"

The truth struck Taylor like another blow. Not Maia. This had to be Maia's mother, Irana. Taylor had seen her once on a comm call before being dishonorably discharged from the Coalition's military. *That's good, right? It isn't Maia. You don't want her anywhere near here.* But some selfish part of Taylor had wanted to see Maia's face one last time.

The second guard shoved Irana to her knees. His bare hand rested on the back of her neck, waiting.

"Who does Sorra report to?" the first guard asked.

"I don't know," Taylor insisted.

Irana shrieked. She twitched in her captor's grip, straining against her cuffs. Her face twisted, and her shoulders pulled at strange angles as she went into spasms.

Taylor's stomach lurched. If she'd had any food in it, she would have vomited. Soldiers dealt with fear every day. They slept with the knowledge that they might not make it through to the next morning. But seeing Irana's tortured expression, so like Maia's...

"Stop!" she cried. "I really don't know. Please, I'll tell you anything else."

Taylor's guard nodded at his partner, who removed his hand from Irana's neck. Irana slumped forward, unnaturally still.

"Sorra has naledai contacts on Nakonum. Where are they hiding?"

"I swear, I don't know," Taylor said.

The second guard reached for Irana's neck again. Her sea blue eyes, so like Maia's, went wide with fear, and Taylor lost her composure. The only thing worse than withstanding torture was watching someone else endure pain on her account.

"You sick fucking cowards," she spat, struggling against her cuffs with what little remained of her strength. "You have to torture someone else just to get me to talk? You can't touch me. You need me—"

She barely knew what she was saying, but she continued spouting off until the first guard did what she wanted. His hand cracked against her face, and she writhed as a fresh shockwave of pain passed through her system. The needles returned, rippling through her skin as the poison spread.

"Great, now look what you did," the second guard said, his voice sounding far away. "She can't talk if she's unconscious, scumbrain."

If the first guard replied, Taylor didn't hear. Darkness closed in around her, and the only noise in her ears was the faint rush of her own blood. Everything hurt. Her face, her side, her chest. Her eyelids fluttered, and she glimpsed a pale silver face hovering a few feet away from hers.

Maia, I'm sorry.

***

Maia pinned her back to the wall, edging along the rounded passageway. She paused at the nearest door, rifle at the ready. As far as dangerous locations went, offices weren't too high on her list, but Teichos Industries' administrative headquarters was crawling with security guards. She and her companions had anticipated resistance, but nothing like this.

Cautiously, Maia pressed the button beside the door. It flashed white, and the door opened in a spiral. She breathed a sigh of relief. Each time she attempted to open a door; she couldn't predict whether the specialized glove she'd stolen off a dead security guard would fool the scanner or alert the enemy to her position...again.

With a quick look to make sure the coast was clear, Maia crept into the room beyond, clutching her rifle close. She scanned her surroundings—a mess of broken terminals and scorched office furniture in twisted silver masses—but saw no other hostiles. Obviously, some of her squadmates had already been through here ahead of her. Relaxing, she continued.

"On your six, Maia!"

Maia whirled and aimed, pumping two quick blasts from her rifle. The guard behind her fell, a smoking hole in his silver Teichos Industries chestplate. Apparently, the coast hadn't been clear after all. "Thank you," she said through the radio in her helmet.

Emerging from behind an overturned desk, Rachel Harris gave a thumbs-up. Like Maia, the human wore light grey armor given to her by the rebels. "Said that automatically. Glad you knew what it meant."

Maia felt a twinge in her chest. "Taylor taught me."

There was an awkward moment of silence, where they avoided making eye contact through their visors. Maia tightened her jaw. There was plenty of blame to go around for what had happened to Taylor, but now wasn't the time. They were here to find Daashu's coordinates and, hopefully, rescue her.

"Kalanis, Harris, what's your location?" Akton's raspy growl came through Maia's helmet.

"Third floor of the facility," Rachel replied. "Two corridors from the elevator."

"Sorra and I are on the fourth floor. We found something."

"Get your asses up here," Sorra added with her usual impatience. The ikthian rebel leader was rarely in a good mood.

Maia left her hiding place behind a partially broken terminal and headed for the door. When she got there, she paused, listening for movement outside. Hearing nothing, she went through weapon-first. "Clear."

Rachel fell into step behind her, watching their rear as they made for the elevator. Maia's stomach clenched when she saw the moving numbers. Someone was coming up from the ground floor.

"Told you we should've deactivated the elevators," Rachel said, reaching for a pouch on her utility belt. "But *nooo.* 'It's faster for us to use them,'" she said, in a snotty imitation of Sorra's voice. She motioned for Maia to pin herself against the wall.

Maia did so moments before the doors spiraled open. A group of ikthian security guards prepared to exit, weapons at the ready. Rachel pulled a biogrenade from her belt and lobbed it inside, her arm a blur of motion.

A loud boom shook the hallway, followed by high-pitched ringing. Maia winced, shrugging in a useless attempt to cover her ears. Her helmet offered protection from loud noises but didn't block them completely. Finally, the smoke cleared. Aside from the ghastly coating of gore and dismembered body parts, the elevator's twisted frame meant it was unusable.

"I suppose we will be taking the stairs after all," Maia said.

Thankfully, they didn't meet any more resistance. Maia was mildly out of breath by the time they arrived on the fourth floor. She cleared the next door, heading down the prefab hallway in search of Akton and Sorra.

"Over here!" a baritone voice called. Maia caught sight of Akton's enormous digging claws waving from another open door. His shaggy coat was mostly covered by armor, but his bulky shape was instantly recognizable. She hurried into the room with Rachel, where they found Sorra standing before a glowing terminal, pointing her rifle at an ikthian employee's back.

"About time you two got here," Sorra said, without turning away from her prisoner. Several inches taller than Maia, with broad shoulders and a narrow waist, the ikthian rebel cut a striking figure in her armor. "I was just finishing a download with this one's login credentials."

In the past, Maia might have protested Sorra's treatment of the prisoner. The ikthian was a worker, judging by her rumpled lab coat. Unarmed as well. The webs between her fingers shook as she used the haptic interface to complete the download.

This is for Taylor, Maia reminded herself. Any guilt she felt evaporated.

"It's finished," the ikthian stammered. She seemed young, and the mottling on her crest was a particularly vivid shade of crimson.

Sorra smirked. "We're done here. Nice suggestion for us to target Teichos Industries, Kalanis."

Maia allowed herself a brief moment of pride. It had been her idea to infiltrate the administrative offices of the private security firm, which staffed Daashu with many of its guards and interrogators. "We really have the compound's coordinates?"

"Assuming they're accurate," Akton said. "Let's get out of here before backup security arrives."

A grin spread behind Rachel's visor. *"Elurin,"* she said over the radio, *"we need a pickup."*

"You got it, Harris," the pilot answered, her voice sounding in Maia's ear as well. *"Meet me on the roof."*

Maia looked at the prisoner, whose trembling legs didn't seem like they would support her much longer. "What do we do with her?"

Sorra raised her rifle. It was bigger than Maia's, with a scope mod for long-range accuracy, but they had the same basic build—black and blocky, like most naledai weaponry. "We can't leave her alive."

Maia began to protest, but Rachel beat her to it. "Come on, Sorra. I know you're in charge, but she's obviously a civilian."

"A *Dominion* civilian," Sorra said. "If they aren't with us, they're against us. And, as you said, I'm in charge."

"With all due respect, she could have valuable intel," Akton said.

"I have intel," the prisoner squeaked, her hands held apart in surrender. "I'll tell you whatever you want to know. Just don't shoot me!"

"Fine." Sorra looked to Maia. "It's your mate we're risking our lives for. Loose ends will only make that rescue mission harder. Still want to bring her along?"

Maia eyed Sorra, then the prisoner. There was no point in killing her if she could be useful. Even though Elurin's stealth fighter was small, it had enough room for one more. "Let's take her with us."

"Fine. Bring her." Sorra shoved the prisoner toward Akton, then headed for the hall, and the stairs that would take them to the roof.

Maia sighed. She was sure to get an earful from Sorra later, but she was too excited to care. *We finally know where Taylor is, and I won't rest until I bring her home.*

Chapter Two

SORRA BRACED HER WEBBED hands on the cold metal table, leaning forward and peering into her prisoner's eyes. "Tell me your name."

The prisoner cringed in her seat, hunching as if to appear smaller. "A...Aeris."

"Your full name."

Aeris averted her gaze, lowering her mottled red head. "Aeris Talekas."

The corners of Sorra's lips almost twitched up. This interrogation was going smoother than expected. Although her squad's minor act of rebellious mercy had irked her, she wasn't sorry she'd listened. Clearly, Aeris was harmless. The cuffs probably weren't necessary, though Sorra didn't offer to remove them.

"Here's the situation, Aeris," she said, pinning the unfortunate ikthian with her stare. "I can make your stay here very comfortable or very uncomfortable, depending on how cooperative you are. Clear?"

Aeris' eyes darted around the room as if in search of help. Not that there was much to see. Sorra had never made use of the base's interrogation facilities before, but they were adequate. The room was small, metal, no windows. No furniture either, except a table and two uncomfortable chairs. Microcameras in each corner transmitted audio and video to Odelle—Sorra's mate, and the rebellion's communications specialist—and the generals next door.

"Yes," Aeris said. "It's...um, I understand."

"Good." Sorra pushed off the table, folding her hands behind her back and adopting a more relaxed posture. Aeris relaxed as well, her shoulders slumping. "What is your role at Teichos Industries?"

"I'm an IT specialist," Aeris said.

"Do you have access to their secure databases?" Sorra already knew the answer, since Aeris had logged them in, but it was useful to establish a baseline for truthfulness. She paid close attention to Aeris' face.

"Yes, most of it." Aeris gave no twitch or nervous dart of the eyes to indicate a lie.

"What do you know about Daashu?"

Aeris recoiled at the awful name. Everyone, even ikthians, feared Daashu. Her mouth worked for several seconds before she managed to speak. "Not much. Teichos Industries supplies the compound with guards and tech. I just maintain the databases and make sure our communications remain secure."

Sorra circled the table. "You don't know where Daashu is?" She stopped, placing a hand on Aeris' shoulder from behind.

Aeris flinched, but the cuffs and Sorra's grip prevented her from escaping. "No," she whimpered.

"Not even the coordinates?" Technically, the prison's coordinates were in the data they'd stolen, but confirmation from a second source would reassure Sorra's paranoid mind. Corporate interests could be wily with their data.

"I swear I don't know anything else about Daashu without looking it up in the database."

Sorra squeezed Aeris' shoulder lightly. Although she wasn't touching Aeris' skin directly, the threat was implicit—she was only a few inches away from the prisoner's bare neck. Ikthian toxins weren't as potent among their own species as they were to aliens, but a moderate dose could still be lethal. "Are you sure?"

"Really," Aeris insisted. "I protect the data—I don't snoop through it! D-didn't you download what you needed when I logged you in?"

Sorra removed her hand, trying to push past her frustration. Obviously, this was a dead end. She could tell Aeris was being truthful, but that didn't help if she had nothing useful to say. "If you don't have any information for me, we're done here." She circled the table once more, heading for the door.

"Wait!"

Sorra kept her gaze calm as she turned to regard the prisoner. She didn't say anything.

"I don't know anything about Daashu..." Aeris trailed off as she stared at the table. "But I know something else."

Sorra waited.

"Teichos Industries has been taking on contracts to provide other high-security compounds with guards and equipment. Especially medical equipment."

Sorra returned to the table, resting her hands there again. "Tell me everything."

***

Odelle turned away from the wall monitor in the viewing room, regarding Kross and Oranthis. The naledai generals matched her stare with equally somber expressions. Aeris' information, though vague, was concerning enough to cause a prickle along Odelle's neck ridges.

From the ruffling of the fur along their backs, which poked out the top of their blue uniform shirts, the generals felt much the same. They stood close together on the left side of the room—a necessity, since it was small—while Odelle took what little space remained on the right, grateful even for that. She would never get used to the close quarters the naledai lived in, especially considering their massive size. If either Kross or Oranthis were to straighten their backs instead of slouching, they'd be taller than her by half, and their heads would almost touch the ceiling.

"Why haven't we heard about these compounds from other sources?" Kross asked.

Oranthis' broad nostrils flared. "Seems like something our spies should have warned us about long before now."

"It must be a recent development," Odelle said. "Otherwise, I would have been told before my defection."

Kross scratched his thigh with a massive claw. "That only makes me worry more. If secret medical compounds are cropping up in Dominion space, in such a short span of time, and you never heard of them before you left..."

A tense pause filled the room. Though Odelle didn't regret revealing her double-agent status and leaving the Dominion, it was disconcerting to know that the empire's wheels continued to turn without her. She was used to having inside information about anything and everything the Dominion and its dictatorial leader, Chancellor Corvis, did.

This time, Odelle had nothing. Information was the only weapon she knew how to use, and she had been thoroughly disarmed.

Eventually, she broke the silence. "The good news is, the data Sorra's squad retrieved has proven incredibly valuable. Not only do we have Daashu's coordinates, layout, and defenses, but we know a lot more about Teichos Industries as well. They work alongside the

Dominion's military to secure high-clearance facilities. Information concerning their methods of operation will give us a considerable advantage."

That put the generals more at ease, but Odelle had spent enough time around naledai to read their furry, heavily scarred faces. They were afraid, and it took a lot to throw off stalwart old soldiers like them.

"Looking into this should be our top priority," Oranthis declared. "As soon as Sorra wraps up, we'll talk strategy."

Odelle prepared to agree, but the sound of a buzzer interrupted her. Someone was waiting in the hallway. She crossed the room in a few steps and examined the door-mounted screen.

Four familiar faces looked back at her—Maia, a Dominion geneticist and fellow 'traitor'; Akton, a brave naledai soldier; and Elurin, the rebellion's best pilot. Rachel—their new human ally, now an official member of the rebellion—stood next to them, slightly off-camera.

Odelle glanced over her shoulder at the generals, who nodded, and opened the door. The four newcomers entered, and she stepped back to let them in. Cramming seven people into this viewing room, especially three male naledai, didn't leave much room for personal space at all.

"Elurin," Odelle asked, "what have we learned from the data download?"

"Daashu's ours for the taking," the ikthian pilot said. Her grey eyes gleamed. "Security's tight, but not insurmountable. The prison's best defense is that no one knows where it is or how it's laid out. Now we do."

Odelle nodded, but her gaze travelled to Maia. The scientist stood near the door; her bright blue eyes consumed by an almost frightening fire. Odelle knew that look all too well—the tight-set jaw, the determined jut of the chin. She had seen it on Sorra plenty of times, usually right before her mate did something stupid and self-sacrificing.

"Be blunt, Valerius," Oranthis said, addressing Akton by his last name. "What resources would we need for an infiltration?"

"That depends on our goal, sir," Akton said. "To rescue Taylor Morgan, and maybe a few other prisoners? Not much. We have enough data to disguise ourselves as a Teichos transport vessel. We could even hijack a real vessel on the schedule and bring that to Daashu. Once we're planetside, we blow our way in with some plasma charges. It won't be subtle, but I don't think we need to be. Because Daashu's security clearance level is so high, there aren't many guards and interrogators on-site."

Kross scratched his chin. "It's a risk. Whoever we send might not make it back."

"I volunteer." Maia stepped forward, squaring her shoulders. Odelle had to admit, Maia had changed a great deal in recent weeks. The meek scientist she'd met three months prior had hardened considerably since then. The confident way she stood. How she spoke. "I agree with Akton's assessment, and I am willing to go as soon as you grant permission, generals."

Kross and Oranthis looked at each other. "It isn't that simple, Doctor Kalanis," Kross said. "Your bravery is commendable, but I hardly think you're in a position to assess strategic merit. We need to go over this data ourselves."

Oranthis nodded his shaggy head. "Even then, the risks might outweigh the benefits. I hate to say this, but you deserve honesty, considering all of your relationships with Lieutenant Morgan. It might be more to our benefit to launch a missile strike on the prison instead."

Cold claws gripped Odelle's gut. *What?* The possibility hadn't even occurred to her. She turned to Oranthis, wide-eyed. "What do you mean?"

He cleared his throat with a gravelly growl. "Several naledai soldiers are imprisoned in Daashu as well. Brave souls, but it would be a kindness to send them to join their Ancestors instead of enduring further torture. More importantly, it would prevent them from revealing dangerous information. Even the best soldiers break."

"Permission to speak, sirs?" Rachel asked. Her eyes burned almost as brightly as Maia's.

"Granted, Harris," Kross said.

"Sometimes soldiers have to make hard decisions, but Akton has the makings of a really good plan here. I think we can do this. I volunteer along with Maia. Elurin will come, too. Right?"

Elurin straightened. "I volunteer as well, generals. I'm the best pilot you've got. Rachel has years of military experience. Akton's a brilliant strategist, and there's no better hand to hand fighter on all of Nakonum. Even Maia's been working her ass off to get her piloting and weapons clearances. She's a certified medic now. Let us try. If we fail, well...then you can do your strike. It won't make a difference at that point."

15

Odelle watched the two generals as they exchanged glances, communicating without words. She understood their point of view, but her heart agreed with Maia and the others.

"Write up a proposal," Kross said. "Present it to us in forty hours."

"Forty hours?" Maia repeated, her voice rising. "Taylor may very well be dead by then! She has already been imprisoned for close to two months—"

"As you say," Oranthis interrupted, "Lieutenant Morgan has been imprisoned for almost two months. Either the Dominion has no intention of killing her, or she has already joined her Ancestors. We can't send some of our best people off without an airtight plan. Especially you, Kalanis. I'm sure you're training hard, but two months doesn't make a soldier."

Maia worked her jaw, clenching her fists. Odelle feared she might argue, but she gave the generals a cross-armed salute over her chest. "Understood. Thank you for your time, generals." Without waiting to be dismissed, she left the room, the doors hissing shut behind her.

"You'll have to forgive her insubordination," Odelle said, offering the generals an apologetic look on Maia's behalf. "She's young."

Kross smiled, showing his sharpened fangs. "I can't blame her for clinging to the hope that her mate's alive." He lifted the patch on his left eye, which was nothing more than a snarled-shut socket. "Lost this because I had the same delusion. Haven't had another mate since."

Odelle filed that information away. She hadn't known Kross had lost a spouse, but almost everyone had lost someone to the Dominion. *It's a miracle Sorra's still alive, with all the danger she puts herself in.*

"I'll make sure Sorra's squad puts together a proposal," she said. "Right, Akton?"

The young naledai seemed like he wanted to protest, but a look from her changed his mind. "Right," he grunted. "With your permission, I'll begin as soon as you dismiss me, generals."

Oranthis nodded. "Dismissed, all of you. We need to meet with Sorra."

With identical salutes, Akton, Elurin, and Rachel left the room. Odelle made her own excuses, saying, "I'll retrieve Sorra for you."

The generals looked at the wall monitor, where Sorra seemed to be finishing her interrogation. Odelle left the room just in time to meet Sorra in the hall. A smile spread across Sorra's face, which Odelle couldn't help but return.

"Kross and Oranthis have requested your presence next door, but I need you more," she said.

Sorra folded her arms, shifting her weight to one hip. "Oh, *really?*" Her smile went from friendly to predatory in an instant as she ran her tongue over the sharp points of her teeth.

Odelle's neck ridges prickled, and her heartbeat sped up. Still, they hardly had the time for such games. "Not like that, I'm afraid. Akton thinks we have enough data to infiltrate Daashu and launch a rescue mission."

"They shot him down, didn't they?" Sorra said, although she didn't seem truly upset about it.

"Unfortunately," Odelle said.

Sorra heaved a sigh. "Then Kalanis and the others are probably sulking. I'll find them after I talk to the generals."

"No, find them now," Odelle insisted. "If I'm right, they're already gathering supplies and preparing to leave. Elurin has the clearance to do it. If I read the situation right—and I always do—they'll be gone before your meeting with Kross and Oranthis is over."

"Fuck." Sorra groaned, pinching the bridge of her slightly crooked nose. "Those idiots. I'd better make sure they survive to endure their punishment."

Odelle cupped Sorra's face, leaning in for a kiss. It was brief, but Odelle ached all the more. Sorra's sweet, warm taste, and the scent of the naledai-inspired leathers she wore, would have to sustain Odelle until she returned.

"If you die this time, Sorra, I'll never forgive you." It was meant to be a joke, but her heart gave a rapid thump out of rhythm. It was the same poisonous fear she felt every time Sorra left—a fear Odelle had no choice but to live with, as long as Sorra lived, too.

"Don't worry," Sorra said, confident as always. "They haven't managed to kill me yet, and they never will."

***

Elurin studied the ship's multiscreen dash with a grim expression. She didn't regret commandeering one of the rebellion's stealth fighters, but guilt roiled in her stomach. This wasn't the first time she'd defied a superior officer's orders—she was a Dominion defector, after all—but Kross and Oranthis had always trusted her in spite of her past. They would undoubtedly ground her when she returned, and she would deserve it.

If I return...

With practice that came from years in two different militaries, Elurin pushed those thoughts aside. Negativity wasn't the answer. Instead, she made sure their ship was still on course to intercept the Teichos Industries transport. There was no sign of their quarry, but it wasn't quite time yet, according to the schedule they'd downloaded.

To distract herself, Elurin glanced at the copilot's chair. Maia sat in silence, chewing her lip and staring at the ship's dashboard. She wasn't the only nervous one. The ship was small, large enough for six—the traditional number for an ikthian seeker squad, from whom Elurin had stolen the fighter—but just five of those seats were filled this time.

Elurin checked on the rest of the squad via the rear cameras. Like Maia, Akton seemed lost in thought, his yellow eyes hidden behind a shaggy fringe of fur. Beside him, Sorra lounged. She hadn't unfastened her chest straps, but she'd loosened them enough to slouch. Sorra was probably the strangest commander Elurin had ever worked under. Her sarcasm and unorthodox methods rarely seemed beneficial, but Elurin couldn't deny that she produced results.

And then, of course, there was Rachel. Rachel, with her warm brown skin and bouncy curls, and that heart-melting grin of hers. She sat in the back, with the final empty seat beside her. "How much longer, Elurin?" she asked.

A smile softened Elurin's face. Rachel's voice bolstered her confidence, reminding her why she'd decided to disobey orders in the first place. *For Taylor, and hopefully all the other rebel prisoners in Daashu. If she's anything like Rachel, she deserves to be rescued.*

That was another source of tension. From her first meeting with the stubborn human, Elurin had felt an unexplained magnetism between them. At first, she'd mistaken it for hostility. But even in the midst of a stressful situation like this, Rachel's presence made her feel lighter.

Stop being stupid. Your little interspecies crush can't go anywhere. There were a myriad of reasons. Rachel sought out males of her own kind, for one. She'd only recently come to understand that not all ikthians were out to kill her. And, of course, there was the fact that one or both of them might not return from this mission.

"Elurin, did you hear me? How much longer until the transport gets here?"

Elurin shook herself. *Great.* This wasn't a promising start to a mission that would require all the focus she could muster. "We're next to their planned route, so it should be any moment, but you know how it is. Schedules change. Transports run late."

Sorra snorted. "For predestined conquerors of the galaxy, Dominion transports almost never have their shit together."

That was true. Over the past decade, the Dominion's attempted conquest of Earth had stretched their resources thin. It was, perhaps, their primary weakness. The rebellion had been quite effective at choking off their supply-lines in naledai space. Fighting a war on multiple fronts drained the Dominion armada of ships, troops, and supplies faster than they could be replaced.

If they gave up on Earth, the Dominion could re-solidify their holdings and wipe out the naledai rebellion, but their pride and thirst for conquest won't let them. It was a discussion she and Rachel had participated in many times. The human's big brown eyes always glinted when she was enthusiastic. Such a curious color for eyes, brown. Apparently, it was common for humans. Sometimes, Elurin felt like she could fall into them.

"Our info's fresh," Elurin said. "I doubt the transport will have had time to reroute."

Akton smiled to show agreement—or, at least, he tried to. Although humans and ikthians had both developed smiling as a nonverbal form of communication, naledai hadn't. When they tried to copy it in the name of interspecies socialization, the results were...disconcerting at best and terrifying at worst, thanks to their large incisors.

"So, we continue sitting here?" Maia asked.

Elurin looked over at her copilot again. Maia's eyes held a sea-storm in their depths, and their intensity made Elurin's scales itch. "Yep. But not for forty hours, at least."

Maia's lips pressed into a thin line of disapproval, but she went back to watching the dash, so Elurin did the same.

The cabin fell into tense silence, until one of the monitors flashed. Elurin tapped it, zooming in with her fingertips. Another ship was approaching at a fast clip, following the transport's expected trajectory. From its size and specs, she felt confident it was their target.

"Here we go," she said, pulling up another screen to recalculate their route. "Buckle up, cowboys."

There was a brief bark of laughter from Rachel and confused looks from everyone else.

"What the fuck does that mean?" Sorra asked.

"No idea," Elurin said. "Harris taught it to me."

"Listening to Harris will only get you in trouble," Sorra said.

Elurin's heart jumped. *She can't know, can she? I haven't been that obvious.*

"Says you," Rachel said. "C'mon, let's go hijack a transport."

Chapter Three

RACHEL REGRETTED HER WORDS less than a minute later. The ship sped forward with a sickening lurch, and even its gyroscopic design wasn't enough to keep her guts in one place. She'd never been a great flyer, no matter how skilled—or cute—the pilot was. *Cute? Not the time, Harris.*

Elurin swooped into a climb next, lifting Rachel's stomach a second behind the rest of her body. It flopped down again as Elurin straightened the ship. When Rachel looked out the left viewport, she saw another vessel speeding alongside theirs–a round, steel-grey transport shaped like a bullet.

"We're in their sightline," Elurin said. "Prepare for fire."

The ship was in Elurin and Maia's hands, which left Rachel to clutch her rifle and pray to deities she didn't really believe in. In the space of several heartbeats, Elurin disabled one of the transport's thrusters with a well-placed shot. Their ship pulled alongside. The decontamination chamber doors hissed as they unsealed.

"Bridgeway connected," Maia said. "You're clear to board the transport."

Rachel unbuckled her harness. Grabbing her helmet, she pulled it over her head until the seals clicked, plugging into her suit's filtration system. Elurin remained in the pilot's chair, and Rachel only spared her a brief glance before joining Sorra and Akton. Sorra carried her usual modified rifle, while Akton wielded his favorite auto-targeting biogrenade launcher. Their faces were grim behind their visors.

"Ready?" Sorra asked.

Rachel and Akton nodded. Together, they entered the decon chamber, a rounded bubble with circular doors on either side. The first door closed, and pressurized air blew through the small space. Beams of white light crawled along Rachel's armor, scanning for hazardous materials.

After a few seconds, the lights turned purple with a cheerful, two-toned chirp. The second door opened, revealing the bridgeway. It was little more than a tube, four meters long and barely tall enough for

Akton to duck through. The other end had attached to one of the transport's hatches.

As Rachel watched, the hatch spun open. The nose of a rifle poked through.

"Back!" Sorra shouted.

Rachel leapt back into the decon chamber. Several plasma shots struck the spot where she'd stood moments ago, leaving dirty streaks of carbon scoring on the bridgeway's silver walls.

"Take cover," Akton barked.

Since there was nothing to duck behind, Rachel flattened her back to the wall and closed her eyes. The bright light from Akton's biogrenade flashed through her eyelids. Her helmet muffled the noise, but it was still uncomfortably loud. When she opened her eyes and peeked down the bridgeway, their enemies had fallen back somewhere behind a cloud of streaming white smoke.

Sorra straightened from a crouched position and waved them forward. She took point while Rachel fell in behind Akton, crossing the bridgeway at a fast prowl.

The ikthians who'd fired on them lay sprawled in the other decon chamber, their armor smoking at the seams. Akton's biogrenade had obliterated their bodies. Only charred chunks remained, barely distinguishable as flesh and bone. Even for Rachel, a veteran soldier, it was a brutal sight. She tried not to look.

Sorra stepped over the mess and touched the terminal beside the next door. It lit up, and the door spun open. "Clear," she said, and they entered the transport.

The bridge alone was large enough to fit their entire fighter inside, but Rachel didn't get much opportunity to learn its layout. A door on the opposite wall opened, and three more soldiers rushed through. They dropped thin metal bars in front of the doorway, and blue electro-shields buzzed to life from the ground up, creating a chest-high glowing barrier.

Shit, they brought cover with them.

Rachel aimed high, sending a round through one of the soldier's helmets. Her target slumped. Akton fired. Hit the barrier. An enemy round clipped his shoulder. He grunted, clapping a paw to his armor. Rachel took a step toward him.

"Stop!" Sorra's voice rang across the bridge. She stood by the pilot's chair, holding her rifle to a frightened ikthian's head. He wasn't wearing a helmet, and his silver skin had taken on a sickly purple hue. "Lower your weapons and cut off those shields, or I kill your pilot."

The soldiers froze for a few precious seconds. Rachel sensed an opportunity, but Akton reacted first. He charged the barrier, getting close enough to angle his shots over the top. This time, he didn't miss. Their remaining enemies collapsed, and everything went silent.

A few seconds passed. No more ikthians rushed the bridge. Rachel's racing heart began to slow.

"How many aboard?" Sorra asked the pilot.

The ikthian's mouth wobbled, but he couldn't seem to answer.

"How many?" Sorra jabbed her rifle against his head.

"J-just my copilot and a prisoner," he replied. "Don't shoot. I surrender—"

"Coward." Sorra dispatched him with a single shot. The pilot slumped in his chair, dark purple blood running down his silver face. In the past, Rachel might have been relieved. Every dead ikthian meant one less enemy. But since befriending Elurin, ikthian deaths struck her somewhere in her gut, more gruesome than before.

Sorra turned toward her. "Harris, secure the bridge. Akton, with me."

Akton obeyed, while Rachel took up position on the other side of the electro-shields. She could use them to her advantage if more hostiles came.

Akton and Sorra returned in less than a minute, with a burly, scarred naledai in tow. He was missing an arm, but it seemed to be in the early stages of growing back. "Ancestors be praised," he rumbled. Judging by his torn grey jumpsuit, Rachel guessed he was the prisoner being transported. "Today's my lucky day."

"Not as lucky as you think," Sorra said in a flat voice. "Hopefully we'll have you back on Nakonum in a matter of hours, but we have to make a stop first."

"Where?" the naledai asked.

"You won't like it," Rachel said, with a note of sympathy.

He snorted. "Pretty much anywhere's better than here."

Akton clapped him on the shoulder. "We're going where you were headed to begin with, cousin."

The naledai's face fell. "Daashu? Seriously? What a fucking cave-in."

While Sorra tipped the pilot's body out of his seat and took his place, Rachel returned her rifle to the strap on her back. She activated her helmet's radio, speaking to Elurin and Maia. "Transport cleared. Sorra's in command. We're headed to Daashu."

We're coming for you, Taylor. Please hang on a little longer.

***

Taylor's eyes fluttered open. Her blistered cheek throbbed, and aching dryness glued her tongue to the roof of her mouth. Every breath, no matter how shallow, felt like the stab and twist of a knife. It made her worry the broken rib was getting worse.

She didn't know how long she'd been strapped into the interrogation room's chair. Instead of regaining consciousness all at once, it happened in stages. Moving shadows at first, speaking indistinctly. Then voices. Sharp questions.

"Where is Maia Kalanis?"

"Who does Sorra report to?"

"Where are the rebel leaders?"

Taylor groaned, too weak and confused to answer—until she saw Irana kneeling on the floor by her feet. The ikthian looked even thinner than before, if that were possible, her yellow dress in shreds. Fear cleared Taylor's cloudy mind. She sat up as straight as her restraints allowed. "I'll talk. You don't have to hurt her."

The first interrogator showed no reaction. Not even his eyes betrayed what he was thinking as he reached for something on his belt–a metal canteen. *Water.* Taylor swallowed. The last bit of moisture she possessed welled in her mouth.

"Answer, and you get water," the second interrogator said. "If you remain silent or lie, I poison her." He put his palm atop Irana's crest, and she flinched beneath the weight of his webbed hand.

Taylor tried to speak. Failed. Sucked her tongue and tried again. "Okay."

"Where is Maia Kalanis?"

Irana cast pleading blue eyes upon her, and Taylor's heart clenched. There was no fighting their captors, but she didn't know the answer. "Maia could be anywhere by now. Ask me something I know, and I'll answer."

To her relief, the interrogator holding Irana's head didn't release his toxins. The other interrogator made no move toward his canteen, though. Taylor's hands clenched in her cuffs, longing to rip the canteen from his belt.

"Who does Sorra report to?" the first interrogator asked.

Taylor gritted her teeth. "I don't know."

The interrogator nodded to his partner, who tightened his grip. Irana screamed like a dying woman, a violent shudder contorting her skeletal frame.

"Oranthis, Kross," Taylor said, unable to tear her eyes away. "Naledai generals. I met them." She'd surrendered those names before, though to her credit, she'd held onto them for several days first. Enough time for her allies to hide, she hoped.

"Useless." The interrogator opened the top of the canteen, holding it inches from Taylor's face. "Who does Sorra report to?"

One last spark of anger flashed within Taylor. She glared into the ikthian's cruel green eyes. "Go fuck yourself."

The interrogator threw the canteen aside. It hit the floor with a clatter, and water spilled onto the metal. Taylor choked on a sob, but the sound became a shout as the interrogator drew his hand back.

Taylor braced herself, but the blow never came. Instead, a loud boom shook the chamber, followed by piercing, high-pitched ringing. She flinched and shut her eyes, but with her limbs restrained, there was little she could do to protect herself.

When she opened her eyes again, one of the walls had been blown open. Two armored figures hopped over crumpled metal and twisted support beams. They carried rifles, but Taylor didn't hear any weapon fire. Only the incessant ringing remained as plasma flashes exploded from the rifles' dark muzzles. Both interrogators dropped to the floor, dead.

Taylor's surge of adrenaline dissolved into a silent sort of calm. Trapped, at the mercy of whoever these soldiers were, there was nothing she could do. If this was her time to die, hopefully it would be with a clean shot. Not the worst way to go. She'd got to see her captors die first.

One of the armored figures approached, pausing only to remove a comm band from one of the dead interrogators' wrists. They rushed past Irana—who had collapsed, breathing heavily—and knelt in front of Taylor's chair, fumbling to unlock her cuffs with the comm band.

"Taylor?"

The sound of her name came through warped. Distant. *Familiar?* The ringing in Taylor's ears waned, and she strained to hear. The soldier unfastened the cuffs and pulled her into their slender, gentle arms.

Wait. They know my name. Is this a rescue?

Taylor's confusion snapped into sharp clarity. If this was a rescue, she needed to give it her all. Summoning her last reserves, she tried to speak, but all the breath rushed from her lungs as her savior's visor retracted into their helmet. A tear-streaked silver face peered down at her, and Taylor only managed one awestruck word—"Maia!"

***

Taylor!

Maia couldn't believe she was holding her lover in her arms. Warm, breathing, alive! She forgot all about the plasma charges they'd detonated, the rifle she'd long since abandoned on the floor, the dead guards, and the live ones who were surely on their way. She hardly noticed as Rachel and Akton ushered the other unfortunate prisoner, an ikthian, through the hole they'd blown in the wall to seek refuge in the hallway.

She'd found Taylor. That was all that mattered.

"Taylor," she sobbed, clutching the human to her. She wept into Taylor's hair, ignoring the smell of dirt and stale sweat. Taylor's buzzed black hairstyle had grown out, short but ragged. Her muscular form had thinned considerably, her skin was pale, and—

"Tides, your face," Maia gasped as she noticed the horrible webbed blister on Taylor's cheek. Her first instinct was to touch, to try and help, but when Taylor flinched, she pulled her hand back, resting it on Taylor's neck instead.

"Your...face..." Taylor stared at her with dark brown eyes, but there was the tiniest twinkle of mirth in them, a small glimmer that hadn't dimmed during her imprisonment.

It took Maia a moment to realize what Taylor meant, but then she laughed. "Yes," she said, crying fresh tears—only this time, they were tears of joy. "I had a little work done on Tarkoht, remember? The nose is too thin, but my new brow line is... how do you humans say it? Growing on me."

"Beautiful," Taylor croaked, with considerable effort.

"Kalanis?" Without letting go of Taylor, Maia turned to see Sorra standing behind them. She pointed her rifle at the hole. "We need to get her out of here."

That was the only thing in the universe Sorra could have said to make Maia move. "Can you walk?" she asked Taylor.

Taylor's brow furrowed as though she weren't sure.

"It doesn't matter. I'll carry you from here to Korithia if I have to." Maia helped Taylor to her feet, but she didn't have to make good on her promise. Taylor was able to walk, though she leaned heavily on Maia's shoulder as they headed for the smoldering hole. Sorra ducked through to help them navigate the twisted slag of hot metal spilling into the interrogation room. It took both of them to heft Taylor's feet clear of the smoking ruins.

In the hallway, Rachel and Akton stood over the bodies of two more guards, one of whom was missing his rifle. The ikthian prisoner held the stolen weapon, and when Maia laid eyes on her again, realization struck like a solar flare.

"Mother!" Shock and relief warred inside her chest. Could it really be Irana, after all this time?

Irana turned and did the last thing Maia expected. She smiled. "You're alive," she said, in a rasp that wasn't much better than Taylor's.

Four more guards rushed around the corner. Two aimed their weapons, taking shots while their companions erected glowing barriers. Irana whirled, firing with deadly accuracy despite her visibly weakened state. Her target dropped the shield they'd been about to place, slumping to the ground. Sorra and Rachel dispatched the other three before they could get their bearings.

"Move!" Sorra ordered, jerking her head toward the other end of the corridor. It was the same way they'd come in, a path clearly marked by the remnants of several small-scale explosions.

Maia broke into a run, moving as fast as she could without abandoning Taylor. *Later,* she told herself. There would be time to process all this once she and Taylor—and her mother—made it out alive. She hadn't come this far, risked this much, just to lose Taylor for good.

***

"Get the engines going! We're headed your way."

Elurin's head jerked up as Rachel's voice came over the ship's radio. She'd spent the last several minutes in strained silence, watching the dash and waiting for instructions. One of the biggest downsides to being the pilot—she often had to defend the ship. For her, the storm-awful waiting was always a hundred times worse than fighting.

"I got you, Harris." She glanced through the viewscreen, wincing at what she saw. Orange-pink flares followed a small group of shadows hurrying toward her ship and the stolen transport.

Grinding the points of her teeth, Elurin spun the fighter and readied the main guns. If Rachel and the others got closer, she could lay down cover fire while they boarded. As soon as Elurin made out Rachel's sprinting form, she let loose, blowing a blackened crater between her group and the pursuing guards. The closest ones went flying, landing in pieces several yards away.

At last, the rescue party reached the ships. Rachel crouched behind Elurin's fighter, peeking around its edge to offer more cover fire as her companions boarded the transport. Elurin counted them off–*Sorra, Maia... they're carrying Taylor?* The view wasn't clear enough to tell, but she hoped so. She caught sight of Akton shepherding another ikthian and two ragged looking naledai onto the transport, where the prisoner they'd rescued in transit waited to help them aboard.

As the transport took off, more lights flashed at the edge of Elurin's field of view. She counted at least four enemy ships preparing to give chase, spherical Dominion fighters much like the one she'd stolen. "Hop aboard, Harris," she shouted into the comm. "Now, or we're both dead!"

No answer.

Elurin's heart sank, but then the ship's doors opened. Rachel staggered toward the copilot's chair, ripping off her helmet and taking great gulps of air. Her curly black hair was wet, plastered to her shimmering brow.

"Go!"

Elurin gunned it, speeding off into the atmosphere. Though she could have outrun the transport easily, she remained behind the larger vessel. Her eyes locked onto the dash as the enemy ships pursued, angles and trajectories racing through her mind.

"Take over the guns, Harris, and keep firing. I'll get you in position."

Rachel did as instructed. She was no great shot, at least not aboard a ship, but she didn't need to be, firing constantly. Elurin veered at an angle, passing in front of an enemy fighter. It went up in a subdued violet plume, much less brilliant than it would have been within a planetary atmosphere.

A shot from another pursuing vessel winged them on the starboard side, and Elurin growled as her ship shuddered. Their shields had deflected it, but Dominion ships like this one packed a punch. A few more hits, and the shields would fail.

"The transport?" Rachel asked, panting.

Elurin checked. "Out of range and moving fast. Should be able to jump soon. The fighters are focusing on us."

She shouldn't have said anything. Two enemy ships sped past her fighter from above and below. The first ship's guns spun around its spherical body to fire backwards, while the second ship pursued the transport.

"Shit," Rachel snarled. "Who do I shoot?"

Elurin dipped, narrowly avoiding another blast. "The one chasing the transport!"

Rachel fired. The distant ship exploded into a purple cloud, while the ship directly in front of them continued firing. Their fighter rocked. Warning sirens screamed throughout the cabin

Elurin checked their shields. Dead. Another hit would kill them. *Hope the others got away safe. At least we won't die for nothing.* But then she caught a glimpse of Rachel's wide, fearful brown eyes.

Determination burned within Elurin's chest. *No. I signed up to die this way, but Harris didn't.* She looped into a spiral, keeping her path as unpredictable as possible, but there were several near misses. Through it all, the sirens wailed.

"Hold on," Elurin said, swiping furiously at the ship's interface. "We're going down."

"Down where?"

That question was answered as a brilliant blue and green sphere rushed into view. A terraformed planet! Elurin had no idea which planet she was speeding toward, but she didn't care. If it had a breathable atmosphere, that was good enough. *If Harris is gonna die, she deserves to go out groundside.*

The remaining enemy ship hastened its pursuit. Elurin did her best to dodge, but a blast struck one of her engines. The fighter spun wildly. She tried to start emergency landing procedures, but it was too late. Their ship hit the atmosphere with a wrenching shudder, nearly throwing her from her seat.

"Elurin!" Rachel cried.

The sharp scent of smoking electrics filled the cabin, and sparks burst like fireworks from between loosened panels, but Elurin's focus remained on the dash. They were going to crash, but if they were really, *really* lucky, maybe she could crash in a way that wouldn't kill them.

Green raced toward them. An entire ocean of green. *A forest? Shit.* Elurin had been hoping for water, but she didn't have much choice in the matter.

"Helmets on," she said as they hurtled toward the emerald sea of treetops. The last thing she saw before impact was Rachel's terrified face disappearing into her helmet.

Chapter Four

RACHEL GROANED, WINCING AS a spike of pain drove through her skull. After a few moments, the stabbing sensation faded to a dull ache. She grinned. At least she'd survived the crash, probably thanks to Elurin's skill as a pilot.

Elurin?

The name caught in her burning throat. She coughed, feeling the jerking motion in every rib. Her mouth tasted like copper and death, but she tried again. This time, she managed to speak, if barely, "Lurin?"

"Harris."

Rachel's heart leapt. She opened her eyes, but all she managed to make out were foggy grey blurs. One of the larger blurs moved, solidifying into the shape of a face.

"Stop squirming, Harris," Elurin grumbled. "You've got a head wound."

Moving hurt anyway, so Rachel obeyed. Something wet and foul smelling smeared across her brow. Gradually, her vision cleared. Two ash-smudged, worried-looking Elurins hovered over her, but they soon merged into one.

Rachel sighed with relief. "You made it," she said as Elurin fumbled with something. A white box. *The ship's medical kit?*

Elurin noticed where her gaze had wandered. "Got it from the ship. Or, what's left of her."

Rachel turned her head, pleased to find that the pain wasn't nearly as overwhelming. Probably because of the ion gel Elurin had smeared across her forehead, and the injection Elurin jabbed into her hip. Elurin had stripped off part of Rachel's armor to reach her skin, but she was too out of it to care.

A few yards to the right, Rachel saw what remained of the stealth fighter. The silver orb was squashed to half its former size, like a giant had stepped on it. It had crumpled inward to protect them upon impact, but somehow, Elurin had managed to get them out through the doors. The ruins still smoked in the grass.

"You hurt?" Rachel asked.

The injection had already done her a world of good. In a few moments, she felt well enough to sit up. Elurin knelt next to her, uniform ripped at one shoulder and sporting scorch marks around one of the cuffs. She had a head wound as well that she had wrapped in gauze, though it looked clean and relatively small. She had also slapped a flesh-knitting patch across the back of her hand.

"A few bruises. No serious bleeding or broken bones. Ancients, Rachel, you lost a *lot* of blood."

Blinking dazedly, Rachel touched the side of her face. She barely noticed how warm and wet it was, and a crimson stain came away on her glove. "Yeah. Head wounds tend to bleed a lot."

Elurin chuckled, shaking her head in amazement. "I knew humans were almost as hardy as naledai, but I had no idea."

"Yeah," she said, feeling Elurin's worried stare upon her. "Humans can even lose limbs and still get on fine...although you won't see us re-growing 'em."

"Good to know."

"So, what's the plan?"

Elurin shrugged. "Hadn't gotten around to that yet. Thought saving your life was more urgent. Tell me off if I prioritized wrong."

"Asshole." Rachel turned her attention back to the ship's wreckage. Maybe there was still something useful amidst the debris. "Think our comm might still work? We could call for help."

Elurin frowned. "Doubt it. There's an emergency beacon in the back that's specifically designed to sustain this kind of impact, but..."

"But?"

"We'd be signaling everyone in the area. *Everyone.*"

Rachel's heart sank. The last thing they needed to deal with while injured and stranded were Dominion forces—the soldiers who'd been pursuing them, or maybe even seekers. "Well. Fuck us, then."

"That sums it up pretty nicely," Elurin said, with a dark laugh.

Rachel sighed. "How about we find some food? Once we've eaten and rested, and whatever good stuff you gave me has some time to work, we'll look at the beacon. If the enemy comes, we'll be in better shape to fight. Maybe we can steal whatever ship they fly in on."

"Assuming there aren't too many," Elurin added, but her eyes lit up. "It's a decent plan. You're smarter than you look, Harris."

Rachel rolled her eyes. "Screw you."

"Hey, I'm not the one who marched through the desert whining about how awful and murderous ikthians are on my first rebellion mission, *to my ikthian commander,* only to stumble right into a squad of seekers. That's twice I've saved your life now, by the way. You're welcome."

Rachel's cheeks burned. "Not how I remember it."

"You can refresh my memory while we strip the ship. Maybe we'll get lucky and find some usable supplies besides the med kit. I'll need your help getting the beacon out through the door. Can you stand?"

Elurin offered her hand, and Rachel took it. Aside from a moment of dizziness, she managed to stand without much difficulty. She smiled at Elurin. It wasn't until they reached the ship that Rachel realized she was still holding Elurin's hand, even though she didn't need the support.

***

"Sorra, are you really all right?" Odelle asked.

Sorra shot her a narrow-eyed look. Though she had no doubt Odelle loved her, the question wasn't the inquiry of a worried mate. That had come when Sorra had first disembarked the transport a few minutes prior, dragging herself into the brightly lit hangar. Odelle had rushed the bridgeway and gasped the same words then, her eyes roaming Sorra's body in search of injuries.

But the initial surge of relief had passed for both of them. Now, the question was a warning, a somewhat sharp response to Sorra's brooding silence the past two minutes. *You're holding something back,* it said. *If you keep lying by omission, you won't share my bed tonight.* She'd been Odelle's lover long enough to read between the lines.

"I'm fine," Sorra whispered. She didn't want others in the hangar to hear, especially Akton, who waited a few yards away. Already, the former Daashu prisoners—including Taylor, with Maia hovering by her stretcher—were being moved to the medical ward.

All but one prisoner.

"So you claim," Odelle whispered back, barely moving her mouth, "but your expression says otherwise."

Sorra busied herself looking around the hangar. They'd all made it back in one piece, with the exception of Elurin and Harris. Their failure to establish contact worried her, but Elurin had outflown better pilots than the scrambling guards on Daashu. She and Harris were probably laying low until they determined it was safe to return to base.

But another big problem waited aboard the transport, locked in the same holding cell Teichos Industries had used to transport prisoners. Irana Kalanis. A woman Sorra had hoped was dead, until they'd locked eyes in the ruined remains of Taylor's cell.

Of course. It had to be Irana. Fuck everything.

Unable to stand Odelle's searching stare any longer, Sorra turned to Akton. "Wait here for Kross and Oranthis. I need to make a quick trip."

Akton nodded his large, shaggy head. "Ikthians. Always have to piss every five minutes."

"Only because we drink more water than you, furball."

"Try digging in one of Nakonum's deserts. Then you'll learn what thirst is."

With a roll of her eyes, Sorra strode across the hangar, Odelle close on her heels. Rebels scurried out of their way, watching Sorra with something akin to awe. Surely rumors that she had returned from Daashu alive were already circulating the warren. It would cement her reputation as a fearless, practically immortal revolutionary, but it would also make things difficult. Routine tasks wouldn't be easy while a pack of awestruck naledai and ikthian defectors swarmed after her.

"Slow down," Odelle demanded, drawing even with Sorra. "This isn't a race...unless you really do need to use the facilities."

"Irana's aboard the transport," Sorra said without preamble.

Surprise lifted Odelle's voice. "You found Irana alive?"

They exited the docking bay, entering one of the warren's many corridors, and continued their whispered conversation as they walked.

"We *rescued* her." Sorra growled the word through gritted teeth. Given the choice, she would have left Irana to rot, but duty came before old grudges. Irana might prove useful—*and shooting a mother in front of her estranged daughter would be a scummy thing to do.* Even if the mother and daughter in question were the Kalanises, neither of whom she particularly liked. *At least Maia's proven somewhat capable. She sees through Dominion propaganda. But Irana...*

Irana Kalanis was, and always had been, duplicitous; not merely one of Chancellor's Corvis's politicians, but a master of spies. She was part of the reason Corvis had remained in power for so long and was the hidden hand behind several attempts on Sorra's life in recent decades, through more than one fake identity.

Odelle stopped in front of a door midway down the next tunnel. It opened when she touched its scanner, and Sorra entered the room without being asked. It was small, with little more than a workstation and terminal—a former office cubicle in use as a storage room, with several metal crates to make the walls feel even more constricting.

"Why is this a bad thing?" Odelle asked. "Yes, you hate Irana—"

Sorra aimed a pointed look at her mate. "She tried to kill me more than once. Hate is an understatement"

"Not personally."

"That's not how Kalanis operates. She gets others to do her dirty work. Then they send her neat little reports without any mess on them."

Odelle heaved a sigh. Her expression reminded Sorra of an exhausted instructor dealing with a particularly rebellious student. In other circumstances, it might have amused or aroused her. Not now. Not while Irana was only a short distance away, ruining her mood merely by breathing.

"If you're quite finished muttering and interrupting," Odelle continued, "I was going to say, your feelings about Irana are irrelevant. You don't need to interrogate her. We have soldiers trained to deal with situations like—"

"But they won't get a crack at her," Sorra said, folding her hands behind her back and pacing the length of the room. It was barely five steps wide, so she whirled frequently. "You're already scheming, I can tell. You'd have been as bad as her if you were on their side."

Odelle grabbed her shoulder on the next pass, forcing her to halt mid-stride. "Sorra," she said, with infuriating calmness. "It doesn't matter who interrogates Irana. You won't have to. In fact, you *can't*, because I don't trust you in the same room with her, and neither will Kross and Oranthis. Isn't that what you want? For her to be kept far away from you? Or do you just want to shoot her instead?"

"Can I?" Sorra pleaded, with mock piteousness.

"Stop being difficult."

"You're talking in circles," she said. "Trying to distract me."

"I'm not—"

"You want to talk to her, don't you?"

Odelle didn't avert her eyes, but Sorra thought she saw a flash of guilt in them. "We have a history, from when I was Corvis' Executive Media Coordinator. I could establish a rapport."

"Absolutely not." Sorra jerked her arm away. Odelle and Irana, in the same room? She wouldn't allow it. Irana never harmed Odelle while they were working together, but only because she hadn't known Odelle was a double agent.

"We could dress you up as a fellow prisoner," Sorra said, already constructing a plan. "Irana might confide in you then—no! It's stupid of me to consider letting you to talk to her in the first place—"

"Sorra." It was Odelle's turn to interrupt, and she did so with considerable indignation. "First of all, this isn't your choice. Second, I'm sure Irana knows I've defected by now. Her interrogators undoubtedly asked for information about me. I'm currently the most wanted woman in Dominion-controlled space, after all."

Sorra forced a laugh to distract from the churning in her gut. "Brag about taking my spot, why don't you?"

"Maia beat you out before I did. Why don't you ever pester her?"

"Why do you think Kalanis the younger annoys me so much? Don't answer that. You'll have to start a list."

Odelle folded her arms, as solid and impassive as a wall. Just about as immovable, too.

Eventually, Sorra sighed. Her agitation calmed, giving way to worry. "I hate Irana, and I don't trust her. The last thing I want is you in a room with someone I don't trust."

"I know." Odelle touched her shoulder, far gentler than when she'd interrupted Sorra's pacing. "But you trust me, don't you?"

"Don't be ridiculous."

Odelle's eyes widened.

"Not that it's ridiculous to trust you," Sorra amended. "It's ridiculous of you to ask the question in the first place. I've always trusted you, even back in university."

"I know," Odelle said again. Her palm slid up Sorra's shoulder and along her neck, stopping at her face. Sorra leaned into the touch, her third eyelids fluttering as she exhaled. In spite of all the tension twisted up inside her, it felt good to be in Odelle's presence.

"You'll be fine," Sorra said, trying to convince herself more than pacify Odelle. "I know you will."

"I might not be a soldier, but I'm not without resources. If anyone can get Irana to talk, I can...or perhaps Maia."

Sorra blinked. "That might be a better idea, although she isn't a trained interrogator. She's obnoxious, but far from stupid. I could teach her."

"'Far from stupid.'" Odelle scoffed. "What a magnanimous way to describe one of the greatest scientific minds of our generation. I'll take first dive at Irana. If I come up without any pearls, we'll use Maia."

"If Maia agrees to be used," Sorra replied. "She might not want anything to do with her mother."

"She will," Odelle said, with absolute certainty. "Don't worry about that."

***

White light shone through Taylor's eyelids, bright enough to burn. She moaned, curling her forearm over her face.

"Hurts," she rasped, but aside from the familiar effects of dehydration, she didn't feel terrible. The pain in her side had dulled, as had the burn on her cheek. When she tested her facial muscles, they moved without aching.

"Taylor." A soft hand stroked her forehead, brushing loose strands of hair away. "You're awake."

Taylor's eyes snapped open. She tensed, preparing for pain, but it wasn't an ikthian interrogator. The figure was silver, with delicate webbing between her fingers, but familiar.

"Maia?" Taylor smiled, relaxing into the touch.

There was no mistaking it—Maia was really here, not merely a figment of her imagination. She looked different than Taylor remembered. Thinner. Older. The silver sheen of her skin was duller, and the planes of her face were narrower. Her movements were hesitant, as though she were unsure of herself, and of how much contact Taylor would permit.

After a moment, Maia resumed stroking Taylor's hair. *Guess my rescue wasn't a dream after all. Maia's with me. And I'm probably on some heavy-duty pain medication.* A sense of peace settled over her, and she almost drifted back to sleep.

"What am I going to do with you?" Maia said. "I spent two months terrified that you were dead."

"M'not," Taylor said, but speaking took a tremendous effort. Still thirsty, her throat burned. "Water?"

Maia left the chair and hurried to a sink in one corner of the room. A hospital room, Taylor noted. Not much different from others she'd spent time recuperating in, although the bed was overlarge. Medical equipment was stacked beside it. Eerie quiet and a strong, sterile smell permeated the place. Judging by the one diagram pinned to a wall, depicting a hulking skeleton and an unfamiliar mass of organs, most of the patients here were probably naledai.

After a moment, Maia returned with a paper cup. She sat in the chair, bringing the cup to Taylor's lips. "Drink slowly," she said as she tipped the water into Taylor's mouth. "Otherwise, you might make yourself sick. We have you on intravenous fluids, so once you wet your mouth, you should feel better."

Taylor moaned with gratitude as the cool liquid soothed her throat. She tried to gulp more, but Maia pulled the cup away. When Taylor reached for it, Maia relented and handed it over.

"Slowly," she repeated.

Taylor tried her best to obey. She held onto the flimsy paper cup even after it was empty, unwilling to let it go.

"Thanks," she said, pleased to note her voice was much stronger. "What do you mean, 'we' have you on fluids?"

"I kept myself busy while you were away. I may not be 'that' kind of doctor, but I have expanded my skillset by assisting in Jor'al base's medical ward. Akton taught me how to use a rifle, too."

Taylor smiled. She did have vague recollections of Maia shooting enemies during their mad dash from the cell and onto the transport. "Good for him. He's okay, right?"

"Yes," Maia said. "In fact, he is the hero of the hour. Before now, anyone would have claimed returning from Daashu with not just one, but five rescued prisoners in tow, was impossible. A suicide mission."

"Five?"

"Two naledai prisoners from Daashu, a third aboard the transport we stole, and you."

Taylor's grin disappeared. "That's four." Maia averted her eyes, and more of Taylor's memory returned. "Your mother. She's here?"

Maia folded her hands in her lap, staring down at them. "Irana was among the prisoners we rescued. Why was she in your cell when we arrived?"

Taylor licked her lips, stalling for time. She wasn't sure how much to reveal, especially while Maia was clearly in a vulnerable state. She decided on the truth. Maia deserved that. "They were trying to make me talk."

Maia looked quietly horrified, mouth opening and brow creasing with worry lines. "Oh."

"I gave them all the information I could," Taylor said. "It was outdated anyway. Once I made it through the first few days without breaking, I knew you and the others would be safe. So I started talking, like the Coalition trains us to do if we're captured. I hope I spared her some pain."

Maia blinked rapidly, fighting tears. "Your own safety is far more important to me. My mother and I have not been on good terms for some time." Her eyes hardened, and she forced a smile, as though to steel herself. "But that's irrelevant now. I'm here to make sure you recover."

"I'll be okay," Taylor said, but she suspected her recovery wouldn't be as simple as Maia made it out to be. She felt exhausted beyond measure and could not dismiss the anxious feeling in the back of her brain that she was still in danger. That was something that could be dealt with later, though.

Maia eyed the paper cup. "I will not press you for details, but please don't lie to me. I saw the state you were in." Cautiously, she reached for Taylor's hand, wordlessly waiting for permission. This time, Taylor was prepared. She took Maia's hand deliberately in hers and didn't flinch at the contact.

Taylor took a deep breath. "I'd do the same thing again if—"

"Please," Maia said, "I doubt either of us would survive another foolish gesture of bravery on your part."

But she squeezed Taylor's hand, and Taylor found that she had enough strength to squeeze back. It felt so nice, holding Maia's hand. The first touches she'd experienced in months that weren't painful. That felt safe.

"I knew you'd come," Taylor told her. "It's what I told myself to keep from giving up. That you'd come for me."

Maia rubbed her knuckles with a tender thumb. "I did. And you survived."

"We survived," Taylor corrected. They sat that way for a long time, holding each other's hands.

Rae D. Magdon & Michelle Magly

Chapter Five

"HEY," ELURIN CALLED AS she caught sight of Rachel emerging from behind the trees. She set down the last crate of the supplies she'd salvaged from the crumpled ship. "Find any water?"

Rachel ambled over, dragging her boots across the heavily rooted jungle floor. She seemed tired, which was no surprise given her recent injuries. That was why Elurin had suggested she do the lighter work of walking the perimeter.

"No water," Rachel replied. "Saw some weird birds with two sets of wings, but nothing dangerous."

"Your birds only have one set? Weird." Elurin sat down, leaning against the ship for a breather. She opened one of the ration kits, grabbing a nutrient bar and withdrawing a water canteen. "Good news is, I managed to rescue the water purifier. If we can find a river, we'll be okay."

"Good, because I'm dying of thirst." Rachel slumped beside Elurin, wiping her hair back from her forehead. "How are you not sweating your ass off right now?"

Elurin chewed her nutrient bar, the sweet taste bursting across her tongue. "Ikthians don't sweat," she said, passing Rachel a nutrient bar as well. Sweat. An intriguing concept. Once, she'd asked Maia about the shimmer that often-covered Rachel's rich brown skin. A human method of thermoregulation, Maia had explained; apparently, sweat also contained salt, which made it taste absolutely delicious.

Elurin tried hard not to stare at the gleaming stripe of sweat on Rachel's brow beneath the edge of her curly black hair. *Does it really taste good, or was Maia exaggerating?*

Rachel accepted the nutrient bar and took a large bite. She didn't even finish swallowing before asking, "How do ikthians cool down, then?"

Certainly not by sitting close to you. "Step one is always finding water or shade, although we have a few small tricks."

Rachel arched a brow. "Enlighten me."

"Ever wondered why ikthian crests have spots?" Elurin dipped her head, showing Rachel the mottled silver-blue pattern on her crest. "Warm blood moves to the dark edges to cool down." She spread the delicate webbing between her fingers. "Same with the webs between our fingers and toes."

"Wild." From Rachel's bemused chuckle, Elurin could tell she didn't mean any offense. She'd come a long way from the bigoted human who'd thought all ikthians were bloodthirsty, mind-controlling monsters.

"No weirder than getting rid of what little water you have to cool off," Elurin said.

"Hey, sweating is a highly effective cooling system," Rachel said, with mock indignation. "Humans used it to outlast all our prey."

It was Elurin's turn to laugh. "Give me a speedy pod and sharp teeth any day. Why do you think the seekers are such effective hunting units? It's in our blood."

"Don't say that," Rachel groaned.

"Fine, but we really should look for water soon. I'll go with you this time." Elurin stood, placing her hands on her lower back to stretch her stiff spine. Though her injuries were mild, the crash had left her sore.

"Let's go now," Rachel said, shouldering her rifle. "Can you grab the water purifier?"

"Sure." Elurin picked it up, where it sat next to the rest of their supplies. The black cylinder, like a thermos with a cap on both ends, represented their best chance for survival.

"What about the beacon?" Rachel asked.

Elurin glanced at the beacon, which she'd also rescued from the wreckage. It was a brick-like silver box designed to withstand trauma, with a few basic buttons. "We'll leave it here for now. We can turn it on later, once we're sure it's safe."

"*Are* we safe?" Rachel asked, scanning the jungle.

Elurin did the same. Intertwined pairs of arecae trees surrounded the newly made clearing, their drooping, segmented leaves swaying in the breeze. Fruit-bearing sativus vines wound their way up the spiraling trunks, while red and yellow thurium flowers with heart-shaped petals grew at their base.

"See those?" Elurin asked, walking toward them. "They're arecae trees, native to Korithia. They're often an ikthian metaphor for lovers, because they grow in pairs, but for our purposes, this is a Dominion-terraformed planet. Don't know whether it's been terraformed for resource production or permanent settlements, though."

"Even if it's just a resource planet, there'll be processing stations and people," Rachel said, following a step behind. "I grew up on one of Earth's lumber-producing colonies."

"Not a homeworld native?"

Rachel shook her head. "Wish I was. You?"

"Wish I wasn't."

"Fair."

"Did I ever tell you why I defected?" Elurin found herself asking as they continued through the trees.

Interest sparked in Rachel's brown eyes. "Nope."

"I was on Korithia for a break between missions and received a classified message." Despite the heat, a shiver coursed down Elurin's spine as she dredged up the memory. "I was being recommended for an award because of my kill score. Let's just say that it was in the high thousands."

She waited for the inevitable judgment in Rachel's eyes as the human drew even with her, but it never came. Rachel's expression remained sympathetic, as far as Elurin could tell. "The number bothered you?"

"Yeah. I sat thinking about that number all night for...Tides, I don't know how long. I couldn't believe I'd been responsible for ending that many lives. So I requested my mission files. Some came with images."

Rachel's breath hitched. "Civilians?"

Elurin hesitated, but here, trapped in the jungle with Rachel, she felt removed enough from her old life to confess. "Some were children. Those were bombing runs, mostly. I never asked questions, just assumed they were hotbeds of rebel activity. Even though I grew up with the whole line about how naledai benefitted from serving ikthians, I couldn't reconcile it in my brain. Bombing naledai pups. How could that possibly benefit anyone?"

"It didn't," Rachel murmured.

Elurin started at the pressure of Rachel's gloved hand on her shoulder. The contact made her feel a small surge of giddiness, and the gesture reminded her of just how far Rachel had come. One touch from an ikthian could spell death for aliens, after all.

She heard what I did, and she isn't pulling away. She's reaching out instead.

"But you left the Dominion," Rachel said.

"Yeah." Elurin took a steadying breath. Rachel's contact had rattled her, though not in a bad way. "Went on a bender on the edge of naledai space. Seekers tracked me down, of course. I was too drunk to fight back, but there were a few rebels at the same sketchy bar. Once they took care of the seekers, they asked why the Dominion was after me. I told them everything, and they made me an offer. I was lucky."

"Just because you were lucky," Rachel said, obviously choosing her words carefully, "doesn't mean you didn't deserve a second chance. Hell, I got a second chance I didn't deserve, too. Did I ever tell you I let a slimy politician get away with murdering my commanding officer?"

That confession sent Elurin's mind awhirl. She stopped in the middle of stepping over a twisted root to glance over at Rachel. "What?"

Rachel sighed. "Short version, my commander helped Taylor and Maia escape from Earth. I ratted him out to Bouchard. Creepiest Coalition councilor I ever met." She pulled a disgusted face. "Just thinking about it leaves a bad taste in my mouth."

Although she suspected Rachel was speaking metaphorically, Elurin offered the water canteen. "Here."

"Not what I meant." Rachel took the canteen and swigged, then passed it back to Elurin. She drank as well, trying not to think about the fact that Rachel's lips had been pressed there mere moments before.

They continued through the jungle in silence. Hidden animals filled the air with chirps and buzzes. Large leaf-beetles with shining rainbow shells, almost the size of Elurin's head, buzzed between branches.

"Whoa," Rachel said. "Those are some big bugs."

"We're lucky it's daytime. There are way more at night."

"Yikes." Rachel pushed aside an overhanging arecae frond, peering around the twined trunks. "Hey, look! A river."

The sound of running water drifted toward Elurin, a truly wonderful noise. She wiggled her toes in her boots. She wasn't stupid enough to go swimming in a strange jungle stream, but maybe she could get away with wetting her feet.

Suddenly, the buzzing and birdsong stopped. The jungle grew eerily silent. Elurin froze, grabbing Rachel's arm and preventing her from approaching the stream. "Wait. Listen."

"I don't hear anything," Rachel said.

"Exactly."

An ear-splitting roar shook the trees, startling several leaf-beetles from their perches. Elurin reached for her back, only to realize she'd left her rifle at the crash site. She'd been focused on the water purifier. *Blood in water, what was I thinking?*

"Run!" Rachel shoved Elurin back the way they'd come just as a giant shadow burst through the trees, leaping toward them with teeth bared.

* * *

Odelle stood outside the interrogation room, smoothing her face into something unreadable. *Be a lake, Odelle. Calm, with hidden depths.* She'd had ample practice, but under the circumstances, she found it more difficult than usual—Irana Kalanis waited for her on the other side of the door.

Her past with Irana was choppy, though not as stormy as Sorra's. Sorra. Another problem Odelle wasn't sure how to deal with. She didn't know what sort of mood to expect from her lover when she returned to their quarters that evening.

With skill born from years of practice, Odelle put those thoughts from her mind. If she was to extract any information from the ex-spymaster, she had to focus on the present. In the present, her position was advantageous. Irana was the rebellion's prisoner, while she was one of its most valued allies.

She opened the door. The room's interior was small, dark but for one dim ceiling light. It was bereft of furniture except for the table and two opposing chairs in its center, all bolted to the floor.

Irana sat in the chair facing the door, her expression as neutral as the best ikthian negotiators. Her blue eyes fixed on Odelle as soon as she entered. "Executive Coordinator Lastra." She gave a shallow dip of her head. "It has been a long time."

Odelle took her time closing the door, striding over to the table, and taking her own seat across from Irana. "Irana Kalanis. I've had the pleasure of getting to know your daughter these past few months."

She knew she'd scored a point by the almost imperceptible widening of Irana's eyes. Her third eyelids flashed into view, as though she were blinking away some irritant.

"I never suspected you to be a traitor before your defection," Irana said, as if she was merely speaking of the weather. "Me, the one with information feeds anchored in every corner of Korithia. You hid your true motivations well."

Odelle leaned back in her chair. "What do you think those motivations are?"

"At present? To debrief me."

"That's a kind word for this process." Odelle glanced at the electromagnetic cuffs around Irana's wrists.

Irana didn't dignify the gaze with something so banal as a snort or roll of her eyes, but the line of her lips did thin out, as though she were amused. "You are clever, Lastra, but you have no idea of the horrors Daashu inflicts upon its prisoners. My imprisonment here has been like a vacation in comparison."

Odelle took a moment to study Irana. In some ways, she looked similar to how Odelle remembered–short and slender, gracefully built. Her face resembled how Maia's had looked before her cosmetic surgery, especially the piercing blue eyes. The mottled markings on Irana's crest and around her temples were a deep shade of azure, more striking than her daughter's faint coloring.

But there were differences. Irana wasn't merely slender anymore— she was thin. Worryingly so. Ugly purple-black bruises marred her neck and one side of her crest. She looked, in a word, exhausted.

"You've been given medical treatment?" Odelle asked, though she already knew the answer.

"For dehydration and long-term exposure to unfriendly toxins, yes." Irana paused. "In any event, I am in much better shape than the human you brought here."

Odelle made sure she gave no reaction when Irana mentioned Taylor. "How do you see your future, Irana?"

"I accepted the fact that I had no future the moment Corvis threw me in Daashu," Irana said, her gaze unwavering.

"That's not true," Odelle said. "As you said, the rebellion hasn't harmed you. We've treated your injuries—"

"And in return, you expect my cooperation."

Odelle frowned. "I think cooperation would be in your best interest. You've always been a pragmatist, Irana. Besides, there's no love lost between you and Corvis. Your loyalty to her was always rooted in what she could provide you. In your current position, the answer is nothing. I, on the other hand, can provide you with quite a lot."

Irana remained silent for several moments, considering. Odelle wondered if taking this tack had been a mistake. The former spymaster was known for her mind games, and Odelle had hoped the easiest way to circumvent them was with simple, reasonable honesty.

After a while, Irana dipped her head again. "Obviously, I wish to be fed and clothed, access to water, medical care."

Odelle knew Sorra would have rankled at that. The Dominion rarely offered its prisoners such dignity. *But we're the rebellion, not the Dominion. And stranglekelp catches fish by offering shelter.* "Obviously."

Irana lifted her gaze. "I also wish to see my daughter one more time. You may monitor our conversation, if necessary. It will be of a personal nature, nothing to do with Dominion secrets."

Odelle worked to conceal her surprise. It wasn't strange that Irana wanted to see her daughter after her near-death experience, but the fact that she'd so easily agreed to monitoring was unusual. However, Odelle knew better than to complain. "I can arrange that."

"In return, I will tell you what you want to know—although I warn you, my information may be outdated."

"I have no doubt it will be useful." A thought tugged at her, and Odelle activated the comm on her wrist, pulling up one of the documents Sorra had retrieved during their infiltration of Teichos Industries. Irana looked mildly annoyed. She wasn't used to being kept waiting. Daashu hadn't completely broken her after all.

"Well?" she asked.

"Before we begin in earnest, I wondered if you might tell me, do you know anything about a series of secret compounds being built and staffed by Teichos Industries in recent months? I have coordinates." Odelle turned her wrist, showing them to Irana.

A flicker of surprise crossed Irana's face. "Perhaps your rebels do have some small chance. What you call compounds are actually research stations. They develop weapons, on direct orders from Corvis."

"What kind of weapons?" Odelle asked, with more urgency than intended. This was more information than the captured IT specialist from Teichos had been able to provide.

"Many kinds," Irana said. "Large and small scale. But your list is incomplete. There are two other facilities that may be of interest to you."

Odelle pressed a button on her side of the table. A hidden drawer opened, revealing several datapads. She slid one across the table to Irana and used her comm to unfasten the other ikthian's cuffs. Irana wouldn't harm her. "Write everything, and I promise to fulfill my end of the bargain."

Irana took the datapad and activated it with a touch of her fingertips. She began typing. "I do believe you will. This arrangement may just benefit the both of us after all."

* * *

"God," Taylor groaned. "I spent weeks starving in Daashu. Now I finally have food, and I can barely stomach it." She set aside the half-empty tube of nutrient paste, which tasted faintly of peanut butter. It was the only comparison she could come up with for the sweet, earthy flavor. It was good, but its smell made her stomach churn.

"You don't need to finish it." Maia hovered close, seated in a chair beside Taylor's bed. A rotating silver tray rested between them, holding a small cup of water and the tube of paste. "We've ensured that your feeding tube will provide enough nutrients."

Taylor forced a smile. "There you go with that 'we' again, Doctor Kalanis. You sure you didn't become *that* kind of doctor while I was gone?"

Maia's eyes darted down, as though she were embarrassed. She raised a hand to rub her neck ridges. "No, but I have been consulting with the team."

The team, as Maia referred to them, were the doctors in charge of Taylor's care. They primarily dealt with naledai and ikthian trauma patients, not humans suffering from malnutrition, but Taylor had been lucky. Somehow, Maia had gotten human nutritional guidelines, which the doctors had used to formulate a treatment plan. The information had undoubtedly saved her life.

With the worst effects of her starvation and dehydration eased, Taylor had a lot more energy. Enough energy, the doctors had decided, to try tasting—if not actually consuming—bland foods again. She hadn't realized just how complicated recovering from starvation was.

I could've been a lot worse off. At least the ikthians gave me enough food and water to keep me going.

Ikthians. That was another pleasant side effect of her stay at Daashu. So far, Maia was the only ikthian Taylor had been able to tolerate in her personal space. There were ikthian doctors on her team, but when one had tried to take her vitals, she'd gone into a panic and attempted to strangle them with her IV line. A nearby naledai assistant had rushed in, and the incident had wiped out Taylor's energy for half a day.

"And what does the team say?" Taylor asked, forcing herself to remain in the present. That was the best way to stay sane. In the present, she was safe, warm, and hydrated. In the present, Maia was with her.

"That your recovery will be a process," Maia said, not for the first time. "I know you want to leave and—"

"Find Rachel," Taylor finished for her. "We've had no word from her and it's driving me nuts. If I could just—"

Maia frowned. "You will be of no help to Rachel and Elurin in your current state. Several rebel ships are already searching for them."

"Or what's left of their ship," Taylor added. But the fact that the stealth fighter's remains hadn't been found amongst the Dominion wreckage was a positive sign. *But I'd feel a lot more positive if I was out there searching.*

Maia placed her hand over Taylor's, giving it a gentle squeeze. Taylor appreciated her slow movements, which offered plenty of forewarning. Sometimes, she couldn't suppress a flinch, even when it was Maia who touched her. Maia's thumb traced over her knuckles. "We shouldn't give up on—"

She was interrupted by the sound of the door. Taylor propped herself up as an ikthian female entered the room.

Taylor's pulse spiked. She curled in on herself, arms flying instinctively in front of her face. Her heart pounded, and her world narrowed to the feel of her own hot, rapid breaths against her chest, ruffling her hospital gown.

"Taylor?" Maia's voice, soft and distant. "Taylor, it's Odelle. Everything is fine."

Although she heard the words, it took Taylor several moments to process them. Her body thrummed with adrenaline and her hands shook. But gradually, Maia's meaning penetrated. She lowered her arms and stopped shaking, but she couldn't calm her breathing entirely.

As her terrified haze faded, Taylor realized that Odelle looked startled. She remained a considerable distance away, just inside the door. "I'm sorry, Lieutenant Morgan. I had no idea my presence would—"

"Fine," Taylor blurted out. "It's fine." Gradually, her body calmed down. *Come on, get a grip. It's just Odelle. She's never done anything to hurt you.*

"Perhaps you should remain where you are," Maia suggested.

Odelle nodded. "Of course. I merely wanted to wish you a speedy recovery, Taylor, and pass along a message to you, Maia. Do you have a moment?"

Maia looked at Taylor. "Will you be all right for a few minutes?"

Taylor considered. Some instinctive part of her didn't want Maia to leave. When Maia was by her side, she felt safe. *But she won't be gone for long...and Odelle will leave.* The feeling of overwhelming panic had faded, and now Taylor couldn't help feeling frustrated and embarrassed.

"Go ahead," she said. "I'll be fine."

And she hoped she would be.

***

Maia closed the door, pausing outside Taylor's room to speak with Odelle.

"I apologize for startling her. I had no idea she would react like that." Odelle kept her voice low, but it wasn't necessary. Doctors and assistants scurried along the halls, darting in and out of patient rooms with glowing datapads in hand and claw, but they were too wrapped up in their work to listen.

"It was an accident. No permanent harm done." Maia added a sense of finality to her tone. Although the subject wasn't awkward for her, she knew Taylor would hate being the topic of private discussion.

Odelle, however, continued on. "I've been informed that it may take some time." There was a question within her statement.

"Two to four weeks is a generous estimate," Maia explained. "They restricted her food and water severely, but humans are remarkably resilient. Her captors gave her the same water rations one would provide an ikthian prisoner of war. She was in a better state because of it."

Odelle shuddered. "I've heard stories about Daashu. I resigned myself to going there if my double-agent status was discovered. But..."

Maia nodded. Ever since she'd defected, Daashu had lurked in the back of her mind, too—a monster in the shadows, stalking her nightmares. Those nightmares had worsened since Taylor's capture. She wrapped her hands around her elbows, tucking her arms in. "What is this really about, Odelle? Rachel and Elurin?"

"I'm afraid not." Odelle worked her lips, and the gesture gave Maia pause. She hadn't known Odelle long, but the ikthian rarely showed such visible hesitation. "We brought your mother back with us from Daashu."

Maia suppressed a sigh. She'd feared it would be something like this. Then again, she'd always feared her mother would become the subject of any given conversation, even before she'd fled Korithia. "And?"

"In exchange for her cooperation, she wants to see you."

"Me?" Maia stiffened, stepping back from Odelle and shaking her head. Seeing her mother once, in the middle of their desperate bid for escape, had already thrown her off. Being asked to meet with her—speak with her—left Maia short of breath.

Odelle's expression softened. "I realize this is difficult. I can't force you to meet with Irana, but I believe she possesses vital Dominion intelligence. As a show of good faith, she already revealed new coordinates related to the secret Teichos Industries compounds."

"New coordinates?" Maia repeated, relieved for something else to focus on. "Have surveillance teams been dispatched?"

"Not yet. We want to go in with as much information as possible."

Maia grimaced. Within a matter of moments, Odelle had brought them right back to the subject at hand. She busied herself staring at one of the supply carts on the opposite side of the narrow hall. It was a simple choice. Help or refuse.

"I don't suppose Irana mentioned why she wanted to see me?"

"She told me her conversation with you would be of a 'personal nature.'" Odelle smiled. "I believe she wants to reconcile."

Maia had no idea how to respond to Odelle's gentle encouragement. *What if Mother does want to reconcile? On whose terms? It has always been on her terms before...*

"Feel free to tell me to mind my own business," Odelle continued, "but might I offer some unsolicited advice?"

Reluctantly, Maia met Odelle's eyes. "Go on."

"People can and do change, especially after facing death," Odelle said. "Sometimes, surviving a traumatic experience can remind us what—or who—we value most."

Maia narrowed her eyes. "My mother actively assisted Chancellor Corvis and her horrifying platform. Enforced her rules. Spread her propaganda—"

"So did I," Odelle interrupted. "Unwillingly, and in the service of a greater cause—but spreading propaganda was in my job description, and I was good at it." She placed a gentle hand on Maia's shoulder, which Maia didn't shrug away. "I think you should hear her out—or, more importantly, give yourself the chance to speak. If she refuses to listen to what you have to say...well, you'll have your answer."

Maia ruminated on the advice, her eyes wandering back to the messy supply cart. She felt a strange urge to go over and straighten the lopsided stack of glove boxes—two for ikthians, two for naledai. *The boxes aren't what I really want to fix. And I cannot fix things by continuing to hide from my mother. If "fixing things" means never speaking to her again, at least I will have context with which to make my decision.*

"All right," she said to Odelle. "Let me say goodbye to Taylor. Then, you may take me to Irana."

Chapter Six

"LOOK OUT!" RACHEL YELLED. The beast lunged, passing close enough for her to smell its putrid breath. She reached for the rifle on her back, but the creature had already whirled to face them. She fumbled, nearly dropping her weapon.

The animal looked like a crocodile merged with a tiger. It was undeniably reptilian, with scaly skin and rows of sharp teeth, but its legs were built for speed. Like most human children, Rachel had gone through a dinosaur phase—but that wasn't quite right, either. It moved like a cat as it prowled around them, cutting off their escape.

Rachel fired at the creature's head. It pounced. The plasma round missed. The beast landed on Rachel's chest, forcing the air from her lungs. She hit the ground hard and her rifle clattered from her hands.

Her world was all teeth as the thing loomed over her. The stabbing pain of its front paws digging into her ribcage made every breath a struggle. She twisted and turned, desperate to avoid the gnashing teeth drawing closer.

"Rachel!" Elurin's shout rose above the creature's growling.

Thump. The creature squealed, scrambling off Rachel and raking her belly with its claws. Thin lines of agony. It faced Elurin, who stood right behind it. She held a dented water purifier in her hand.

"Shoot it!" Elurin shouted, her eyes wide with panic.

Rachel searched desperately for her rifle. It had skidded a few feet away, but she grabbed for it and fired.

The round struck the beast's shoulder. It wheezed in pain and hesitated, seemingly unsure which of them to attack. Before it could decide, Elurin grabbed its neck.

The beast went rigid, then collapsed without another sound. Its body twitched, then went still. Rachel sucked in heaving breaths, heart racing. She was pretty sure she'd just seen death incarnate, and it had been about to eat her.

"Fuck," she said, crawling shakily to her feet.

Elurin hurried over. "Don't touch my hands," she warned, offering Rachel her armored forearm instead.

"What was that thing?" Rachel accepted Elurin's elbow, rising to her feet.

"Vilodent," Elurin said. "They're fast, mean fuckers. Flesh-eaters."

Rachel looked at the vilodent's corpse. Big was an understatement. If it had stood on its hind legs, it would have been taller than she was by half again.

"Did you poison it?" she asked, remembering Elurin's warning. Elurin nodded, so Rachel continued, "Glad I didn't shoot a second time. If my aim had been bad, I could've blown your head off."

Elurin gave her a slightly wild smile. "I knew you wouldn't."

"That would've been something." Rachel gave a groaning laugh. "Shooting the first ikthian who made me think shooting ikthians was a bad idea."

Elurin started to reply but closed her mouth and tilted her head in the direction opposite the crash site. She tapped her gills; a gesture Rachel didn't understand. Rachel gave an inquiring look, so Elurin put her hand flat over her mouth instead.

Rachel recognized that one–a naledai gesture similar to a shushing finger for humans. She remained silent. Elurin crept behind a nearby tree with drooping fronds, and Rachel followed.

As she crouched beside Elurin, she heard the sound of footsteps. Three helmeted ikthians in lightweight purple armor entered the clearing, carrying weapons. One of them gestured at the dead vilodent.

Cold fear shot down Rachel's spine. She exchanged a look with Elurin. *Do I shoot?* She nodded at her rifle. Seekers usually travelled in pods of six, which meant there were likely three more somewhere nearby. But since they were concealed, it was the ideal time to attack.

Elurin nodded back.

Rachel took a steadying breath, as she'd been trained to do, and fired. The ikthian closest to the vilodent went down with a smoking hole in their chestplate. The remaining seekers stiffened, searching for whoever had fired on them. Rachel dispatched another ikthian, this one with a shot to the head. The seeker crumpled.

The final seeker managed to reach for their weapon. They shot at the tree where Rachel and Elurin were hiding, and Rachel fired back. Both missed. The tree shuddered, and the smell of burnt wood filled Rachel's nose. Her own shot went wide, firing somewhere over the remaining seeker's shoulder.

"Run!" Elurin yelled.

This time, she was the one who pulled Rachel out of danger. The tree groaned, then toppled directly onto the third ikthian. Its trunk thudded to the ground, and a shower of leaves drifted down, but the seeker clambered back up. Rachel fired another shot for cover and raced for the crash site.

"We should use the beacon," Elurin panted, running alongside her. "Too late to worry about discovery—they've already found us. Our only chance is to hide until help gets here."

Rachel grimaced. She heard more footsteps crashing through the trees. Their chance to hide was slipping away by the second.

***

Maia hesitated outside the interrogation room, resisting the impulse to pick at the webbing between her fingers. Such an action would be childish, particularly while Odelle stood beside her. But Maia couldn't help feeling childish. It had been years since she'd seen her mother. She hadn't even bothered to say goodbye before fleeing Dominion space.

"Are you all right?" Odelle asked, her brow knit with concern. "If you don't want to do this—"

"What I want is irrelevant," Maia answered, unable to dull the edge of bitterness in her voice.

Odelle frowned. "No, it isn't."

"Would you be able to live with yourself if you refused to participate in a single conversation, which might reveal essential Dominion intelligence?"

"No, but the offer to refuse stands. I won't force you to speak with Irana."

Dragging it out would only worsen her anxiety, Maia decided. She squared her shoulders and nodded. Odelle opened the door, but Maia entered alone. The room was small, its only furniture a table with two chairs. Maia glanced to the corners, trying to see the cameras, but mostly avoiding looking at the seated figure waiting for her.

"Maia." Irana's voice reached toward her, curling under her skin.

Reluctantly, Maia turned toward the table. Irana looked less than well. Though she had clearly received better treatment in Daashu than Taylor—perhaps something to do with their perceived usefulness—she was thinner than Maia remembered. Waifish. Her silver skin flaked at the edges of her crest, and it had no sheen at all. She made a note to ask Odelle what medical treatment her mother had been given.

Or I could ask her directly. It was as safe a topic as any to start with. Maia sat, finally giving into the urge to pick at her fingers. She did so under the table, where her mother wouldn't see. "Hello, mother. Have you received proper food, water, and medical care during your stay?"

"'My stay' makes it sound like a vacation." Irana's voice held the same amount of practiced detachment as Maia's own. "But yes. I currently have everything I need. Thank you for asking."

Silence reigned. Maia chewed her lip, then stopped. It would be yet another thing for her mother to disapprove of. "Taylor, the other prisoner we rescued, was severely malnourished. I wanted to make sure."

To Maia's immense surprise, Irana's face softened. There was even a hint of a smile. "The dark-haired human? I remember her."

Maia had no idea how her mother had interacted with Taylor while in Daashu and wasn't sure she wanted to know.

"A brave human," Irana continued. "She threatened the guards, goading them to poison her into unconsciousness so they would stop torturing me."

Maia's heart clenched. "That doesn't surprise me at all."

"You know her well?" Irana asked.

"My mate," Maia explained. After everything Taylor had sacrificed, Maia refused to acknowledge her as anything less. She was surprised yet again when Irana merely nodded. "Well?" Maia asked, once the silence became oppressive once more. "No admonishments for bonding with an alien? A 'lesser being'?"

Irana shrugged, partially. "I have lost almost everything, my station and reputation included. There is no one left to think poorly of me due to your choice to bond with one of the lesser species." Her tone presented this as a simple statement of fact rather than a reprimand.

Maia sat back in her chair, trying not to appear bewildered. This woman hardly seemed like her mother. Irana had always been an exacting parent, with high standards and higher expectations. To hear her so casually dismiss the revelation that her daughter's mate was an alien left Maia off-balance, like a ship struck by an asteroid.

Irana continued, "But it is my hope that one thing remains."

Maia snapped back to the present. "Yes?"

"My daughter." Irana's arm twitched, as though she wanted to reach across the table, but had forgotten the cuffs she wore. She stared at Maia with doleful eyes. "I was not the parent you needed. I was often away, and I discounted many of your wants and desires. But now, after being held in Daashu...I am relieved to find you alive and unharmed."

Unharmed? Though she hadn't sustained the same physical injuries Taylor had—or even Irana, for that matter—Maia doubted that. Her old life had not been happy, but it had been relatively safe. Familiar. Routine.

The current Maia had none of those things. Any day, the Dominion might discover the coordinates of the hidden Jor'al base and bomb it. She had been through multiple firefights, and it was only due to luck, Taylor's protection, and Akton's training that she'd come out alive. Nightmares still plagued her sleep.

Some harms cannot be undone. That includes the harm my mother has done to me.

"It will take more than a single expression of remorse to mend our relationship. You contributed to a regime that subjugated other sentient beings." A lump formed in Maia's throat, and her eyes stung with the bitterness of shame. Even though she had never been part of Corvis' inner circle herself, to have such a person for a mother horrified her, however reasonable Irana's behavior seemed now. "I stand against the Dominion and everything it represents. What do you stand for?"

Irana's eyes widened. "To be honest, I have not considered it. I never thought I would leave Daashu alive. When I arrived here, my only goals were my continued survival and to see you again."

Maia blinked tears from her eyes. She couldn't break down—not now. "Then, for me, will you help Odelle? Will you answer all her questions honestly, and tell her everything you know that might be useful?"

"Yes," Irana answered.

Maia remained unconvinced. "Just because I asked?"

"Children are a poor mother's pearls," Irana said.

Maia sucked in a breath. Her mother had often recited ikthian proverbs in her youth, but never that one. Most ikthian proverbs having to do with family were about loyalty and obedience, usually from youths to their elders, children to their parents. Irana had been fond of those.

But this one was different. *Children are a poor mother's pearls.* It struck her in an unexpected way. She gazed at Irana for a long time, trying to decide if there was anything selfish in her demeanor, but came to no solid conclusions. *Does she really mean what she says, or am I simply all that's left to her? Would she care the same if she could return to her old life?* Those were questions Maia was not ready to ask, let alone receive answers to. But, for now, it would have to be enough.

"I will visit again," Maia said, rising from her chair.

Irana seemed disappointed but held her tongue.

"I need to watch over Taylor," Maia added, to soften the blow. "She is still recovering."

"Swiftly, I hope."

"Odelle is outside, monitoring our talk."

"Send her in," Irana said. "I will fulfill my part of the bargain."

"Thank you." Maia managed a genuine smile before she left the room, but still heaved a sigh of relief when the door closed. She slumped against the wall to regain her bearings. Her hands trembled. Her mind whirled. *Go back to Taylor. You are most at peace with her.*

Odelle entered the hallway through a door slightly to the left—the observation room, Maia assumed. She stood straighter when she noticed Generals Kross and Oranthis were with her.

"Generals," she said, offering a cross-armed salute.

"Kalanis. Good work."

Maia waited, expecting a "but" in that sentence. It never came. "Thank you? I suppose I might be making my own life more difficult by asking, but...aren't I going to suffer consequences for stealing a stealth fighter and going to Daashu against your direct orders, sirs?"

Kross actually smiled. "You returned with several valuable prisoners. I don't think punishment is in order...at least, not for you. When Elurin gets back, I'll certainly be having stern words with *her.*"

His use of the word "when" buoyed Maia's mood significantly. "Then I hope for her safe return."

"As do we all," Oranthis said. "Dismissed, Kalanis. Go look after your human."

With one last glance at Odelle, who gave her a grin, she headed back to the medical ward and Taylor.

***

Rachel popped her rifle's heat sink, barely hearing the hiss of steam above her own pounding heart. She and Elurin were crouched behind the makeshift barricade they'd constructed from one of the ship's warped outer panels, where they had been for the past several hours. Shaking with fear and exhaustion, she tried to maintain focus. She'd been in combat before, but never for so long outside of training simulations.

Meanwhile, the seekers seemed content to wait them out. They had taken refuge behind the trees on the edge of the clearing, firing every so often to make sure Rachel and Elurin never let their guard down.

A little too often, lately. Their rear was safe, with their backs to the ship, but on a hunch, Rachel checked their right flank. There! A flash of silver and black amidst the foliage. She fired, but the lone seeker retreated behind another tree, their ambush ruined.

"Thanks, Rachel." Elurin fired off another shot, but she missed as well, ducking before any returning rounds could hit her.

"I have your back," Rachel said. For how long, though, she couldn't say. She and Elurin had cover, but they couldn't hole up here forever. Eventually, they would get tired, thirsty, and desperate. Then the seekers would strike in earnest. Their only chance was if someone friendly got the signal from their beacon, which Elurin had activated right before the seekers caught up with them. "How are we doing on power?"

Elurin checked the readout on the side of her weapon. "My weapon's charged, but they're bound to try something new sooner or later. We've been awake and pinned down for almost twenty standard hours. Sleepy soldiers miss things..."

Rachel gritted her teeth. That probably meant an ambush—and she suspected there was more than one squad of seekers in this jungle. She had no doubt their enemies had radioed for reinforcements. *If I go out like this, at least Taylor and the others escaped. I accomplished my final mission...I think.* She wanted to believe the others made it safely to Nakonum.

"Harris!" Elurin yelled.

Rachel whipped around, bringing the nose of her rifle with her. Damn! Her suspicions had been right. Reinforcements had arrived–a fresh squad of six seekers in heavy, black plated armor—far sturdier than the armor the scouts they'd encountered in the forest were wearing. Rachel wasn't sure their rifles packed enough power to bring them down.

"Where are *our* people?" Rachel snarled, firing a shot at the nearest seeker. As she'd feared, her round didn't penetrate the black chestplate. *Fuck.*

Elurin shot her a resigned look. "No idea."

Rachel inhaled, drawing upon all the courage she could muster, remembering every soldier she'd ever befriended who'd died in combat. If it was her time to join them, she'd take as many seekers with her as possible.

She opened fire.

The rounds bounced off harmlessly as three seekers breached the makeshift barricade, tearing the paneling away and pinning Rachel against the wrecked ship. She jammed her rifle into the nearest seeker's gut, earning a low grunt, but it only delayed her enemy for a moment. They grabbed her rifle, tearing it from her grasp and tossing it out of reach.

Rachel thrashed, trying to crawl after it. Cold hands grabbed her by the throat.

She froze. The palms of the seeker's gloves had a strange, porous texture. *For the toxins.* Her burst of rage and determination fizzled out, replaced by a sense of resignation. This was it, then. One wrong move, and she'd be flooded with poison.

Her darting eyes met Elurin's. Her companion had been restrained by two other seekers, who had removed her weapon. Sadness stabbed Rachel's heart. She'd accepted her own inevitable death, but the thought that Elurin would die here, too...

Fwoosh!

A burst of wind screeched overhead, and Rachel looked up in spite of the seeker's hold on her. A gleaming silver ball swooped through the air, firing thin beams of light. Rachel felt the heat of a beam streak by, mere inches from her face. To her complete shock, her captor let go, collapsing to the ground with half their body smoldering. Beside her, one of the seekers restraining Elurin fell with a gaping hole in their chest, while the third dove away and hit the ground.

"Get down!" Rachel shouted to Elurin, taking cover behind what remained of the warped panel they'd been using for protection. The other seekers, who had begun to emerge from the jungle, retreated into the trees.

Elurin joined Rachel in a crouch. "Help's finally here," she panted, looking relieved.

The spherical ship landed a few yards away. A door opened on one side, extending a short metal bridgeway.

"Climb aboard," a naledai woman called. With her broad shoulders, long digging claws, and standard grey resistance armor, she was unmistakably an ally.

Rachel ran for the ship. It fired its rotating guns to cover their escape, and she and Elurin arrived safely through the doors and into the decon chamber. The naledai made sure the doors closed. The ship took off, causing Rachel to stagger and slap a hand on the wall for balance. She sagged with relief. Moments before, she'd thought she was about to die. Now, she was safe. None of it felt real.

But it was real, because the decon chamber hissed open, revealing their savior. "Elurin," the naledai chuckled, removing her helmet. "Why is it your ass I always end up rescuing?"

A big grin spread across Elurin's face. "Jethra Kertamen! What're you doing all the way out here?"

"Looking for you, rockhead. I hoped you'd grown out of the whole death wish thing, but apparently not." The naledai opened her huge arms, and the two embraced.

Watching the whole ritual made Rachel feel strangely queasy. *Definitely the ship,* she told herself.

"Jethra," Elurin said, "this is Rachel Harris. Human. Rebel. Vilodent slayer."

"Vilodent slayer?" Jethra's eyebrows rose into the mop of yellow fur on her head.

"Well, Elurin helped with the vilodent," Rachel confessed, but the moment of admiration snapped her out of her funk. *She rescued us. Be grateful!*

"A mutual kill is still a kill," Jethra said. "I've seen those things wipe out entire squads."

"Including you?" Elurin prodded.

"Oh, yeah. I've been eaten by vilodents twice. Makes it into my top ten worst deaths for sure." The naledai gave Rachel a hearty pat on the back, and she felt the thump through her armor. "Come on, let's get you hydrated and cleaned up."

Rachel grinned. She and Elurin had made it out alive, and not much the worse for wear. Her adrenaline dropped off, leaving her limbs shaky and her steps unsteady. She was grateful when Elurin offered a supportive arm.

"Deep breaths," Elurin said. "You'll feel better after you get some water."

Rachel nodded. When they got back to Nakonum, she needed to find whatever passed for alcohol and have a lot of that, too.

Chapter Seven

TAYLOR CLUTCHED MAIA'S ARM, summoning the strength for one more step. The movement wasn't painful, but after walking the hospital corridor for several minutes, she felt like she was dragging her feet through cement. Nevertheless, she felt a sense of pride as well. She was up and moving, if only in short bursts.

"Well done," Maia said, offering a tender smile. "Your endurance is returning."

Taylor squeezed Maia's forearm, pausing to catch her breath. She hadn't realized how much she'd missed walking until Maia had helped her take her first tentative steps the day before, under a naledai doctor's supervision.

"So, can a woman who walked down the hall almost entirely by herself get a kiss, maybe?" she asked Maia.

Said hall was mostly empty, due to the late hour. Only a skeleton crew of doctors and assistants remained to staff the medical ward, which meant the path was clear and silent.

The mottled blue spots on Maia's crest deepened to a faint purple color. She leaned into kiss Taylor's cheek, but Taylor turned, catching Maia's lips instead. It was a soft kiss, but it lingered.

"You know I would give you anything, Taylor," Maia murmured when they withdrew.

Taylor squeezed Maia's arm again. "I'm the one who owes you, I think."

"There is no 'owing,'" Maia said in English, shaking her head. "To be honest, I've lost count of how many times we've saved each other."

"Your English is getting better," Taylor noted.

Normally, Maia spoke in her own language, which the subdermal translator behind Taylor's ear interpreted automatically. Still, she was touched that Maia had taken an interest in her language.

"I completed several English training modules while you were gone. If your jailers had removed your translator, I wanted to be sure I could communicate with you, at least on a rudimentary level."

Taylor felt an uncomfortable swell of guilt. *Maia learned some English, how to shoot a gun, and how to provide basic medical care, all while I was locked away.* While it was impressive that she had learned so many new skills, it also cemented the fact they were at war. Maia was deeply involved in a war against her own people—in no small part because of Taylor. *She'll never be the same as she was, and I'm part of the reason.*

"Taylor?"

She turned, realizing Maia had noticed her sudden silence. "I'm fine. Not in pain. Just thinking."

"Unpleasant thoughts?" Maia asked gently.

"It doesn't matter. I'm okay."

Maia's forehead furrowed. "I know I've suggested it before, but I think you should consider speaking with one of the trauma counselors on-base."

"I know," Taylor said, without much enthusiasm. *How well would a naledai understand human mental health issues? And what does it matter, if I get killed next time? Because I have to go back into the field eventually. I'm a soldier.*

Her identity as a soldier was one of the few things that had remained to her in Daashu. Something to cling to, something they couldn't strip away. Even now, she couldn't see any other option but to return to war.

Is that fair to Maia? She risked her life to rescue you—are you going to risk it again? Maybe not just because you're a soldier, but because dying in battle would mean no more nightmares?

They were, ironically, exactly the kind of thoughts she should process with a trauma counselor. Just the idea put her hackles up.

"Hey, Loo! You beautiful son of a bitch."

The sound of her old rank pulled Taylor away from her thoughts. She turned, and her mood leapt when she saw who had called out. She dropped Maia's arm, walking quickly back the way she'd come without a second thought to her tired, trembling legs. There, standing in the medical ward with a doctor and two assistants, was someone she hadn't expected to see again–Rachel Harris. She didn't seem to be missing any important body parts, either.

"Harris," she said, pulling Rachel into the tightest hug she could manage. "You smell awful."

"Well, sorry I stink after crash landing in a jungle while trying to save you. You're welcome, by the way."

Tears sprang to Taylor's eyes, and she hugged Rachel even harder. She hadn't realized how much she'd missed her friend, or even just seeing another human. Finally, she let go of Rachel. "Where's Elurin?"

"Alive and well," Rachel said, with an odd sort of smile that Taylor couldn't quite interpret. "The generals wanted a word, since she didn't have any major injuries. I assume she's getting her head bitten off. By the way, I shot a crocodile tiger."

"A what?" Taylor asked.

"Well, Elurin called it a vilodent, but I killed it," Rachel said, her eyes dancing. "Huge. Sharp teeth."

"How big was it?" Taylor frowned. Surely Rachel didn't mean a centaur-like animal that was literally half-crocodile and half-tiger, but something more like a large, reptilian cat. The resulting image in her brain was surprisingly cute.

"Bigger than three of you, and you're built like a brick shithouse," Rachel explained. "At least, you used to be."

"Excuse me?" Maia said.

Taylor stifled a laugh. She doubted Maia's language modules had covered idioms like that.

Rachel clapped her on the shoulder and turned to Maia. "Good to see you too, Kalanis."

Taylor glanced between them in mild disbelief.

"You were gone for a while, remember?" Rachel said. "Who do you think kept pushing for permission to go save your ass? The two of us, that's who. We're the Taylor Rescue Squad."

They high fived, and Taylor's jaw almost dropped. The old Rachel never would have spoken kindly to an ikthian, let alone touch one bare-handed. Obviously, she and Maia trusted each other to a certain extent and had even formed a friendship.

I guess we are a hyper adaptable species, and Rachel's always been smart. If it had been her assignment to guard Maia on Earth instead of mine, I'm sure she would've changed her mind as fast as I did.

"Is this a good time to say 'I told you so,' Harris?"

"Elurin and I infiltrated Tarkoht together, remember? I've been cool with non-Dominion ikthians for a while."

Taylor offered Rachel an upward nod of approval. "Cool enough to teach Maia how to high-five, apparently."

A nearby assistant cleared their throat, an ikthian wearing blue scrubs and a rather no-nonsense expression. "I realize the two of you must be glad to see each other, but we have other patients who are sleeping. Also, we still need to take a look at Harris here."

As the assistant drew closer, Taylor's heart sped up. She took a step back. While Maia no longer triggered her panic response, other ikthians—especially ones she didn't know—still evoked deep feelings of fear that disgusted her. *Rachel's fine with ikthians now, and I'm the xenophobe. Great. Maybe I should talk to a trauma counselor.*

Rachel's brow furrowed, but she didn't say anything.

"Go on, Rachel," Maia said, smoothing the interaction over. "Let the professionals give you a clean bill of health. Taylor should get some more sleep anyway. It's late."

"Ugh. Sleep. Need me some of that." Rachel leaned in for another hug. "See you tomorrow, okay?"

Taylor hugged back. Rachel's embrace was warm, solid, and reassuring, even if she did smell like plasma rounds and day-old sweat. "I'll be here."

***

"Okay, you're finished," the ikthian field medic said, offering a friendly smile.

Elurin didn't feel the least bit encouraged. Yes, she'd been lucky. Of course she was grateful to have escaped the crash and the seekers, but the prospect of leaving the docking bay, where the field medic had met her with a cart of supplies, was terrifying. That meant reporting to the generals.

"Thanks," she mumbled, forcing a smile in return. She stood, took a deep breath, and straightened her shoulders. *Okay, Elurin. If they discharge you or bump you down to copilot on some backwater supply runs, you'll just have to deal. You disobeyed, even if it was for the right reasons.*

But she couldn't force herself to move. She stared stubbornly at her own feet, trying to summon her willpower, when a voice calling her name served as a welcome distraction. She looked up to see Sorra approaching at a fast clip, wearing a sharp, brown-gold rebel uniform without any decorations. As long as Elurin had known her, Sorra had never been fond of medals. Too ostentatious, Elurin supposed, although she'd never asked.

"I'm on my way to see the generals," she said, before Sorra could offer any instructions. "Just gathering my nerve. What'd they do to you?"

"What *can* they do to me?"

Elurin gave Sorra a skeptical look. Sorra liked to play the fearless defector, but that didn't mean she could go around doing whatever the fuck she wanted. *Or maybe I'm wrong. Maybe she can, and her attitude isn't all for show.*

"Have any idea what they'll do to me, then?"

One corner of Sorra's mouth quirked. "You owe me," she said, then nodded for Elurin to follow her.

Elurin tried to focus on the relief she felt instead of the annoyance. *Sorra wouldn't have smiled if I was really in deep waters, right?*

She clung to that hope as she followed Sorra out of the docking bay and into the network of tunnels beyond. "Hallways," technically but naledai were comfortable in extra-close quarters. Elurin always found them cramped and unsettling.

Sorra led her unerringly through the complex network. Before she knew it, they'd arrived at a pair of metallic doors near the heart of the warren. Two armed naledai guards surveyed them, holding rifles. Upon seeing Sorra, they stepped aside, allowing them both to pass.

The interior of the round room buzzed with activity. Glowing monitors circled the perimeter, attended by naledai in jumpsuits. When she entered, eager gazes darted her way. *Great. On top of everything else, my dressing-down has to be public.*

A large, oval-shaped table took up the center of the room, and it was there that the generals stood, obviously awaiting her arrival.

Oranthis looked up when the doors opened. Elurin snapped to attention and saluted. "Generals, sirs!"

Kross continued reading his datapad for a few seconds more before deigning to look up. "At ease."

Elurin dropped the salute, but her spine remained stiff. She couldn't help it.

Sorra didn't bother saluting, but she gave the generals a respectful nod.

"Report, pilot," Oranthis barked.

"Disobeyed direct orders and used my high-level clearance to commandeer a stealth fighter for a secret mission to Daashu. Retrieved five prisoners, alive—including a naledai prisoner in transit, Irana Kalanis, and Taylor Morgan. When we were pursued off-planet, Harris and I hung back to buy Sorra's transport vessel more time. Ended up wrecked on a terraformed Dominion world, far from civilization. Activated a distress beacon—was picked up by pilot Kertamen and her crew during a firefight with seekers. After medical evaluation and immediate debriefing, I reported straight here. No losses to report, other than the fighter."

She was out of breath by the time she finished. Her nerves stretched thin, but she forced herself not to quiver. Somehow, standing before the two naledai who would decide her fate reminded her of staring down the vilodent.

To her immense surprise, Kross gave Oranthis a sly look. "I heard she killed three vilodent bare-handed."

Heat rushed to Elurin's head spots. *The rumor mill's already going.* She couldn't help flashing back to that moment. Rachel had looked like some kind of vengeful goddess, half-sprawled on the ground, hair tossed, dark eyes flashing. Clutching the rifle. The sight was burned into Elurin's brain.

"Well?" Oranthis asked, and Elurin snapped back to the present, mildly bewildered when she noticed the twinkle in the general's eye. "Did you kill three vilodent during your unapproved rescue jaunt?"

Elurin gulped. "Just the one vilodent. I only poisoned it; Harris shot it. I was carrying the water purifier."

Kross and Oranthis exchanged glances. Unsure, Elurin looked to Sorra, who wasn't even trying to hide her smirk.

"Your flagrant disregard for our orders will not be ignored, nor will it go unpunished," Kross said, but Elurin could hear the warmth in his voice. "Your pilot's access to rebellion ships and supplies is hereby suspended. You are also grounded until further notice, with some exceptions."

"Exceptions, sirs?" she asked, tentatively.

The generals looked to Sorra.

"You answer to me now, flygirl," Sorra drawled, with no small amount of glee.

"Odelle has proposed a series of stealth missions, based on intelligence given to us by Irana Kalanis," Oranthis explained. "We believe this information to be genuine, as well as vital. You will escort Sorra to and from the given coordinates, so she may assess any potential threats and report back. This is only reconnaissance."

In spite of Oranthis' warnings, Elurin couldn't contain her bubbling excitement. *This doesn't sound much like a punishment, even if I do have to keep working with Sorra. Is this...a promotion?*

Apparently so, because Kross said, "Dismissed, pilot. Sorra will brief you on the mission tomorrow."

Elurin couldn't stifle a grin. "Sirs, yes, sirs!"

"And one more thing," he added, before Elurin could get too cocky. "Next time you pull a stunt like this, it won't just be you who pays for it. You wouldn't want your friend Valerius demoted, would you? Remember, rocks roll downhill."

Elurin's smile fell. "With all due respect, sirs, I talked him into going. I take full responsibility—"

"Yes, and Kalanis talked you into going," Oranthis said, waving a dismissive claw. "At this point, I don't care whose idea it was. If any of you pull unauthorized stealth missions in Dominion space again—and that includes you, Sorra—it will irreparably damage the alliance the naledai and Dominion defectors have worked so hard to establish. Is that clear?"

Sorra nodded. "Clear as a windless lake, generals."

"Good," Oranthis said.

"And Elurin," Kross added. "Try not to strangle any more dangerous animals. Poison won't always work fast enough to stop teeth. Dismissed."

***

Odelle scanned the terminal again, blinking the blur from her eyes. She wasn't sure how long she'd fended off sleep, but it was becoming a losing battle. Her head sank every few lines she read, and she was hard-pressed to stay standing. The bed in the opposite corner of the room called to her, and she was sorely tempted to continue her reading tucked beneath the covers.

She refocused on the problem at hand. While she felt confident in her latest course of action—sending Sorra and Elurin to investigate the coordinates Teichos Industries' databases and Irana had so generously provided—this latest development put a snag in her plan.

Two other sets of coordinates, buried deeper in the Teichos data, were right on top of rebel bases. Those two rebel bases had been uncommunicative for the past week or more. One was from Altos, Nakonum's fifth moon, which hosted a small but stable naledai community; and another, Xedos, a few planets' jump from the naledai homeworld. Mostly farmers. *Relatively safe places, considering they're occupied by the enemy...and no word at all.*

She had gone over both locations' final transmissions too many times to count but could find nothing odd. Not a single clue as to why the rebel cells had stopped all communication. She closed her eyes and rubbed her neck ridges. An ache was brewing, one that pounded all the way up her skull.

The sound of the door caused Odelle to open her eyes. She turned, smiling as Sorra entered. "You're back. How did it go?"

Sorra removed her brown and gold uniform jacket, slinging it onto the bed. "Well enough, but you knew it would, so why are you asking?"

"If you're going to be difficult, I'll be more specific. How did Elurin take the news?"

"How do you think?"

Odelle rolled her eyes. "Sometimes I'm sure I'll pass on to the ocean of stars before you ever give me a straight answer to a simple question."

"Elurin's fine." Sorra prowled over, placing both hands on Odelle's hips. "Don't worry about her."

"Should I pay attention to you instead?" Odelle asked, leaning into her mate's touch. She rested a moment, letting her eyes drift shut.

Sorra tilted her head. "You might enjoy that more than whatever else you're thinking about," she said, a note of concern in her voice.

Odelle sighed. "I've been looking at the coordinates that have stopped transmitting. We need to send someone to investigate."

"Do the generals agree?"

She nodded. "They're as concerned as I am. For all we know, the cells might have been compromised."

Sorra's brow furrowed. "I've been meaning to send Valerius on a new errand. Could be a chance for him to spread his wings as a team leader. That naledai's got the makings of a first-class officer, spy, or anything else he sets his mind to."

Odelle managed another weary smile. "Indeed, he does. Do you think the generals would agree to send him?"

"Why not? It could be a reward doubling as a punishment, and it might solve a problem for them. But what to do with Harris."

"She only just got back, and they almost died!"

Sorra snorted. "When did that ever stop someone like her?"

Odelle did not deign to give rhetorical question an answer.

"Harris will be clamoring to tag along with me and Elurin—and in no possible universe will the generals let her after their last little excursion. I'll tell them to send her with Akton so he has to deal with Harris' bullshit. Bet the generals will consider that—"

"Judicious punishment?"

"I was going to say hilarious, but sure." Sorra leaned past her, switching off the monitor's screen.

"Excuse you," Odelle said, although she was far too tired to muster up much indignation. "I was using that."

"It's late. You almost yawned in the middle of that sentence. Come to bed."

"But—"

"Let Valerius and Harris worry about it."

Odelle hung her head. Her limbs felt far too heavy, and she could hear the white hiss of the waves in her head—the blood rushing through her own ears, she knew, but that was what it sounded like. "I'm not sure I can sleep."

"You'll sleep," Sorra said, already steering her toward the bed. "I have a lot of weapons in my arsenal."

Chapter Eight

"SO, ARE YOU AND Harris fucking?"

"What?" Elurin looked up from the dash and turned toward Sorra, who leaned back in the copilot's chair. The rebel leader stared out the ship's viewport with an air of bored disinterest, not even bothering to glance in Elurin's direction.

"Just a question to pass the time," Sorra said. "No need to get all offended."

The spots on Elurin's crest burned. She understood the impulse to make conversation, especially during the tense moments before a mission, but Sorra's manner was a bit much.

Not that it matters. Me and Harris fucking is about as likely as an asteroid strike. While Elurin had definitely taken notice, she was positive the human didn't return her interest. *Rachel might be friendly with non-Dominion ikthians now, but it's a long way from friendship to fucking.*

"If this is your way of easing the tension, it sucks." Elurin returned her attention to the ship's dash. They were using a repurposed Dominion fighter, which she'd restored herself and tentatively dubbed the *Riptide,* but if anyone asked for security codes, their cover would be blown.

So far, their plan seemed to be working. They were only a few minutes out from the coordinates Odelle had given them and hadn't encountered any hostile vessels—or any vessels at all. Unfortunately, neither the Teichos Industry data, nor Irana, had been able to tell them exactly what to expect upon arrival.

"This is what I get for trying to be sociable," Sorra muttered.

"Demanding to know whether I fucked an alien isn't being sociable. It's being an asshole."

Sorra's laugh grated like metal against metal. "I won't deny that."

They flew onward, approaching the programmed coordinates at a fast clip.

"So, did you?" Sorra asked.

Elurin rolled her eyes. "You really *are* nosey today."

"I'm not hearing a no."

"Why do you care? We aren't friends."

A smirk played about Sorra's lips. "Elurin, I'm hurt."

I won't react. It's just Sorra trying to get under my skin. "So, what did you do to land someone like Odelle, anyway? She's so far out of your quadrant it isn't even funny."

Sorra's smirk grew wider. "Do you really want to know?"

To avoid answering, Elurin checked the dash again, noting their progress. "Almost there. I'll do a fly-by to get some readings, then pull in somewhere relatively safe."

Sorra merely nodded.

To Elurin's relief, there were no other ships around Askari, the tiny, uninhabited and un-terraformed moon Irana had told them about. That in itself was strange. If the Dominion had a compound here, there should be some kind of defense. She pushed through the atmosphere, speeding through a series of reddish rocks and canyons.

"Pretty," Sorra commented.

Elurin agreed. Pity this moon didn't have colonists. The landscape was lovely.

Soon, Elurin spotted what appeared to be a terraforming bubble on the *Riptide's* dash. She activated the ship's cloak, one of the many upgrades she'd added during her downtime. Being a former Dominion pilot had its advantages, like knowing which parts of the electromagnetic spectrum the Dominion's defensive programs monitored.

Before long, they reached the bubble. It was smaller than Elurin expected, only large enough to house three spherical silver buildings. She landed the *Riptide* behind a large outcropping of rock and began her readings.

There were definitely ikthians inside the base. The *Riptide's* cameras and VI had even put together some projected schematics for the three buildings. But the bubble would present a problem. The only way in was through the top, and it needed to be opened from inside.

"There's only one thing for it," Sorra said, sounding far from enthused. "Wait for someone to fly out and hope the cloak you designed is as good as you say."

Elurin sighed. It wasn't a great plan, but there weren't many other options besides an outright assault. That wouldn't work with one ship. "Guess this just turned into a stakeout," she said, unfastening her harness and getting out of her seat. At least they'd brought food along.

***

Rachel shifted uncomfortably in the copilot's seat as Akton steered their small ship toward Altos, and the secret rebel base they were bound for. So far, things were unnervingly quiet. Akton had tried contacting Altos Base several times already but received no reply.

It's just like Odelle said. What could have happened down there?

"K3 Oserion to Altos Flight Control," Akton repeated into the ship's radio. "Requesting permission to land."

No response.

Rachel jiggled her knee, burning nervous energy. She should have been pleased about being back in the field. Sitting around recuperating had always left her twitchy. But the nature of this mission unsettled her. *Is it because there's been no communication from the base we're checking, or because Elurin isn't here?*

Since leaving Earth, Rachel had shared Elurin's company far more often than not. The ikthian had been her guide to the alien worlds beyond the Coalition's colonies, and Rachel hadn't realized how reassuring her presence had been...until it was gone. She considered Akton a friend, but it wasn't the same.

Before she could spare any more thoughts for Elurin, they breached the moon's atmosphere. Low vibrations coursed through the ship. She held onto her harness through the minor turbulence.

"K3 Oserion to Altos Flight Control," Akton repeated. "Requesting permission to land."

No answer. Akton looked at Rachel, concern on his shaggy features. "I've got a bad feeling that everyone's dead or fled."

"Let's hope fled," Rachel said, but her hopes weren't high. If anyone had escaped Altos alive, surely they would have contacted Nakonum for assistance.

Their descent became eerier as they dipped groundward. At first, the landscape consisted of furrowed crop fields tucked between symmetrical sand dunes. Naledai farms. It was ingenious, how they managed to grow things in such dry climates. Rachel wondered how the humidity-loving ikthians had conquered the naledai in their own territory. *Guess better weapons beat better agriculture.*

Gradually, the farms condensed into a small rural community. The round lumps of the naledai dwellings gave way to taller buildings. Not as tall as skyscrapers, but Rachel hadn't expected that. Naledai preferred digging down instead of building up.

"This is wrong," Akton said, studying the ship's dash. "I'm not seeing any signs of life in the colony. Are you?"

Rachel's heart sank. Looking out the viewport, she couldn't see the movement of tiny people. There wasn't even any air traffic for Akton to steer through. Altos was, for all intents and purposes, abandoned. "Should we land? I know we aren't at the rebel base yet, but this is wrong."

Akton answered by doing so. The ship touched down on an area of scrubby grass between several buildings. *Had it once been a park?* A place for naledai children to play, maybe.

"Stay sharp," Akton said. "It seems quiet, but that doesn't mean we're safe."

Rachel unfastened her harness and put on her helmet. Akton depressurized the ship, and they headed through the narrow decon chamber before disembarking. A soft, warm wind blew across the scrub grass as Rachel stepped onto the field. A distant animal's call sounded, reminding her of a bird cry. Other than that, it was quiet.

"Where is everyone?" she murmured, glancing between the nearby buildings. Most were two-story, hump-like affairs, with round tops and flat foundations, although they had been constructed with reinforced steel rather than dirt and rock.

Akton lifted his rifle. "Let's find out."

Rachel followed Akton away from the field and along a nearby street. There, they found their first naledai, an adult male, dead. He looked thin, almost emaciated. Patches of his fur had fallen out, and the bare parts bore nasty-looking blisters. When Rachel knelt to examine him, she didn't note any obvious injuries.

Guess you were unlucky. I'm sorry.

"Harris, over here." Akton pointed to the building.

Rachel rose to catch up. Akton had peeked inside one of the larger buildings, and when he pulled his head back through the doorway, his face was crestfallen behind his visor. She steeled herself before peering inside.

There was no telling what purpose the building once served. All the furniture had been removed or pushed against the walls, leaving the enormous room bare. Bare except for hundreds of cots, and the bodies lying on them.

Lined up in neat rows much like the farm dunes, in each cot lay a body, some of them painfully small. Children. There were corpses dressed in decontamination suits on the floor, too—sprawled as though they'd collapsed. The place smelled like a hospital under the unmistakable scent of death.

"If so many people were...sick? They had to be sick or poisoned, right? Why didn't they go to the hospital?" Rachel asked.

Akton heaved a deep sigh. "I saw a sign for a hospital down the road. I have a feeling if we go there, it'll be the same story. They probably brought emergency services here because the place ran out of room." He regarded Rachel with sad brown eyes. "They weren't prepared for whatever did this."

"We should report back to Nakonum. Get a biohazard team out here. Do the rebels even have something like that?"

"I don't know," Akton said, "but we aren't equipped to handle it. We don't know why the people here didn't seek help off-moon. Did the Dominion intercept all ships and transmissions requesting aid, or..."

Rachel caught Akton's meaning. A shiver ran down her spine. "Or whatever killed them works really fast."

＊＊

"Hey, someone's leaving." Elurin's voice cut through the silence.

Sorra looked up from the idle game she'd been playing on her comm. She put the slim black wristband in rest mode and checked the viewport. The large, silvery-white bubble surrounding the spherical buildings had opened, allowing a transport ship to emerge through its roof. She strapped herself back into her seat and nodded to Elurin. "Go."

Elurin did. As copilot, Sorra helped her activate their cloaking devices—one to fool any short-range scanners and another to bend the light into a reflective shimmer around their ship. The first was more effective than the second, because if someone studied the sky closely, they might see a telling shine.

Lucky tides were with them, and Elurin sped through the bubble's entrance moments before it closed. She touched down behind the largest of the three buildings, amidst several other parked ships. Mostly transports, only two fighters. Apparently, this base wasn't prepared for an attack. Was secrecy supposed to be its main defense? If so, what was Chancellor Corvis hiding here?

"Let's disable those fighters," Sorra said. "If we have to leave in a hurry, I'd rather be running from transports."

"Good idea." Elurin powered down the ship and stood, checking her armor and weapon.

Sorra did the same. The standard Dominion gear was made of black, lightweight polymer, able to withstand basic fire and better for being stealthy. She checked the camera feed going from her helmet to her comm. She'd promised Odelle she would record everything, to help unravel the mystery.

They exited their ship, checking for anyone who might have caught a glimpse of their landing. Their luck held. There was no one around to notice them.

"Where are the guards?" Elurin whispered through the helmet's radio. "A place like this must have some."

As it turned out, the guards were posted at the entrance to the hangar. Two stood at the gate leading toward the buildings, conversing. One laughed, but Sorra remained unaffected. Years ago, she might have felt a twinge of regret. Not anymore. There were plenty of "nice" Dominion sympathizers, but evil didn't always look the part. Her job was to stamp it out regardless.

She exchanged a meaningful look with Elurin, gesturing at the nearest guard's head with the nose of her rifle. Then, she took aim and fired, while Elurin did the same. The guards fell in unison, and Sorra scurried along the shipyard wall, grabbing one of the limp corpses under the arms and dragging it back out of sight. She and Elurin stashed the corpses underneath one of the empty fighters.

"That will be a fun surprise if anyone tries to follow us," Sorra remarked as she took her guard's comm. She used her own comm to scan the guard's face and hands, in case they were needed.

Elurin ducked around the other side, and Sorra kept watch as Elurin did something to the ship's downward-facing plasma propulsion units. She soon peeked back into view, smirking. "I almost hope they try to chase us now."

"No, you don't. Let's go." Sorra headed for the buildings, Elurin matching her stride.

"So, don't look at anyone, don't say anything, and act like we're supposed to be here?" Elurin asked.

Sorra nodded. "That's how it's done. If we get stopped, let me do the talking."

They returned to the gate where the two guards had stood watch. Sorra fiddled with the comm she'd stolen, sending through a series of security codes from the Teichos databases. The gates opened, allowing entry to the first building.

Scientific outposts resembling this one—bubbles on otherwise un-terraformed planets—were usually bustling with people. Armed guards, scientists in lab coats, other support staff. A reception desk.

Not so here.

They had emerged into a smallish round foyer, with three clear elevator tubes at equidistant points around the room. Silence greeted them.

"Spooky," Elurin muttered.

Sorra agreed. She approached one of the elevators. Fiddling with the dead guard's comm caused it to activate, and the elevator arrived at their floor with a chirp. An ikthian man in a lab coat, presumably a scientist, was already inside, and they joined him. Sorra gave him a polite nod as she entered, with Elurin a step behind.

"Which floor?" he asked.

Sorra noted that he'd already pressed one of the buttons–1BG. "Same, thanks."

The scientist didn't question her, and the short ride passed in silence before the tube opened again, revealing a brightly lit, blue-tinted hallway lined with clear walls. He exited, and Sorra watched him go through one of the nearby doors without a backward glance.

After all these years, it still surprises me how many layers of security you can breach just by staying quiet and pretending you belong. She left the elevator, picking up the scent of filtered air and disinfectant. Elurin followed.

The lights within the clear-walled rooms on either side of the corridor were brighter than the lights on the ceiling, and it took a moment for Sorra's eyes to adjust. A large room to her left contained large machines—medical equipment, if she had to guess—and more scientists in lab coats, lost in the glow of terminal screens and datapads. Some kind of laboratory.

A series of smaller, divided rooms to the right caught her gaze next. She had seen plenty of awful things. Dead bodies. Prisoners of war. A few comrades had died in her arms. But she'd never witnessed anything like this.

They were adjacent to what looked like hospital rooms, visible through what Sorra assumed were one-way mirrors. Silver, sterile, with impersonal-looking exam tables that had shackles on them.

Naledai were lashed to the tables. Their condition ranged from healthy-looking specimens who struggled and screamed, though Sorra couldn't hear it, to still forms who looked half-dead. Most were missing feet, or in the early stages of growing them back. The reason hit Sorra like a blast of ice, to ruin any possible chance of escape, were any prisoner to do the unthinkable and break their bonds.

But that wasn't the worst. All the naledai were visibly malnourished, missing large chunks of fur. Angry-looking blisters covered their bodies, and their hollow chests jerked with visible coughing fits.

As Sorra studied the rooms, she realized several of the exam tables also bore humans. She hadn't met that many humans, but even from a distance, she knew their skin wasn't supposed to look so angry and raw. Some of them looked worse than Morgan after her stint in Daashu.

And in the rooms further along...ikthians. Perhaps thirty of them. As disgusted as Sorra was by the treatment of the naledai and human test subjects—for they could be nothing else but test subjects—seeing her own people weak, blistered, and half-rotting made Sorra tremble.

She never trembled.

As she stood in place, trying to collect herself and decide how to proceed, an ikthian in a full-body protective suit entered the nearest room from an adjoining one. They started taking the vitals of a blistered, unconscious ikthian as if it were an everyday occurrence.

Sorra forced herself to keep watching. Her immediate instinct was to help, but there was nothing she could do while surrounded by enemies. Not to mention other dangers. The scientist's protective suit spoke volumes, and Sorra's mind leapt to contamination or disease. She could only hope that filming the incident would provide some insight for the rebellion.

"Fuck," Elurin said. Sorra could tell by the quiver in her voice that her companion was similarly horrified.

"Yeah," said an unfamiliar voice. "It's hard to stomach sometimes, especially our people. Even if they don't have any lineage to speak of."

Sorra's heart leapt into her throat, but she forced herself to turn to the speaker at a normal rate rather than whirling around. An ikthian in a lab coat stood behind them, a woman. Her mottled crest had a pinkish tinge, not all that different from Odelle's. The resemblance didn't help Sorra's nerves, but she managed a nod, grateful her visor was tinted.

"Newbie here," she said, nodding casually at Elurin. "Just rotated in. Giving her the tour. Thought I'd show her the aliens."

To her relief, the scientist bought it. "I was curious at first, too," she said, with a look of bored disinterest. "Now, the novelty's gone. Data is data no matter the species."

"Same shit, different day?" Elurin said.

Sorra gritted her teeth. *I told her to let me do the talking!*

"Pretty much." The scientist's brow furrowed in confusion, or perhaps concern. "I didn't know they were bringing in a new rotation of guards. I thought we were about to wrap up here, since we moved onto environmental distribution. They sent about twenty of you home yesterday, didn't they?"

"Yes," Sorra confirmed. While undercover, it was usually best to agree with whomever she was talking to. More pieces tended to fall into place that way. "Newbie's just a last-minute fill-in."

"Wish I could get someone to fill in for me. I haven't been off-base in months." The woman shuddered, glancing about before whispering to them. "Considering what we're working on, I'll consider us lucky if they *let* us leave."

Before Sorra could formulate a response, Elurin chimed in. "Why wouldn't they let us leave?"

Sorra nudged the side of Elurin's boot, but it was too late. The scientist's face clouded with suspicion. She glanced at them, then the row of testing rooms, and took a step back, reaching for her wrist.

"That's above your clearance level," Sorra barked at Elurin, but it was too late.

The scientist had activated her comm. "Security—"

Sorra grabbed Elurin's arm and hauled her toward the elevator. They almost bowled over another scientist trying to disembark, but Sorra shoved him aside. The lift doors closed, sirens wailed, and two real guards rushed around the far corner of the hallway.

"This is why I told you not to talk!" Sorra snarled as the lift sped back to the ground floor. "Now we have to shoot our way out."

"Well, sorry for not being a master of espionage on my first undercover mission. I'm the pilot—"

"Exactly! If you'd done your fucking job and let me do mine, we wouldn't—"

The doors opened, revealing another contingent of armed guards behind glowing blue barriers. Sorra ducked out of their sights, aiming her rifle around the edge of the door. Together, she and Elurin opened fire. Their rounds bounced harmlessly off the barriers, and Sorra heard someone shout, "It's only two of them. Advance!"

She gritted her teeth. If she wanted to get back home to Odelle and tell the generals about their grisly discovery, they had no choice but to fight their way out.

Chapter Nine

IN A MATTER OF hours, medics and scientists from Jor'al swarmed the abandoned town on Altos. Rachel watched them scurry from within the clear-walled tent where she was currently being held. When they had called for backup, she hadn't expected a reaction like this.

"Why so many people?" she asked Akton, who stood beside her in a pair of green scrubs. "I didn't even know the rebellion had so many scientists."

Akton shrugged. His digging claws had been bagged with something like loose gloves, and so had his feet. Every inch of his large, furry frame was covered except for his head, and he wore a mask over his muzzle. Not that she could judge. She'd been forced to strip off her armor without any concern for modesty before enduring extremely thorough decontamination procedures.

"Don't ask me, Harris," Akton said, his voice muffled. "Guess they figure the risk of…whatever this is…is bigger than the risk of attracting the Dominion's attention."

Rachel sighed. She didn't envy whoever made the call.

Two doctors entered, sealed in stark white biohazard suits and protected by face shields. "Rachel Harris? Akton Valerius?" one of them said, glancing at a datapad. "I'm Doctor Tyche. I need to take your vitals."

Someone else already did. Don't you guys communicate? Nevertheless, Rachel submitted as Doctor Tyche—ikthian, judging by her size and shape—and the other doctor, a male naledai, took yet another series of vitals with scanners and handheld equipment they'd brought on a silver trolley.

"Do you have any idea what happened to these people?" Rachel asked as Tyche opened the back of her suit, pressing a sensor between her shoulder blades. She shivered at the cold metal on her bare skin.

"Not yet," Tyche said, "but I promise, we're working on it as fast as we can."

After two minutes, during which Rachel bit her lip to keep from asking more questions the doctor probably wouldn't, or couldn't, answer, it was over. She was permitted to readjust her "clothes," while Tyche typed on her datapad with gloved fingers.

"Good news," she said, smiling through the screen of her helmet. "We've run every test we can think of, and there's no evidence that whatever killed the civilians here has gotten on or in either of you."

"Does that mean we're free to go?" Akton asked hopefully.

Rachel was doubtful.

"We're going to observe you for a while just to be extra careful," Tyche said, "but we don't think any foreign agents have affected either of you."

"Foreign agents?" Rachel repeated. "So you do think they were infected."

Tyche hesitated. "It isn't that simple. A large number of things could have caused this. Poison, some kind of virus—"

"We get the idea," Akton said.

"We'll figure out what it is," the naledai doctor, who had been examining Akton, said in a reassuring tone. "Once we know, we'll come up with a plan to make sure this doesn't happen again."

The image of tiny naledai bodies lying on rows of cots flashed into Rachel's mind. A shudder ran down her spine. *Fuck, I hope so.*

* * *

Sorra gritted her teeth. With their backs against the wall, pinned down by a squad of security guards, there was only one option. She closed the elevator door, firing until the last possible moment. "Second floor, flygirl."

Elurin pushed the button. With a lurch, they sped up. The clear nature of the tube allowed Sorra to watch the guards. Several broke away from the blue barricade, hurrying to cut them off.

Sorra's mind raced. Going down was out of the question, but she thought she'd seen tinted windows amidst the building's many facets. They were structural weaknesses.

"Find a window, then jump."

"Jump?!"

"We're wearing armor." Leaping from a second story window wasn't an appealing prospect, but they were running out of options.

Elurin stared at her in disbelief, but if the pilot had any further arguments, she didn't get the chance to voice them. They arrived on the second floor to find it deserted. Shouts and footsteps approached their position with frightening speed.

The second floor almost reminded Sorra of a university dorm. There was a hall lined with several doors, most decorated with small personal images. Off to one side were a few couches and chairs, several large terminals, and a gaming station. A circular window glinted at the end of the hall. Sorra ran for it at full speed, already aiming her rifle.

"Wait!"

Sorra came to an abrupt halt.

Elurin arrived beside her, panting lightly. "Why not just open it?"

Sorra rolled her eyes. *For once, the kid has a good idea.* She forced open the window with a grunt. Whoever designed this building had obviously focused on securing the lower levels, where the research was being conducted, rather than the upper ones where people lived. It probably helped that these prefab stations were only meant to last short-term.

The sound of footsteps came closer. Behind her, the elevator chirped. More guards from downstairs. "You first," she ordered, shoving Elurin for good measure.

Elurin already had one leg out the window by the time the first wave of enemies rounded the corner. One tried to open fire, but Sorra shot first. Her target fell. A second guard tried to erect a blue barrier, but Sorra's next round caused them to retreat behind a corner.

She spared a brief glance at the window. Elurin was gone, and Sorra didn't wait to see whether she'd landed safely. She hauled herself over and out, feeling a shot hit the back of her armor just before she dropped. Pain burst between her shoulder blades, although it didn't pierce the protective plating.

"Fuck!" she groaned.

Sorra hit the ground in a cloud of reddish-brown dust. Her helmet prevented her from breathing it in, but it obscured her vision for a moment. Then she saw Elurin, extending a hand. She took it and started running. Pain throbbed behind her right shoulder, and an ache burned in one of her knees, but she hardly noticed as she headed for the shipyard.

Rather than hurl themselves out the window, the guards retreated to use the front door, which bought Sorra and Elurin precious time.

They arrived at their concealed ship, and Elurin climbed in, hitting the emergency bypass for decontamination.

Sorra stumbled in after her, panting. She flopped into her seat without bothering to fasten her restraints. "Go!"

Elurin sped toward the top of the dome. Sorra realized they were going to smash their way through mere seconds before it happened, when Elurin fired the guns to weaken the spot she was aiming for. A horrible grating sound filled Sorra's ears as the *Riptide* spiraled, veering wildly from whatever course Elurin had intended.

Sorra screamed. Pain ripped through her. She picked herself up off the floor by the copilot's seat—*when the fuck did I get here?*—and clambered back into her seat, fastening her restraints. Her armor held. Barely. She'd definitely have bruises underneath.

To her relief, Elurin had the ship back under control, heading into the welcoming arms of space.

"Didn't anyone tell you to always buckle up?" she said, with a manic laugh.

For once, Sorra swallowed any smart remarks. "I can't believe we survived."

"Me neither," Elurin said. "Two near-death experiences in six days."

"Anyone following?"

Elurin checked the displays. "Nope. Guess their ships aren't cooperating." She laughed, and Sorra did, too.

"Make the jump back to Nakonum as soon as we're clear."

"You got it." Elurin hesitated. "What *was* that back there? You know, the scientists and..."

Test subjects. Sorra had recorded footage of the lab, but she could remember it clearly without. The bodies. The blisters. The sight of death. Naledai, humans, ikthians. She was grateful she'd only seen it instead of having to smell it.

"Definitely test subjects. Testing for what, I don't know."

Elurin's expression became grim. "Me neither. But whatever it is..."

Sorra nodded. Whatever it was had to be extremely dangerous.

***

Maia woke in the middle of the night, jarred awake by a knock upon the door. With only a brief glance to check on Taylor, who remained sound asleep, she rose from her chair to answer it, blinking the bleariness from her eyes.

She had expected a nurse, or perhaps one of Taylor's doctors, but Odelle stood there. The ikthian's brow was creased, her expression grave.

"Maia, may I have a word?" she asked in a quiet voice.

Maia glanced over her shoulder. Taylor stirred slightly beneath the covers, rolling from one side to the other. "Of course," she whispered.

Maia stepped out of the room and into the hallway, empty due to the late hour. There was someone at the reception desk, and a skeleton crew of doctors and assistants, but no one close enough to hear their conversation.

"Yesterday, I sent Sorra and Elurin, as well as Akton and Rachel, on separate covert missions. The first pair went to investigate the coordinates Irana provided. The second pair went to find out why one of our satellite bases stopped responding to transmissions from Nakonum. Both teams have returned with alarming news."

"Alarming?" Maia's chest tightened. Judging from Odelle's expression, "alarming" might be an understatement.

Odelle produced a datapad. Maia took it, scanning the lines of text. *Biological weapon...airborne virus...diversity of hosts...ten-day incubation estimated in naledai.* There was a video clip beneath the first several paragraphs. With growing fear, she pressed it.

The audio was low, but she made out Akton's low, growling voice. *"Harris, over here."* The clip showed the interior of a building crammed full of cots. Each cot contained the withered, blistered body of a dead naledai. Old and young, large and small. Too many to count.

"Tides," Maia whispered.

"There's more," Odelle said.

Maia desperately wanted to look away, but she continued. She read, scarcely processing the words, until she reached a series of images. A laboratory. Sterile silver rooms. More wet, raw bodies. *Test subjects?* Naledai, human, ikthian. *Multiple species. Diversity of hosts.* Her breaths came short as cold realization struck.

"I did this, didn't I?" she whispered.

"No, Maia." Odelle took the datapad. "You didn't cause this."

"But I did," Maia protested, with growing horror. Her words became fast, pleading, although to whom she wasn't sure. "Viruses capable of infecting multiple species from different solar systems are vanishingly rare, despite the Ancients' influence on our genetics. I have never heard of such a thing occurring naturally."

And that was it. Why it was her fault. Surely the Dominion had developed this virus, this weapon, and in order to do it, they needed data. *Her* data. The most comprehensive genetic record of the Milky Way's sentient life, in all its diversity. There was no other explanation. *Corvis took my data on Tarkoht, and this is the result.*

"We only know of two small-scale launches so far," Odelle said.

"Only two." This nightmare had already happened. People had died because of her. An entire naledai colony, wiped out. The proof was on the datapad Odelle held.

"But why?" Her rising voice sounded through the hall, but she was too upset to lower it. "Why does the Dominion want to kill colonists? Wrong as it is, the subjugated naledai supply Korithia and the inner planets with food, cheap labor, everything! Aside from a few rebel pockets, naledai space is already conquered. Why would the Dominion wipe out one of their own resources?"

Odelle lowered her gaze. "Perhaps they intend to use it as a warning, or cause deaths wherever they suspect rebel activity. Maybe they've decided eliminating some of their own resources is a worthwhile price to pay to end the rebellion once and for all."

Another terrifying thought struck Maia, almost too frightening to consider. *Nakonum may have been conquered, but Earth hasn't. Not yet anyway.*

"We have to warn Earth. There were humans among the test subjects." Instinctively, she glanced back at the closed doors. Although she couldn't see inside Taylor's room, she could picture her lover, still asleep in her bed. Peaceful and oblivious. *Oh, Taylor. I'm so sorry.*

Odelle nodded. "We're trying but getting a message through has proven difficult."

"What do you mean?"

"The Dominion has strengthened its blockade around Earth's solar system. Naledai transports have been unable to get through. According to reports, the humans have held Earth and their closest colonies with surprising effectiveness..."

The "but" at the end of Odelle's sentence made Maia's heart sink. Her voice shook as she replied, "But that will change if the Dominion uses this bioweapon against the Coalition. The humans will be decimated."

Chapter Ten

MAIA WANDERED THE HALLS of the Jor'al base. She passed several naledai soldiers, hardly taking notice of them. They didn't seem to notice her, either. At this time of night, everyone who wasn't asleep had a specific task to perform. Still, as one young naledai shot her an apologetic smile while squeezing past in a narrow corridor, a chilling thought struck. *A naledai warren is the worst possible place for disease to spread. They're overcrowded, and everyone is always in such close contact...*

She tried to push those thoughts away by force of will but was utterly unsuccessful.

No one spoke to her until she arrived at the small section of the base reserved for housing prisoners. There were few in residence. Only two nighttime guards stood watch outside the nondescript door. Capturing live prisoners was not one of the rebellion's main objectives. Her mother and the scientist from Teichos had been anomalies.

Mother.

That was why she'd come here, Maia realized. To speak to Irana. She had to know whether her mother had known about—or, worse, helped develop—the bioweapon. *I acknowledge my guilt, but will she acknowledge her own complicity? Will she tell me the truth?*

Those were questions she couldn't answer standing outside She approached the guards, who arched their bushy eyebrows at her, nodding their recognition. That thought made her extremely uncomfortable, since she didn't want to be associated with the prisoner they were guarding, but she addressed them, nonetheless. "My name is Maia Kalanis. The generals have granted me ongoing permission to speak with the prisoner Irana."

The prisoner. It was easier to say than "my mother."

"You're on the list," one of the guards said. He stood aside, and his companion opened the doors.

Maia entered. The room contained a single, sturdy-looking cot, and a toilet and showerhead had been installed in the left corner. It was nicer than the cells in Daashu, though not as luxurious as the repurposed officers' quarters Maia had been imprisoned in on Earth.

Irana, seated on the cot, turned as the door shut. "Maia?" She started to stand, but Maia motioned for her to remain where she was.

"Irana."

The use of her name caused Irana's eyes to widen. "To what do I owe the pleasure?"

Maia searched for words, struggling to force them past the rapidly forming lump in her throat. "Did you know?"

"About?"

"The bioweapon the Dominion developed with my data."

"A bioweapon." Irana tilted her head. Her voice and expression were, as usual, frustratingly neutral. "So, that's what Corvis had those scientists working on."

"You didn't know?" Maia asked, afraid to hope.

"I knew weapons of war were being developed, but not their specific nature. By the time the base began operations, I had...lost Corvis' trust." The *"because of you"* remained unspoken.

In spite of everything, the primary emotion that welled in Maia's chest was relief. Her mother was still a war criminal, of course, but at least she hadn't actively participated in developing a murderous biological weapon. *What low standards I have for her. Would she have participated in the weapon's development, had she known? If Corvis had still trusted her at the time?*

"Why did you ally yourself with Corvis?" she found herself asking. "How could you support a leader, a society, that committed such atrocities?"

Irana remained silent for a long moment. "I doubt you will find my explanation satisfactory. Nor will you understand it."

Maia stared into Irana's eyes without blinking. "Try me."

"Very well." Irana held Maia's stare, unflinching. "You were a fortunate child. You grew up with the Kalanis family name, as well as significant wealth. When I was young, I only possessed the former. I had a respectable lineage, but by the time I was born, the Kalanis family fortune had dried up. I rebuilt it for you and our descendants."

Maia scoffed. "That's it? You grew up titled but poor, so you decided to become a fascist?"

"You're oversimplifying—"

"Because it is simple, Irana." Maia clenched her fists, trembling with rage at her mother and herself.

She had grown up on Korithia, swimming in the cesspool of Dominion propaganda–ikthian superiority, their Ancients-given destiny, their duty to subjugate other species for the advancement of the universe. For the "lesser species" own good, even. But she had seen the inconsistencies in that worldview that had inspired her to pursue the sciences and directed her research.

I don't know what's worse. Mother being fooled by the same shallow propaganda or seeing through it and supporting Corvis' regime for personal gain. It must be the second. She's far too intelligent for the more generous explanation.

"How could you?" she snarled, still shaking with anger. "Surely you knew our privileges came from the subjugation of others. Didn't that ever bother you?"

For the first time in Maia's recent memory, Irana took on an expression of hurt. "I am not a monster, Maia."

"You rebuilt our family's empire on the backs of conquered slaves and paid its price in blood," she replied.

"It was a price I paid for you," Irana protested, but Maia spoke over her.

"I'm ashamed you paid it. Securing your family's legacy is no excuse."

"No," Irana said, softly and without bitterness. "I suppose it isn't."

Maia's eyes brimmed with tears. She blinked her third eyelids rapidly to clear them away, then turned without another word. Irana said nothing as she left, but Maia felt her mother's eyes boring into the back of her crest long after the doors closed.

* * *

Something felt off as soon as Taylor woke up. The sterile scent and soft beeps of the machines, which she was lucky enough not to be hooked up to anymore, hadn't changed. But something felt different, so she opened her eyes.

For the first time in a long time, the chair beside her bed was empty. Maia's familiar shadow wasn't there. Taylor felt a stab of panic in her gut. Maia calmed her and kept the nightmares at bay. *Where is she?*

She didn't get the chance to worry for long. Just as she was gathering her strength to get up, the door opened. Maia entered, her silhouette drooping in the dimly lit doorway. Upon noticing Taylor, she switched on the light, albeit to the lowest setting.

"You should be asleep," she murmured, returning to the chair.

"Not sleepy," Taylor said.

Something was wrong, she was sure of it. Maia's voice was tired, her eyes haunted. Taylor knew that expression. It reminded her of her own—or, at least, what she'd glimpsed in the mirror since her arrival on Nakonum.

"Whether you're tired or not is irrelevant. You need sleep," Maia said gently.

"Can't sleep while you're upset." Taylor patted the edge of the bed, and Maia abandoned the chair to join her. "Wanna talk?"

Maia's gaze remained downcast, as though she were ashamed. "No, but you will find out sooner or later. Better you hear it from me." She twisted her hands in her lap. "Sorra and Elurin have returned from their latest mission. According to their reports, as well as reports from Rachel and Akton, the Dominion is developing a bioweapon capable of infecting multiple Milky Way species."

Taylor took a moment to process. "How is that possible? I've never heard of a disease that can infect such different hosts. Have you?"

"Never outside of a laboratory," Maia said. Taylor couldn't miss the tremor in her voice. "Taylor, they used my research to make it. Corvis got her hands on a copy of my data before Tarkoht was destroyed."

Taylor's heart sped up. She remembered running through grate-floored hallways, the slap of her boots and her own heavy breathing drowned out by the blare of security alarms. That was before she'd handed herself over to the seekers to secure her friends' escape. Before she'd been taken to Daashu.

"She must have assembled a team of Dominion scientists to make this," Maia continued, with growing distress. "It's my fault—"

Taylor blinked, shaking off the memory. Maia needed her. "No." She reached into Maia's lap and took her hand. "You didn't make whatever this thing is."

"My data led to its creation." Maia raised her chin, staring at Taylor with tear-filled eyes. "Good intentions cannot erase disastrous results."

"Bullshit."

Maia leaned back. "What?"

"It means you're wrong." Taylor brought her other hand to Maia's cheek, swiping away a tear. "Intentions matter. You're far from the first scientist whose discoveries were used for war. Humanity's had several."

Maia shook her head, weeping.

Taylor continued, "Ever read about a scientist called Einstein? I know you read some human books back on Earth."

"Who were they?"

"A famous human physicist. His discoveries led to more discoveries that allowed other scientists to make the first atomic bomb. Basically, my American ancestors bombed my Japanese ancestors. At least two hundred and fifty thousand civilians died. America claimed they wanted to end the war. Really, they wanted to seize whatever power they could through the threat of annihilation. They didn't care about the cost."

The heartbreak on Maia's face was instantaneous. "Taylor."

"It was generations before I was born," Taylor assured her. "All Einstein did was write a letter advocating for scientific research, but after the atomic bomb, he devoted the rest of his life to anti-war and civil rights efforts." She squeezed Maia's hand. "What are you going to do?"

"What am I going to do?" Maia stared at her. "What *am* I going to do?" It seemed the question hadn't occurred to her.

"You're unbelievably smart," Taylor said, offering Maia the most encouraging smile she could muster. "There's no one better equipped to combat this bioweapon, but you can't figure out how while you're wrapped up in your own guilt."

Maia sniffed, and her tears slowed. "I suppose this is a selfish reaction, isn't it?"

"It's, pardon the phrase, a *human* reaction." Taylor sighed. "English really needs a more inclusive word for other sentient species. My point is, it's natural, but you have to push past it."

She was gratified and more than a little relieved when Maia leaned into her arms, seeking an embrace. "Thank you," she murmured, nuzzling her nose into the crook of Taylor's neck.

Taylor held her, enjoying the feel of Maia's trembling body pressed against hers. Maia had comforted and cared for her day after day, but she hadn't been able to do the same until now. It made her feel good. Useful. Her trauma hadn't taken away her ability to give love and support.

Maybe I'm not as broken as I thought.

The sudden surge of confidence, combined with her returning strength and Maia's closeness, awakened unexpected feelings. Taylor kissed the top of Maia's crest—the fine, soft silver scales there made Maia's skin both like and unlike her own.

Maia looked up, and Taylor understood the longing in her eyes. She didn't lean forward, but she parted her lips in clear expectation. *She's waiting for me to kiss her first. Letting me keep some control.*

Taylor drew Maia's face to hers and brought their lips together. It felt like finally coming home.

***

Maia hadn't realized how much she'd missed Taylor's kisses until their mouths met. They had exchanged soft pecks, kisses of relief and reassurance, but nothing like this since Daashu. Taylor tasted like salt, and it wasn't merely the pleasant brine of her skin. It was something almost bitter, and Maia realized she was tasting Taylor's tears.

She pulled back, even though it pained her to do so. "Why are you crying?" she asked softly.

Taylor smiled. "Happy."

Under other circumstances, Maia might have questioned Taylor's statement. She might have considered it inappropriate, even callous, to steal a moment of happiness amidst such dire circumstances. But she had learned a lot from Taylor. One of those lessons was to seize happiness whenever and wherever she found it, because it was never a guarantee.

So Maia clung to happiness and to Taylor and kissed her again. Taylor was her anchor while the waves threatened to drag her down. *If she still sees goodness in me after what I've done, perhaps there is something of me worth salvaging.*

"Please." Maia ran her fingers through the soft black strands of Taylor's hair, letting them tickle her webbing. Her hair had been buzzed short, and it made her look more like her old self. She also made the same, familiar sounds of pleasure as Maia stroked it.

"Are you sure this is okay?" Taylor asked.

Maia lost herself in Taylor's warm brown eyes. "Please," she whispered again. "Just be careful."

"I won't hurt you," Taylor said, her brow knitting with a look of soft hurt.

Maia laughed. "Of course not, but you are still recovering. Resist the impulse to be athletic."

Taylor pouted, but only for a moment. She tipped Maia back onto the bed, stripping her shirt over her head with almost unbearable slowness. Maia shuddered as Taylor's fingertips slid reverently along her stomach. The thought that Taylor could still view her as something to be treasured and admired and protected shook her to her core. She kissed Taylor again, long and deep.

Eventually, Taylor had to pull away for breath. Maia barely had a chance to whimper—and remember that humans needed to breathe far more often than ikthians—before Taylor spoke. "You mean everything to me," she said, with the tenderness of love and the strength of sincerity. "You always will, no matter what."

Maia's lips trembled so much that all she could say was, "Taylor." The name that had become her universe.

Taylor paused, and the dear worry line that wrinkled her brow almost made Maia cry again. "Are you sure you're okay?"

"I will be, because I am yours."

Taylor made a gentle noise of understanding. She bent her head, and Maia parted her lips for Taylor's tongue. Familiarity untangled the tight knot in Maia's chest. The pressure there moved downward, becoming a tingle in her belly rather than a ball of stress. It reminded her of a memory, one that felt much further in the past than it actually was.

She pulled back from the kiss. "Do you remember back on Earth, when you found me crying in the shower?"

From the bright sheen of Taylor's eyes, Maia could tell that she did indeed remember. "Of course."

"I was broken. You put me back together." Allowing herself one more stroke of Taylor's hair, Maia removed her hand, lacing her fingers through Taylor's. She guided Taylor's palm to her breast, urging her to squeeze. "I need you to do that again."

"You weren't broken then," Taylor insisted, "and you aren't now. Or if you are, so am I. We'll be broken together. Not so bad, right?"

Although she didn't entirely believe those words, Maia allowed them to find a home within her. When she repeated them inside her head, they almost sounded true.

Maia wasn't sure what sort of signal she gave for Taylor to continue. Whatever the reason, Taylor resumed exploring her torso, kneading her breasts, caressing her shoulders and stomach. Taylor's hands travelled the landscape of her body. To be known so well, yet re-learned with such thoroughness, was Maia's undoing. Her tears came quietly, and she smiled, allowing Taylor's hands to heal her.

"There she is," Taylor murmured, her voice full of affection.

Maia ran her hands along Taylor's back, sighing as the muscles there tensed. It wasn't the bad kind of tension, like flinching—rather, a rolling bunch of anticipation. When she reached the small of Taylor's spine, she urged Taylor closer. Several frustrating layers of clothing remained between them.

"Clothes off," she gasped.

Taylor shifted, putting only enough space between them to strip off her oversized hospital gown. Maia shucked her pants and underwear before allowing herself the privilege of admiring Taylor's naked body.

Her heart throbbed in her throat, forming a lump of joy and sympathy combined. Taylor's body looked similar to the vivid images in Maia's memory, and yet noticeably different. Her limbs were leaner. Her hip bones, too prominent. Scars marred the otherwise smooth landscape of her chest and shoulders, similar to the fading one on her face.

"Oh, love." Maia felt more injuries as she ran her palms along Taylor's triceps, winding around to stroke her back. Her body felt different, ridged and uneven.

"Don't you dare." Taylor caught Maia's wrists, holding them in a loose grip. "Feel sorry for me later. Stay here in the now with me."

Maia gazed into Taylor's eyes, so full of love. When Taylor looked at her that way, she couldn't descend any further into dark thoughts. She took Taylor's hand, which still braceleted her wrist, and guided it along her inner thigh.

Taylor's fingers delved between Maia's outer lips, seeking her clit and stroking either side of the swollen ridge. Her head lolled back, and she moaned as Taylor's mouth sealed around the peak of her left breast. Taylor's other arm slid beneath her, wrapping around her waist, strong and secure. *I see Daashu didn't take all your strength away.*

Her eyes fluttered as Taylor focused more intently on her clit. The circles shrank until they touched the tip, and Maia's pelvis jerked. She couldn't remain still, but Taylor didn't seem to want her to. Low, possessive moans vibrated around Maia's nipple each time she bucked, and from the gentle tug of Taylor's teeth, Maia knew she liked the reactions.

At first, Maia wasn't sure what to do with her hands. She needed to grip something—Taylor, preferably—but she didn't want to touch somewhere off-limits. Before, Taylor's whole body had been open to her. Now, things could be different.

Taylor noticed her hesitation, kissing across to the opposite breast. "It's okay. You can touch me," she whispered.

Maia took Taylor at her word, teasing her right hand through Taylor's hair and sliding the left down her back to grasp a handful of her rear.

As soon as she squeezed, Taylor's fingers skimmed her entrance, lightly at first, asking permission. Maia gave it by twining her legs around Taylor's. She was ready, so slick that her muscles didn't resist. Their bodies came together as fluidly and naturally as ever. Heat blossomed within her core as her muscles stretched around Taylor's knuckles.

Taylor set a rhythm that matched the slow pace of her breathing. Although Maia could predict when the thrusts would hit its apex, each one made her see stars. She wasn't prepared—not for how good it was, nor how much it made her feel. She shivered, clutching Taylor's back as her inner walls clenched.

A single thought broke through–*Taylor is inside me.* Taylor was alive, and safe, and loved her.

"So warm." Taylor's lips skimmed up from Maia's breasts, gliding toward her throat.

When her lips latched onto a tender place beneath Maia's neck-ridges and nibbled, Maia went stiff, releasing small slips of wetness into Taylor's hand. She bit her lip, trying to breathe through the sudden pressure, but it quickly overwhelmed her. As much as she wanted to live in this moment, where Taylor was making love to her and her guilt didn't matter, her body had other ideas.

When the heel of Taylor's hand rubbed against her clit, Maia came. She shuddered, unable to choke back her cries. Taylor's fingers curled harder against her front wall, probing the perfect spot, and Maia released all she had.

The last time she'd come had been with Taylor, back on Earth. They had only hidden on Tarkoht for a short time, and then...she hadn't felt much like touching herself while her lover was imprisoned, possibly dead. Something had broken open inside her, revealing all the vulnerable and hurt places. But Taylor was there to shield her, to let the healing begin.

"I love you," Maia sobbed against Taylor's lips. She hadn't realized she'd pulled Taylor's mouth to hers until she tried to speak.

"Love you, too."

***

Taylor kissed Maia until she calmed and long after, cradling her through the aftershocks. "I love you. You're everything to me," Taylor whispered. Eventually, Maia's tears dried and her sobs were reduced to sniffles. She made eye contact, clearly a little embarrassed, and Taylor hastened to reassure her. "You're okay. You're okay."

"I am," Maia whispered. "Thank you."

Taylor smiled. Maia's strength never failed to amaze her. "You've got nothing to thank me for."

"You're wrong." Maia cupped a hand over hers. "I have everything to thank you for." Gently, she tugged Taylor's wrist, urging her to withdraw. Taylor did, albeit reluctantly. However, when Maia tapped her stomach, gesturing for Taylor to lie on her back, she did so without protest.

There wasn't a trace of fear as Maia rolled on top of her and began kissing down her chest. Part of her had worried there might be, somewhere deep down, but she felt completely safe. She was immensely grateful that the universe had left this one thing, sex as a source of solace, untarnished. Her breath hitched as Maia's tongue flicked her nipple before dragging down her abdominal muscles. It was warm and soft and long.

Maia ducked beneath Taylor's knees, scattering kisses along her inner thighs. "Is this all right?" she murmured, glancing up.

"More than all right." Taylor spread her legs, and Maia dipped her head.

Worshipful. That was the only way Taylor could describe Maia's tongue. It delivered worship with each soft stroke, never hurried. Taylor grasped Maia's crest in both hands. She didn't push but offered encouragement by scratching her fingers against the spikes and grooves there.

"Maia, more," Taylor groaned.

Maia seemed all too happy to deliver. Her lips sealed around the tip of Taylor's clit, and Taylor tensed at the abrupt tug of sensation. Pure pleasure. Her toes curled, and she dug her heels into Maia's back.

Maia seemed in no hurry. She made a game of it, easing off until Taylor relaxed, then sucking until her limbs stiffened. Her head spun. The rocking of her hips became more desperate, and Maia's mouth followed the motion, never once releasing even as her rhythm sped up.

"Please!" Taylor hadn't meant to beg, but she was immensely glad she did.

Maia's tongue dragged down to Taylor's entrance, thrusting lazily at first, then with more pressure. Taylor tightened her grip and gasped out encouragement. "Maia, please, you—you feel so good. So fucking good."

Maia pressed her thumb to Taylor's clit, rolling it in slow circles as her tongue continued swirling. It was more than enough. Taylor arched, consumed by powerful shudders. Her nails scratched Maia's neck, but Maia didn't let up, riding the waves with her as they swelled.

"Maia!" Taylor called her lover's name one last time before she was lost for words.

There was only bliss. Connection. Love coursed through every fiber of her being, bringing with it such relief that a few tears escaped her eyes. She came hard and long, and completely for Maia. No one else had ever, or would ever, touch her so deeply.

It took a long time for Taylor to descend. Maia was in no hurry to stop, and Taylor, though exhausted, had been in desperate need of release. She collapsed onto the mattress. Her inner walls gave a few weak twitches, but Maia soothed the aftershocks with a kiss to Taylor's hip.

"I had forgotten how pleasant this feels," she said, running her fingers through the trimmed nest of curls between Taylor's legs.

She chuckled. "Glad you like it. Shaving it all off makes me itchy, but so does growing it out. I'm lucky the caretakers let me trim it."

Maia's eyes grew wide. She gasped, as though suddenly remembering where they were, and yanked the covers over their naked bodies, hiding her face in Taylor's stomach. "Tides! This is a hospital room. Someone could have come in to check on you."

Taylor's chuckle turned into outright laughter.

Maia groaned into her belly. "Stop that. Someone might hear you."

"It's the middle of the night. I think we're okay."

Maia made another embarrassed noise before peeling herself away and burrowing amidst the sheets in search of their discarded clothes. Reluctantly, Taylor allowed Maia to re-dress her in her hospital robe, but she didn't permit her lover to leave the bed. "Stay. Sleep with me."

"Are you sure?"

So far, Maia had kept to the chair every night. Partially because the bed was small, Taylor assumed, but perhaps also to give her space. To allow her time to regain some autonomy. But Taylor no longer needed nor wanted space, and she hooked an arm around Maia's waist, refusing to let her leave. "You aren't going anywhere. Now, c'mon. Sleep with me. Tomorrow, we'll figure out the next step."

Chapter Eleven

ODELLE TILTED HER FACE into the shower spray, letting water run down her neck and shoulders. Pretending it was rain didn't work. The smell was pleasant, but wrong—the sweetness of soap rather than the scent of damp earth. She hadn't been outdoors in weeks. She missed the sky and the feel of the breeze. *A luxury I cannot afford at the moment.*

She stopped the shower and stepped out, draping herself in a towel without bothering to dry off. When she entered the bedroom, shivering at the drop in temperature, she was pleased to see Sorra there, lounging on the bed with one leg braced on the opposite knee.

"I'm surprised to see you here," Odelle said, making her way to the bed. "Wouldn't you rather work somewhere with a terminal?"

Since space in the Jor'al warren was at a premium, their bed was the only furniture in the room aside from shelving built into the walls. Even their private, adjoining bathroom was a luxury.

"And miss the view?" Sorra lowered the datapad she was examining and sat up, offering a smile. "Enjoy your shower?"

Odelle returned the grin. "Well enough. What are you reading?"

Sorra's smile melted away. "Picking a target, actually."

"For?" Odelle asked.

Sorra patted the thick green comforter. "I hate to say it, but we're running out of time. Elurin and I were exceptionally lucky when we infiltrated the base on Askari, because their security was minimal. I think that's because they were about to pack up and leave. The scientist I talked to practically told us so."

Odelle joined Sorra on the bed, sighing. Their banter had lasted all too briefly, but Sorra was right to be worried. "You think Corvis will make her next move soon?"

"Considering the test site Valerius and Harris found? I'm positive. Meanwhile, Jor'al hasn't any luck getting a message through the blockade to Earth, and there are innocent civilians all over the galaxy who don't know about this bioweapon."

"Despite that long list of negatives, I assume you have a plan?"

"A series of broadcasts," Sorra said. "You've said in the past that information is the only way we'll win this war. Right now, I see the wisdom in your approach."

"The broadcast won't reach everyone," Odelle warned. "Many will dismiss it as a hoax, or a conspiracy. The belief that one is superior to others can be intoxicating, even to intelligent people, especially when instilled in childhood. No one is immune, not even us."

"Enough people will listen. I've never been an optimist, but part of me has to believe that finding out the truth about Corvis, the Dominion, and the bioweapon will inspire some ikthians to change their minds, and others who always silently disagreed to take real action."

Odelle's eyes widened. It was unlike Sorra to be so hopeful, especially about their own species. For decades, she had expressed open disdain for ikthians who lived under the Dominion's rule. She had often written Korithian civilians off as a lost cause—future casualties of the inevitable rebellion—while Odelle had favored trying to reach those who would listen. To hear Sorra agree with her point of view encouraged her.

"We have nothing to lose by trying. What the people of Korithia and the inner planets do with the information is up to them. And, of course, we'll warn the naledai colonies about the bioweapon. That's even more important."

"Exactly." Sorra placed a hand on Odelle's thigh, reminding her abruptly that she was still naked. The towel had long since pooled around her waist. "So, how turned on would you be if I said I've started planning a mission to capture one of the Dominion's outer communication stations, on a moon called Hakkar? We can prepare and transmit your broadcasts there."

"My broadcasts?" Odelle sensed where Sorra's mind was going. She wouldn't go so far as to say that spreading truthful propaganda instead of the Dominion's lies—if only to preserve her status as a double-agent—turned her on, but it certainly intrigued her.

"That was always the plan, wasn't it? I'll steal you a station, you make the best damn propaganda you've ever made—only for the right side this time. How do you feel about that, Miss Executive Media Coordinator?"

Odelle had never been so happy to hear her formerly hated title. She gave Sorra an enthusiastic kiss, knocking both her towel and Sorra's datapad to the floor. They lay forgotten for a long time, while far more important activities took place on the bed.

***

Rachel bounced the heel of her boot against the *Riptide's* floor, brimming with energy. A week and a half in quarantine had just about driven her crazy. There had been nothing to do but sleep, watch naledai movies on the datapad she'd begged her doctors for, and text Taylor and Elurin. To their credit, they'd almost always texted back. It had been the one bright spot of her miserable isolation.

Finally, after running just about every test they could think of, the doctors had released her and Akton from their sterile white prisons and declared them fit for active duty. Even better, her first post-quarantine mission was with her new favorite ikthian.

"I hate the last few minutes before a mission drop," Elurin complained from the pilot's chair. "They feel too long and too short at the same time. Gives me a stomachache."

From one of the fighter's rear seats, Rachel made a noncommittal noise of agreement. The final minutes before a drop usually left her jittery as well—and now that Elurin had mentioned it, she felt her energy transforming into far less pleasant nerves. It didn't help that Akton, the chosen leader of the operation, had selected someone else to accompany them to Hakkar.

Sitting a few spaces away, with a few other naledai soldiers between them, was Jethra. The same Jethra who had rescued her and Elurin after the crash. *I should like her, so why don't I?*

Jethra looked in Rachel's direction, piercing yellow eyes searching as though she'd felt the stare. Her large shoulders bunched under her light armor, and her shaggy, sand-colored fur fluffed on the back of her neck, like a cat trying to make itself look bigger.

"Maybe it makes me weird, but I like the feeling right before a drop," Jethra said. "Gets me all tingly."

I definitely should like her. There weren't many soldiers who openly expressed what she felt—the excitement of combat. Some, like Taylor, fought for a sense of duty and identity, because they were protectors. Rachel liked to imagine she was a protector type, but she'd always had a taste for adventure, too. It was why she'd left home and joined the Coalition military as soon as she came of age.

And yet, despite the relatable sentiment Jethra had expressed, it made Rachel's stomach sour. A stomachache, only higher up, somewhere in her chest. She leaned forward and addressed Akton, seated in the copilot's chair. "How much longer, boss?"

Akton glanced back at her, offering a sharp-toothed smile. "Another five minutes, Harris. Keep your pants on."

At that, Rachel couldn't help laughing. "Taylor taught you that, didn't she?"

"And a few others. Elurin, bring up the schematics, please."

"You got it." Elurin pressed a few buttons.

A holographic image shimmered into view between the front and rear seats. Rachel, Jethra, and the other four naledai soldiers, whom she'd only become acquainted with minutes before departure, looked at the glowing yellow image–3D blueprints of a spherical building, surrounded by a circular wall with guard towers.

"This is the comm station," Akton said. "It's only a small one, but it'll serve our purpose. Sorra chose Hakkar because it's relatively close to Nakonum. It bounces Dominion messages and data from Nakonum to some of the outer naledai colonies that the Dominion controls, but it has enough range to broadcast messages to inner Dominion planets, including Korithia."

The schematic grew, focusing on the building rather than the wall. Akton continued, "Elurin will bring us in from above. I'm sure the towers will fire on us, but...well, you've met our pilot."

Scattered but confident laughs echoed around the bridge, and Rachel joined in. She had no doubt Elurin would be able to dodge anything the tiny station threw at her.

"Once we land, we'll split up and infiltrate from multiple points. Elurin and Harris from the east, Jethra and Turvis from the south, Kelin and Rekan from the west, me and Drago from the north. Keep in contact via radio."

The ache in Rachel's chest transformed into a curious fluttering sensation. *Elurin's my partner. Good!* She couldn't resist tossing a smirk at Jethra, who was still studying the schematics. Nevertheless, Rachel felt almost giddy.

"The Dominion doesn't consider this outpost a high defense priority, so it shouldn't be heavily guarded, but use stealth for as long as possible," Akton said. "First objective is taking the station with minimal losses. Second is capturing the civilians running it alive, so they can give us access to the equipment and show us how it works. But if you have to shoot, don't hesitate."

Rachel nodded. This mission was going to be a lot less depressing than the last one. A brief shudder ran through her as she pictured the room full of dead naledai, and she forced the image from her mind. *I'm gonna keep remembering that sight until I die, aren't I? But that won't be today.*

***

"On your six!" Rachel's voice came over Elurin's comm.

Elurin froze, hit by a bolt of panic. *What?* The sound of rapidly approaching steps behind her answered that question. She whirled, then fired into the squad of guards approaching from the other end of the narrow hallway. They retreated, but it bought her enough time to follow Rachel around the corner at the opposite end of the corridor.

"Just say 'behind you,'" she panted as she crouched beside Rachel. Elurin risked a quick glance, but the hall remained empty. "It takes me a second to remember what 'on your six' means."

"Sorry." Rachel grinned behind her helmet's visor. "Habit."

Elurin shook her head in mild bewilderment. She didn't know why Rachel was enjoying this. Their mission to seize the comm station had gone, as Rachel liked to say, "tits up" shortly after landing. Their infiltration was discovered only a few minutes in, and several firefights had erupted throughout the building—including the one she and Rachel were currently caught in.

Maybe ground combat makes her feel like space combat makes me feel. Exhilarated. But without a ship, I can't steer.

The guards made an appearance again, setting up their trademark blue energy shields and making a steady advance down the hall.

"Fuck," Rachel grunted, firing a few shots. The rounds bounced off the shields, leaving black smudges of carbon scoring on the barren metal walls to either side.

"Retreat?" Elurin suggested. "We can meet up with one of the other groups."

"Looks like we have to," Rachel said, though she didn't sound pleased.

"Retreat nothing," Jethra said behind her, taking Elurin by surprise.

"Jethra!" she cried, standing up to clap the tall, willowy naledai on the shoulder. "Where's Turvis?"

"Took a shot to the chest. Injured but not dead. Left him with Akton's team."

Relief flooded through Elurin. She didn't know Turvis well, but she was glad he hadn't died—and extra glad Jethra had come to offer assistance. "We've got a squad advancing down the hall. Ideas?"

Jethra's answer was a toothy grin. "Who needs ideas when you have grenades?" She unhooked one from her belt and tossed it to Elurin, who caught it.

"Careful with those things," Rachel grumbled. "They explode, remember?"

"Not until they're activated," Jethra drawled. She pushed past Rachel, stealing a quick glance around the corner. "They're in range now. Give it to 'em, Elurin."

Elurin passed the grenade to Rachel. "You like this stuff more than me."

Rachel took the grenade and activated it with the press of a button. After a silent count of three, she threw it down the hall toward the advancing line of guards. Elurin threw herself to the ground, covering her head.

The hall shook. Metal screeched. Something wet splattered. Smoke and electricity scent filled her nose, and her mouth took on a foul taste. After another silent count, Elurin peeked around the corner. The advancing squad had become various purple smears on the wall. She shuddered. That was another thing she disliked about ground combat. The muted fireball of a ship exploding wasn't quite as...messy.

Nevertheless, it meant she had one less group of enemies to deal with.

"Nice, Harris," Jethra was saying.

Rachel shrugged. "We're still alive, so thanks."

Elurin frowned. There was an odd sort of tension between them, at least in Rachel, that Elurin couldn't understand.

"How are the other pairs doing?" she asked Jethra.

Jethra spoke into her comm. "Akton, what's your status?"

"All clear on the west side," said Akton, his rough voice coming in through their helmets. Elurin smiled. She'd had no doubt her wily friend would be fine. *"We're mopping up a few stragglers now, and we have a few captives."*

"We're clear on the east," Jethra replied.

"Do another sweep," Akton said. *"Make sure you haven't missed anyone. After that, report to my position. We'll secure anyone still alive and tell Sorra the station is ours."*

Elurin breathed a sigh of relief. The mission had been a success. She returned her weapon to her back then hugged Rachel, who returned the embrace. Then, she gave Jethra a hug. "Thanks for towing us out of the deep."

Jethra gave a rumbling chuckle. "Any time, pebble." She started back the way she'd come, heading for Akton's position.

Rachel gave Elurin a questioning stare. "Pebble?"

Elurin's head spots heated. "Um. It's a naledai diminutive. We're old friends."

"Right. Friends."

Rachel started off in the opposite direction, toward the remains of the guards, but Elurin caught her arm. "Yeah, friends. Why? Is that a problem?"

"It isn't a problem," Rachel replied—too insistently.

"Your tone of voice makes it sound like a problem."

Rachel turned and sighed. "Can we not do this now? If we missed anyone, we might end up in another firefight."

Elurin frowned, but Rachel was right—the mission wasn't officially over. There would be time to talk about it later, although she still didn't know what she'd say. *Why is Rachel so pissy around Jethra? She's been nothing but nice.*

"Fine. But later, we're talking about this. I can't let one of my friends be a dick to my other friend."

"I'm not a dick," Rachel muttered.

Before Elurin could respond, the human removed her weapon from her back and stomped off to check the corridor. Elurin followed, though she wasn't looking forward to moving through the mess Jethra's grenade had left behind.

***

Sorra stepped back and folded her arms, admiring the station Akton's team had secured and the landscape beyond. The rust-red sunset cast a stripe of purple-blue light along the station's wall. Shadows were already lengthening in the dust. Like most naledai terraformed planets, this one was mostly desert, beautiful despite the lack of humidity.

"So, what do you think?"

"It's incredible," Odelle said, craning her neck to better see the prize they'd captured.

The base itself was simple. Only one spherical, three-floored building, surrounded by a circular wall and guard towers. Nevertheless, it held all the necessary equipment for long-range broadcasts, including its crown jewel–a giant laser that rose through a hatch on the top floor. Aimed at the sky and the vastness of space beyond, it awaited any message its owners chose to send.

Standing outside in the late evening heat, her boots dusted with sand, made the laser seem even more awesome in Sorra's eyes. She had only read of its existence, seen a few images, but this was what connected the galaxy–the exchange of information over incredible distances.

"Do you know what you're going to send yet?" she asked Odelle.

"Besides attempting to warn Earth?" Odelle answered. "No, not yet. That's my goal for tonight and tomorrow. I'll need to cut together the footage you, Elurin, Akton, and Rachel collected into something provocative."

Sorra tore her eyes away from the laser to glance at Odelle. "Provocative?"

"Perhaps provocative wasn't the right word," Odelle said. "Something inspiring. But footage of dead bodies isn't exactly inspiring."

"It can be," Sorra said. "Death can inspire anger, fear—"

"But we want to inspire hope as well," Odelle said.

Sorra shrugged. "I suppose...the hope that if enough people rise up, things will change."

A smile played at the corners of Odelle's mouth. "Anger, fear, hope. A tall order for a single broadcast. I would love to do a series, but who knows how long we'll be able to hold this station? Surely the Dominion will try to reclaim it."

Sorra turned and placed her hands on Odelle's shoulders. "Make what you want to make. Whatever your experience tells you will be most effective. We'll hold this station as long as we need to."

Odelle gave one of Sorra's hands a squeeze. "I know you will."

The moment was interrupted by the sound of someone clearing their throat. Sorra sighed, withdrawing from Odelle and turning to glare at whichever unfortunate underling had decided to intrude. It was Akton, and her annoyance faded a little.

Sorra lifted her chin. "Did the broadcast to Earth go out? The prisoners are cooperating, right?"

Akton frowned. "The prisoners are cooperating. We have full control of the laser, and we sent the data broadcast to Earth without any problems, but we don't have a response."

"That doesn't mean it wasn't received," Odelle said, ever hopeful. "Perhaps Earth simply isn't in a position to answer?"

Sorra shook her head. "A message this urgent? They'd answer. The blockade must be interfering with incoming communications."

"Which means they know we know about the bioweapon," Odelle murmured.

"I already assumed that," Sorra said. "I always assume Corvis knows everything we know. Except where the main base on Nakonum is, of course, or she would have infiltrated it long ago."

"Let's hope it stays that way, ma'am." Akton stomped his boot once on the ground, a naledai gesture to back up a statement with luck.

"Let's hope." Sorra fixed Akton with a stern look. "I've asked the generals to post you here, and they've agreed. It's your job to make sure we hold this station for as long as Odelle needs to distribute her broadcasts. Understood?"

Akton crossed his arms. "Understood. It's an honor."

Odelle gave Sorra's arm a soft nudge. "Stop being so military about it. Akton's our friend." She offered him a smile. "I couldn't be in better hands. Er, claws, I suppose."

Akton chuckled. "Thanks, Odelle."

Sorra sighed but didn't protest their informality any further. She wasn't exactly a stickler for protocol or the rules, either—especially recently. *As long as he takes his job protecting Odelle and this station seriously, I don't care.*

"So," Akton continued. "When are you starting on the first broadcast?"

"In a few minutes," Odelle said. "We don't have time to waste."

"You're dismissed, Akton," Sorra said. "I can watch Odelle until she's ready to head inside and get started."

"I don't need a constant bodyguard," Odelle protested, but went quiet when Sorra gave her shin a light kick.

Akton saluted. "Understood. I'll be inside." He departed at a swift lope, leaving the two of them alone.

Odelle fixed Sorra with an inquiring look. "Well?"

"Well nothing," Sorra said. "Is it a crime to want to watch the sun set on a beautiful world with a beautiful woman?"

A pleased flush spread across Odelle's head. "I see."

She sidled closer, and Sorra took the hint, putting an arm around her shoulders. They watched the sun set for the next several minutes, and Sorra tried her best to think only of the present, instead of the future looming before them.

Chapter Twelve

DESPITE PROMISING TO SPEAK with Elurin, Rachel spent most of the next day avoiding her. Not intentionally. First, she took some well-earned rest in one of the comm station's bunks. Once she'd slept, she volunteered for guard duty. Akton had been only too happy to assign her a post in one of the guard towers. She looked out over the dusty red desert, comm at the ready in case she needed to sound an alert.

At least, that was what she told herself.

Unfortunately, spending several hours alone, with only the occasional radio chatter to confirm all was well, gave her time to think. Her thoughts weren't comfortable ones. *Why does Jethra piss me off so much? And why have things gotten so weird between Elurin and me?*

Rachel had never imagined she'd become such fast friends with an ikthian, but that was the way things had gone, and she wasn't sorry about it. About plenty of other things, yes—considering all ikthians enemies, listening to that idiot Bouchard, failing to rescue Taylor sooner—but not meeting Elurin. That, she'd gotten right.

So, why does everything feel wrong?

She slumped in the rotating chair in the middle of the guard tower used for controlling the defense cannons. It felt more like a human-sized fishbowl than anything. By the time she noticed someone approaching from within the compound, she'd scanned the circular viewing area several times.

Akton strode away from the lone building, headed in her direction. She activated the comm on her wrist. "Coming for a visit, Valerius?"

Akton's reply came through with a low chuckle. *"Right, Harris. A nice visit with a picnic lunch."*

Rachel watched him disappear into the base of the tower. The hatch in the floor opened, and Akton stuck his shaggy head through, clambering into the viewing station alongside her.

"Where's that picnic?"

"I've got half a nutrobar if you want it." He reached into his pocket and tossed it to her. Even though it wasn't particularly appetizing,

Rachel unwrapped it and took a bite. She knew better than to let herself stay hungry in the field.

"Fank oo," she said around a mouthful of the tart, chewy grains.

He nodded. "Anything to report?"

"Nope." She looked out at the wide expanse of red desert. It was mostly barren, aside from a few shadowy rock formations and a couple of towering plants that reminded her vaguely of cacti. "It's a wasteland."

Akton joined her. "Not quite. There's all kinds of life in the desert, if you know where to look."

"Underground, I suppose," Rachel mused.

"Exactly. That's where most sensible creatures go in a climate like this. I could survive in this terrain for weeks without supplies, and so could most other naledai soldiers."

It was meant to be a joke, but something about Akton's comment rubbed Rachel the wrong way. Perhaps it was his unwavering confidence, when she felt so unmoored herself.

"Well, goodie for you," she grumbled. "Brag some more, why don't you?"

Akton fixed his yellow-eyed gaze on her. "What's got up your ass, Harris?"

Rachel sighed. "Sorry. Just have a lot on my mind."

"Elurin?" Akton asked.

Her face flushed. "What makes you think it's about Elurin?"

Akton snorted. "When is it not about Elurin with you?"

"I don't..." Rachel's protests died on her lips. "You know her friend, Jethra? She called Elurin 'pebble' the other day. At least, that's how my translator phrased it. Some kind of nickname."

"Ah." A smirk spread across Akton's thin black lips. "That nickname isn't always romantic, you know. I think the humans have one that's similar—'infant,' or something. It can be romantic or platonic."

It took Rachel a moment to understand. "Infant? Oh! You mean 'babe.' Yeah. But why would I care if Jethra was flirting? None of my business."

Akton's gave her a flat look. "Do you want it to be your business?"

"Elurin's a female ikthian. I'm straight." But the words didn't come out with much confidence. *Of course I'm straight. What else would I be? Surely, I would have known if I was something else before now.*

"You're what?" Akton tilted his head curiously.

"I'm...mostly straight," Rachel declared. "I have sex with men. Human men."

Akton chuckled. "Say that a little louder so the whole base can hear you."

She scowled, buying a few seconds by polishing off the nutrobar. "You're straight, right? You would've known if you were attracted to, like, male naledai or aliens or whoever else."

"Why would you assume I'm not?" Akton's smile spread.

Rachel blinked, trying not to look too outwardly stunned. "Fair point. Guess I'm used to assuming."

"Is it possible that you're making some hasty assumptions about yourself, too?" Akton asked. "Some people have a clear picture of who they'd like to partner with, but exceptions are possible."

"Sure, some people. But..." *What am I trying to say? But not me? How do I know for sure?* She bit her lip then said, after a moment's hesitation, "I've never been attracted to an alien or a woman before."

Akton shrugged. "Elurin is more than a female ikthian. She's a pilot, a soldier, a friend. She's clever and brave. Perhaps you admire those things more than you expected to. Perhaps you haven't been attracted to women or ikthians before now because you hadn't met one like Elurin?"

His straightforward statement made Rachel feel a little less like vomiting. *I'm attracted to Elurin.* Framing it that way was easier.

"I can't help wondering if I'm faking," she mumbled. "At least Taylor was attracted to human women before she ran off with an ikthian. I fully admit I was a bigoted ass about ikthians before I left Earth, but they can still kill with one touch. How is sex supposed to work when your partner can literally poison you?" Another thought struck her. "Oh god, I don't even know what's in her pants. What if it's tentacles?"

"Do you *want* it to be tentacles?" Akton asked.

"No!" Rachel paused. "I mean...I guess it doesn't matter?"

She found herself surprised by her own answer. She had never thought much about whether or not she had a preference for a certain type of anatomy before. All the men she'd ever been with had had penises. Now that she considered the possibility, a vagina—or something a bit more alien—wasn't unappealing, when imagined in combination with Elurin.

"It's not tentacles," Akton said, with more than a hint of mirth in his low, rumbling voice.

"Okay," she said, trying and failing to keep a straight face. Akton's amusement made her want to laugh, too.

"Your face, Harris." Akton couldn't contain his laughter. "Anyway, why does it matter what's in Elurin's pants if you like the rest of her? Surely you can work around it."

"Yeah," Rachel said. "Wait. Are you saying I should tell her how I feel?"

"Why not? If she isn't interested—which I doubt—I'm sure she'll say so and that'll be that."

Rachel's brain stopped somewhere in the middle of Akton's sentence. "Does that mean you think she *is* interested?" The note of hope in her own voice took her by surprise. Until that moment, she hadn't realized how much she wanted Elurin to feel something for her in return.

"I've known Elurin a while," Akton said. "She likes spending time with you. I think she'll be flattered at the very least."

"Really? You think she might be into humans?"

"I think she might be into you," Akton said. "You won't know unless you ask."

"This is the worst timing," Rachel groaned. "We're in the middle of a fucking war. Next time one of us goes on a mission, we might not come back."

Akton put a heavy claw on her shoulder. "That makes it the most important time to tell her. We only get so many chances. So many moments with friends and loved ones. Did you know I had a mate once?"

"No," Rachel said, frowning.

"I did. Oh, don't look at me with a face like a drooping branch. I miss her, but it was years ago. She was a fighter, too. One day, she didn't come back. But if I could do it all over again, I would."

Akton reached into his pocket again. He pulled out a small statuette. It was a carved likeness of a male naledai made of red stone, not dissimilar in color from the desert rock. "We pass these along in my culture. Good luck tokens. It was her brother's, then hers. Now it's mine. I always keep it with me."

Rachel took the statuette when he offered it. "It's beautiful." Its texture was polished smooth, and there was an astounding amount of detail in the fur, especially around its muzzle. "Looks a bit like you."

"Maybe," Akton said. "But anyway, we fight harder when we love harder. Bad things happen. People die. But those things are going to happen anyway. Hear some wisdom from a scarred old battler. When you have the chance for something good, take it."

Rachel passed the statuette back. "With how many scars you have, that's gotta be a lot of well-earned experience. I know that's what the naledai believe, and I'm inclined to agree."

He rumbled in approval. "So you have been learning a little about aliens after all."

"Hey, I've always liked naledai. All the ikthians I ever met before Elurin were trying to kill me."

"Fair," Akton said. "You're relieved of duty, Harris. I'll cover your last half-hour. I'm taking the next shift anyway."

"You don't have to do that," Rachel protested. If anyone deserved a break, it was Akton. He always worked twice as hard as everyone else around him.

"Maybe I want to be alone with my thoughts."

Rachel sighed, realizing she wouldn't win this argument. Despite his friendly and easygoing demeanor, Akton could be stubborn.

"Fine," she said, making for the hatch in the floor. "Do you know where Elurin is?"

"Not sure, but I do know where another friendly face might be found."

"Oh?"

"Taylor's here," Akton said. "Fresh out of the Jor'al medical bay. Odelle wants Maia to be part of her broadcast series, so Taylor tagged along. I assume you don't mind sharing a room? Only so many to go around in a station this small."

That slapped a smile on Rachel's face. "Hell no! That's the best news I've heard in a long time. I'll go find her."

Akton looked quite pleased with himself. His fur even fluffed up. "See? I had my reasons for letting you go early."

"So you did," Rachel said. "And Akton? Thanks."

"You're welcome."

***

"Are you ready?" Odelle asked, fixing Maia with a searching look. Apparently, she wasn't satisfied with what she found there, because she continued. "I appreciate your willingness to help, but if you don't think you're ready, I'll understand."

Maia rubbed her neck ridges. She doubted she'd ever feel ready—and she did want to help, desperately. That was why she'd taken the short jump from the Jor'al rebel base to join Odelle in this room, full of terminals and projectors. She would observe the first broadcast as a test viewer, as well as participating in future ones.

This isn't your fault, but what are you going to do about it? Taylor's words.

She searched inside herself until she found her nerve. "Please, show me."

"The footage may be disturbing," Odelle warned her.

Maia's jaw tightened. "Show me anyway."

Odelle activated the terminals via her wrist comm, and several screens started to play the same message. An image of Odelle's face appeared, grave but trustworthy. "My name is Odelle Lastra. I used to be the Dominion's Executive Media Coordinator. Then, I discovered something."

The image changed to an abandoned field. Empty streets. A deserted town. Odelle's voice spoke over it all. "Chancellor Corvis's administration has developed a bioweapon, capable of mass casualties."

Rows of cots filled with bodies spanned the screens.

Maia's stomach lurched. *Tides, some of them are children.*

"Corvis and her inner circle think they can fool you. That they can convince you mass murder and bioterrorism are justified because the targets are aliens."

The image changed to a laboratory full of divided rooms. Maia noted several different species—naledai, human, ikthian. The viewpoint lingered on one of the ikthian test subjects.

"They are even willing to sacrifice our own people to develop this weapon. Innocent ikthians."

A chill ran down Maia's spine. Those who were less affected by the naledai and human images would likely be swayed by this, assuming they believed what they were seeing.

"We have shown you the truth. Now, we must choose—will we allow the Dominion to kill civilians in our species' name?"

Footage of naledai children, running through a different field. Footage of a human family, laughing. The ikthian test subject, for added emphasis and juxtaposition.

Odelle's face appeared. "Or will we rise up and resist? These are not the acts of a superior species. They are the acts of murderous tyrants."

More footage of dead bodies, some sprawled between cots. Masked naledai health care workers, collapsed due to sickness and exhaustion. Maia's eyes were drawn toward the blisters. *What a horrible way to die. How long did they suffer?*

"They do not speak for me," Odelle said. "Will you let their actions speak for you? Or will you chart your own course?"

A simple symbol took over the screen—a stylized white ship, made of very few lines, atop three waves. The text "Chart your own course. Join us." appeared beneath it.

Maia stared at the screen, even after the audio and visuals stopped. She strained to process what she had just seen. "Those test subjects and the naledai civilians must have died in horrible pain," she finally whispered.

Odelle made a sympathetic noise. "I know. I must admit, using images of the dead for propaganda is...not something I have done before. But I have to believe that, if these people were alive, they would want others informed about the bioweapon. Those who won't dismiss our evidence as a hoax, that is. There will always be some stubborn people we can't convince, no matter what evidence we provide. They will assume it's some great rebel conspiracy."

A lump rose in Maia's throat. She tried to swallow around it, but it only burned. "Yes," she said, but she drifted further from the conversation. Further from Odelle and the room full of terminals, to the images she had seen.

She had seen death in combat, had shot people herself—quite capably, thanks to Akton's training. But this was different. These weren't soldiers who had chosen to follow the Dominion's lust for conquest. They were children. They had died to something long and slow and agonizing.

"Have our scientists learned any more about the virus?" Maia asked.

Odelle's answer came as though from far away. "I'm surprised you didn't ask sooner."

Maia had been too afraid to ask.

"I'll have the reports sent over to you," Odelle offered. "I'm sure you'll understand them better than me. From what I read, there's a lengthy, asymptomatic dormancy period, to allow the host opportunity to infect as many other potential hosts as possible. About ten days for naledai. We aren't sure how long it lasts for ikthians and humans yet.

After that, it happens quickly. Hours, for the old and weak. Perhaps two days for the young and healthy."

Two days. It took some of them two days to die.

"Are there treatment guidelines in place, in case we find any more infected civilians? What about a vaccine?" Maia's hopes for the latter were half-hearted at best. Vaccines took time and resources to develop, and while the rebels possessed samples of the bioweapon, they didn't have the scientific data behind its creation.

Odelle's somber expression confirmed Maia's suspicions. "Procedures for quarantine have been developed, and there are guidelines for end-of-life comfort measures, but I'm afraid that's it."

Disappointed but unsurprised, Maia replied, "Surely the scientists who developed the bioweapon have a vaccine. They wouldn't make one without the other."

"Probably," Odelle said, "but I doubt they'll hand it over if we ask nicely. The generals sent soldiers to the coordinates Sorra and Elurin investigated first thing, but it was too late. The base had already been moved."

Maia pulled a face. "The Dominion does tend to do that with their secret bases, as I recall." She suddenly remembered that she was supposed to be commenting on Odelle's broadcast, but her efforts to articulate her reaction failed. Her mouth worked for several seconds before delivering a wholly unsatisfying response. "About your broadcast. I wish I could help, but you were right. I'm too close to this. All I see is what my research caused. I'm afraid my opinion will be of little use."

Odelle's expression was tender concern. "It's all right," she said, placing a hand on Maia's shoulder. "I thought that might be the case. There's no obligation for you to offer your opinion or participate in future broadcasts. This isn't your fault, Maia. Those deaths are on Corvis and the Dominion's hands, not yours."

Maia forced a weak smile. "Taylor says the same."

"Taylor is a smart human," Odelle said. "You should listen to her."

"She came here with me, you know. The doctors released her. She's eating and walking on her own now." Talking about Taylor comforted her in a way all the reassurances in the galaxy could not. The lump in her throat softened, and her stomach stopped churning with quite so much guilt. "I do want to appear in future broadcasts," she added, feeling a little stronger. "I just need time."

"You'll have it," Odelle said. "Now, about Taylor. Has she settled in? Does she have everything she needs?"

"As far as I know. I left her in our room, but I'm sure she'll seek out Rachel Harris at some point."

Odelle laughed. "I imagine they're quite the pair."

That caused Maia to smile as well. "I imagine you're right."

* * *

Taylor sighed happily, folding her hands behind her head and sprawling on her temporary bunk. There were four similar beds in this room, but it wasn't a hospital bed, so she was extremely pleased. The space reminded her of the military barracks at San Diego base, although the rusty red view through the window was decidedly different.

She felt good. Strong. Although she still needed to watch her diet and drink lots of fluids, she was essentially cleared for duty. She drummed her heels on the mattress before climbing down onto the floor for a few impromptu crunches.

Soon, she had a satisfying burn in her stomach muscles. *Now that I'm relatively safe, I can start conditioning again. Get some of my old body back.*

The sound of the door opening interrupted her. She sat up, pausing as Rachel entered the room. Rachel looked the same as always, dark skin, bouncy hair, big smile. A mischievous twinkle in her brown eyes.

"Harris! Glad to see you out of quarantine."

"Morgan! Glad to see you out of the hospital."

Rachel offered Taylor a hand up, and she took it, standing and pulling her friend into a tight embrace. It felt like forever since they'd reunited in the med bay.

"I heard you were around here somewhere," Taylor said. "Maia told me you helped take the station. I'm glad they approved you for active duty again."

"Wasn't too difficult, since I never showed any symptoms of the virus," Rachel said. "As for the mission, it was easy. There were only a few guards protecting this station, since the Dominion's spread pretty thin thanks to the blockade around Earth. Let's hope they go the way of the Romans and break off into pieces."

Taylor's good mood faded a little. "Have you heard any more about the blockade?"

"Not much. Just that the naledai still can't get a message through about the bioweapon. It's a total blackout."

"Then they have to send someone," Taylor insisted.

"It'd take one hell of a pilot to get through."

"So? We have amazing pilots, like Elurin."

"Yeah." Rachel took a step back, her eyes darting away. "Anyway, I agree. If our messages keep getting blocked, the generals have got to send someone. Hell, I'll volunteer."

"Whoa. Did you chug a gallon of coffee or something? If so, where are you hiding it? Because I want some." Taylor studied Rachel, trying to isolate what was so strange about her behavior. She made less eye contact than usual and spoke rapidly. *Like she's nervous. But what about?*

Rachel floundered for a response, then sat on the edge of Taylor's bunk. Her knee bounced up and down, and she frowned. "When did you realize you were interested in Maia? Like, sexually."

It was Taylor's turn to flounder. She blinked, completely taken aback by the question, but eventually, she summoned a truthful, though awkward, answer. "From the start, I guess. Why?"

Rachel stared at her for a long time, as if searching for further answers in Taylor's eyes. "Did it ever bother you? Being attracted to an alien."

Taylor's brow furrowed as she thought back to her stint as Maia's guard on earth. It felt like years had passed since then, even though it had only been a few months. Part of her felt like a completely different person now, but the memories were still fresh. During the darkest moments of her imprisonment, she'd thought a lot about Maia, and the time they'd shared together.

"It was weird at first. I'd never been attracted to an alien before, and there were all these little moments where I suddenly remembered, 'Oh crap, she isn't human.' But it was surprisingly fast. It just sort of happened." She hesitated. "I was more upset about the fact that she was my prisoner and I was her guard. She tells me I never hurt her, but it still makes me feel like garbage sometimes."

"You aren't garbage." Rachel seemed almost relieved, Taylor noted, to be side-tracked by a subject change. She flung an arm around Taylor's shoulder. "I've gotten to know Maia better. She'd die for you. Not that you'd want her to—I know how stupidly self-sacrificing you can be—but trust me when I say, I'm positive she doesn't have regrets. She went through hell and high water to get you back."

Eclipse

The earnestness in Rachel's words gave Taylor her spark back. She grinned. "Hell and high water. Maia will like that one."

"Yeah."

"So," Taylor asked, "are you going to tell me why you're asking all these questions?"

Rachel's lips twisted into a scowl, like she'd tasted something terrible. "Mmm."

"C'mon. You brought it up. Is it about Elurin?"

Rachel rounded on her. "Did everyone figure it out before me? I've barely seen you since you've been back!"

"Lucky guess." Taylor winked. "You two were trapped in the wilderness together."

"You read too many books," Rachel grumbled.

"I thought you were straight and only interested in humans?"

Rachel heaved an exasperated sigh. "So did I."

"Until you met Elurin," Taylor finished for her.

"Yep."

Taylor paused to consider. Despite her lucky guess about Elurin, she couldn't deny that this was a surprise. Plenty of "straight" women were more flexible than they assumed, but she hadn't pegged Rachel for one of them. She had clear memories of the many flings her friend had shared with men at the San Diego base, including their mutual friend Andrew. As far as she knew, that had been Rachel's last "relationship."

"C'mon," Rachel said, almost pleading. "Say something. Don't just leave me hanging."

"Dunno what you want me to say," Taylor said. "Obviously I'm happy to have you batting for Team Queer, but what are you going to do about it?"

"I don't know," Rachel admitted. "Akton says I should tell her."

"Wait, you told Akton before me?" Taylor said, more to lighten the mood than from actual distress.

"He guessed. Also, I didn't know you were here until he told me."

Taylor rolled her eyes. "Fine, fine. You're forgiven. What did Akton say?"

Rachel twisted the sheets. "That it's worth the risk, especially in wartime."

She nodded. "He would know."

"You knew he lost a mate?" Rachel asked.

"He mentioned her once. For what it's worth, I agree with him. Love is worth the risk."

"What if Elurin doesn't feel the same?" The question, and Rachel's soft tone of voice, made her look several years younger, more like a hesitant teenager than a hardened soldier. She tugged at one of the tight coils of hair by her cheek. "There's this other woman. A naledai."

From the worried look on Rachel's face, Taylor made some assumptions. "Are she and Elurin a thing?"

"No idea. What if they are, and I tell Elurin I'm into her? Then I went through it all for nothing."

"Not for nothing," Taylor said. "Sometimes you have to express yourself to grow, even if you don't get the outcome you want." She gave Rachel's shoulder a playful nudge with hers. "But Elurin might not turn you down. You're a catch, Harris. Before I met Maia, I wouldn't have said no to you."

Rachel smiled, showing a dimple in one of her cheeks. "Asshole."

"I compliment you, then get called an asshole? On top of gossiping with Akton instead of me? Some friend you are." Taylor folded her arms in mock offense.

It felt good, bantering with Rachel like in the old days at San Diego base. Made her feel normal. It was really nice to focus on something as lighthearted as Rachel's love life instead of the war, or the trauma she'd endured.

"Hey, I saved your life," Rachel protested. "You don't get to bitch."

"I was a prisoner of war. I can bitch about whatever I damn well want."

They burst out laughing. Taylor leaned her cheek against Rachel's shoulder, back heaving, stomach cramping. It was the first time she'd ever joked about her trauma, and it felt surprisingly freeing. Maybe that was fucked up, but she was too happy to care.

After a while, Rachel took a deep breath. "I'm really glad you're my roommate."

"We're roommates?" Taylor repeated. "Nice!"

"For the next few days, anyway. I assume Maia's sharing a bunk with you?"

"Good assumption."

"About that. I don't want to be gross, but…"

Taylor had to stifle more laughter. "Sex questions?"

Rachel winced. "How do they—how does it work?"

Taylor's smile widened. "I don't normally kiss and tell, but under the circumstances..." Rachel hung onto her words, looking equally nervous and hopeful. "Maybe I can make an exception."

Chapter Thirteen

ELURIN EXAMINED HER RIFLE, making sure all the proper components were in place. The slender black weapon was fully charged. Heat sink worked. Plasma chamber active. No damage to the framework. She'd checked the rifle before and after all her recent missions; it paid to be thorough.

So why do I feel uneasy?

Because Rachel hadn't sought her out yet. That had to be the reason. Elurin never coped well with the knowledge that an important conversation needed to happen sometime in the fuzzy, indefinite future.

Sighing, she placed her weapon back in its holster. She should probably leave the cluttered, second floor space that had become an impromptu weapons room and return to her assigned bunk on the first floor. Rachel was bunking with her—Akton's doing, no doubt—but Elurin hadn't seen her the night before. Either Rachel had been given an assignment that'd kept her up, or she'd made herself scarce.

Is she avoiding me? Elurin couldn't come up with a reason why. Rachel had been snappy since their last mission. Moody and unpredictable. *But that doesn't mean she gets a free pass for being a dick to Jethra and hiding from me.*

As she left the temporary weapon room, passing a few naledai on the way, Elurin couldn't help but wonder if her annoyance was rooted in more than Rachel's odd behavior. *Come on. If you can't be direct with yourself in your own head, you have no right to be pissed at Rachel. You have feelings for her. Dumb, inconvenient feelings.*

They had crept up on Elurin over the past few months. Somewhere along the way, Rachel's stubbornness, brashness, and bravery had become not just admirable, but attractive.

Elurin took the elevator to the first floor, the communal area of the base, mostly empty of broadcasting equipment. It had living areas, as well as a mess-style kitchen and storage rooms. She headed toward her bunk, trying not to pin any hopes on what, or who, she might find. Hope found her, however, when she opened the doors and saw two humans waiting inside. Rachel was sitting on the bed, with Taylor close beside her.

"So, their clits, right? They have them, but they're different. Kinda curve-shaped, and they don't have a hood. It's in the same place, but not like a mini penis." Taylor pulled a face, as though what she'd just said was embarrassing.

Rachel belted out a hearty, uninhibited laugh. "Isn't penis the *worst* word in the English language? Penis. Who came up with that?"

The spots on Elurin's forehead burned like miniature suns. This definitely wasn't the kind of conversation she'd expected to walk in on, but it did make her heart race. *Why is Rachel asking Taylor about interspecies sex?* With ikthians, she presumed. She recognized the description.

Suddenly, Taylor locked eyes with her from across the room. The connection hit Elurin like a blast to the gut. She stepped back, though not far enough for the door to close in front of her. The two of them exchanged identical panicked looks.

"Do ikthian males have dicks? Am I going to have to order a fake one to have sex with her?" Rachel continued.

"Rachel," Taylor interrupted.

"I'm way too far from home to place that kind of order—"

"Rachel!"

Rachel paused when Taylor jabbed her in the side with an elbow. At first, she looked like she might complain, but then she noticed where Taylor was looking.

Elurin felt the exact moment Rachel locked eyes with her. If Taylor's gaze had been a plasma blast, Rachel's would've taken her head clean off. Startled, then clearly embarrassed.

"Elurin?" she squawked, at the same time Elurin said, "Rachel?"

"That's my cue." Taylor leapt from the bed like it had caught fire. She fast-marched past Elurin and out of the room, but not before flashing Rachel what seemed to Elurin like an encouraging grin.

The doors closed at long last, but the wait for one of them to speak was even longer. Elurin looked at Rachel. Rachel looked back at her.

Elurin's head swam. *Do I say something? Wait for her to say something? What's the protocol?* Alarms went off in Elurin's brain. "Maybe I should go."

"Don't!" Rachel shot up from the bunk almost as fast as Taylor. She reached out, as if to prevent Elurin from leaving, but seemed to catch herself a moment later. Elurin felt vaguely disappointed beneath the frantic pounding of her heart. "I mean, stay. Please."

Rachel gestured toward the bed, and Elurin approached with considerable hesitation. To buy herself time, she unstrapped her rifle and placed it a safe distance away, atop one of the cheaply made metal dressers. Only after she'd taken a deep breath did she join Rachel on the bed.

They sat a good two feet apart, so their knees didn't touch.

"I don't know what to say," Rachel blurted. She groaned, slapping her forehead with her palm. "Stupid."

A desire to comfort Rachel emerged from the confusing swirl of embarrassment and hope in Elurin's gut. Regardless of the situation, they were friends.

"Hey," she said, offering Rachel a smile. She wondered if she should reach out but refrained. "You aren't stupid."

"How much did you hear?" Rachel asked.

There was a plea in Rachel's eyes, but Elurin couldn't tell what kind of answer Rachel wanted. *Or maybe an answer isn't all she wants.*

"Enough to know there's an ikthian 'she.'" Elurin pressed her fingertips into the webbing on the opposite hand. "That ikthian wouldn't happen to be me, would it?"

Rachel's brown eyes went wide. Brown. Not a typical color for ikthians, but for a moment, Elurin feared she might fall into them and drown.

"Um," Rachel paused. "What if it was?"

"I…" Elurin steeled herself. "I won't lie and say I'm not interested. But I thought you didn't like ikthians? I mean, not all ikthians, but—"

"No, you're right," Rachel said, with a note of self-reprimand in her voice. "I hated ikthians because the only ones I met tried to kill me. But then I met you, and…well, you're awesome. I started feeling things. Things I still don't understand, but I'm not unhappy about. Just confused."

She said I'm awesome. Elurin couldn't help it. She grinned. *She's attracted to me!* Elurin's heart did a dizzying flip. "Because I'm an alien, or an ikthian specifically?"

"Both," Rachel admitted. "And you're female. I don't know about your culture, but in mine, same-gender pairings are rarer. Not taboo, but they aren't the norm. I guess I felt like, if I was attracted to people other than human men, I would've known."

Elurin felt like she was floating on sea foam, leaping like the fizzy white top of a breaker. "Only one way to find out for sure, right?" she said.

On a hunch, she scooted closer. The distance closed from two feet to one, and though Rachel's chest hitched, she didn't pull away. She leaned closer.

"You'd seriously be okay with that?" Rachel blurted. "Wait, just to be clear, you're offering to kiss me, right? To see if I like—"

Elurin ran out of patience. She cupped Rachel's cheek, and Rachel leaned the rest of the way in to meet her.

Their mouths didn't meet dead-on at first. Both of them tried to adjust, but in the same direction, which only made the disparity worse. After a moment of awkwardness and soft laughter, they finally got it right, and Elurin realized she tasted the softest, fullest lips she'd ever encountered.

Different. Good-different. Warm, with something salty. She recalled Maia's comment about sweat. *Oh, Tides. Does all her skin taste this good?* She desperately wanted to find out.

* * *

Rachel had kissed plenty of people before. Fellow soldiers, mostly. Nice guys. She'd even had feelings for some of them. They'd usually cared about her pleasure, and she'd tried to return the favor.

All of that experience became utterly irrelevant the moment Elurin's mouth met hers. The odd angle and her own fast, nervous breaths reminded her of her first kiss back home. She'd been ten and they'd done little more than smush their faces together behind a fence to find out what all the fuss was about.

Then, something clicked. A spark. Passion, or maybe something softer. Something Rachel wouldn't have been open to without a solid foundation of trust. She couldn't name the feeling, but it rushed from the roots of her hair to her toes.

Elurin's tongue brushed Rachel's top lip, and a shaking hand came to rest on her hip. It fluttered, asking, *"Is this okay?"*

Rachel put her hand over Elurin's. Her fear of skin contact with ikthians was long gone, and present-Rachel was fully distracted by Elurin's lips. She tasted more like heat than any particular flavor. Her tongue was dexterous and long in a way that gave Rachel absolutely filthy ideas. She moaned, sliding her hand up Elurin's thigh.

Fuck. This was supposed to be just a kiss. What am I doing? But she definitely didn't want to stop.

She broke away only when her lungs started burning. Elurin chased her lips, whimpering. Her eyes fluttered open, revealing a flash of milky white eyelid. She seemed befuddled, like she wasn't sure what had just happened.

"Why're you breathing so fast?" she asked. "You're not panicking, right?"

Rachel's eyes flicked down to Elurin's chest to check the ikthian's breathing. It was slow and steady, alarmingly so at first, but Rachel laughed as she realized what Elurin meant.

"Humans always breathe fast compared to ikthians," she said, but then she noticed Elurin's breasts, a firm swell beneath her dark grey shirt. Once Rachel started staring, she couldn't tear her eyes away.

"Ahem." Elurin cleared her throat, and Rachel realized she'd been caught. "Hoping my shirt will come off if you keep staring?" Elurin asked, her lips turned up in a smirk.

"Sorry." Rachel started to remove her hand from Elurin's leg, but Elurin stopped her.

"Wait." There was an awkward beat, but then Elurin said, "I could take it off, if you want."

Rachel's heart hammered in her ears. She wouldn't have been brave enough to make the offer first, but since Elurin had risen to the challenge...

"Yeah. I want."

Elurin stripped her shirt over her head, revealing a tight white undershirt beneath. It showed the hardened points of her nipples with mouthwatering clarity.

"Fuck." Rachel hadn't meant to say anything, but she couldn't help it.

The next minute was slow, breathless torture. She trailed her fingers along Elurin's stomach, gathering her courage. Elurin's skin was soft. It had less give than Rachel's own, but it was pleasantly supple. The tiny scales left a tingling imprint of texture against Rachel's fingertips.

"You okay?" Elurin stared at her with wide blue eyes, urging her to do...something.

The shirt. Right. Cautiously, Rachel pulled it off. It ended up somewhere on the floor as she cupped Elurin's breasts, testing their weight. They were heavier than they appeared, but soft. Rachel had to admit, she enjoyed the sigh Elurin spilled into their next kiss when she gave the right nipple a gentle twist.

"More, please...wait, let's get more comfortable first," Elurin murmured into her mouth.

Elurin rolled onto her back, dragging Rachel down with her. She ended up sprawled on top of Elurin, and a shudder raced through her as the line of their bodies met. Elurin's mouth found her neck, and Rachel stiffened at the graze of sharp teeth above the collar of her shirt.

Right. Predatory, carnivorous species. But Elurin wasn't the only one with fangs. Rachel nuzzled Elurin's collarbone, searching for a place to suck. Ikthian collar bones were slender and flexible compared to human ones, but apparently, they were sensitive. She got an even better reaction when she ran her tongue along the ridges that lined the side of Elurin's neck.

"Are you...sure you've never...done this before?" Elurin panted, obviously struggling for words.

Rachel glowed with pride. She could do this! Be with a woman. Be with an ikthian. Most of all, she wanted to be with Elurin. "Never."

Elurin used her distraction to reverse their positions, pinning Rachel's back to the mattress. Her tongue peeked out, rolling over her lower lip, and Rachel felt a sudden wave of dizziness. *If she goes down on me with that tongue, I might pass out.*

"Tell me what you like." Elurin trailed her fingers up Rachel's belly, beneath her shirt, lifting the hem several inches. "What you don't like." She planted a warm kiss on Rachel's stomach, slightly above her navel. "And if you need to stop at any point, it's okay. I won't be upset."

Rachel appreciated the safety net, but there wasn't a single part of her that wanted to stop. She'd always been a do-or-die kind of woman. "Same for you. But no way in hell do I want to stop."

She lifted her shirt, making short work of her bra as well. Goosebumps erupted on her arms, but not from the chill of the air against her bare flesh. Elurin was staring at her with what looked like awe.

"Do all humans have breasts that big?"

Rachel didn't know whether to laugh or blush. It wasn't the first time a lover had complimented her assets, but coming from Elurin, it made her stomach flutter.

"Not all," she replied.

They could be both a blessing and a curse, but she appreciated the admiration in Elurin's wide blue eyes.

Elurin's hand twitched on Rachel's stomach. "Is it okay if I touch them?"

Rachel's nipples stiffened at the mere thought of Elurin's fingers grazing them. "Please." Elurin leaned in but didn't use her fingers. Rachel gasped as Elurin's mouth wrapped around her right nipple. She tensed at the silky heat, and the light pressure that followed. "Oh, shit."

"Hmm?" Elurin drew back, releasing Rachel's nipple to the air. "Did I do something wrong?"

"No," Rachel mumbled, pushing lightly on the back of Elurin's crest. "You did something very right. Please, do that again."

Elurin smirked as she took the peak of Rachel's breast back into her mouth. Unable to resist, Rachel tightened her hold on Elurin's crest. Elurin moaned around her nipple, rocking forward against Rachel's hip. *Sensitive crest? Okay.* Rachel ran her fingers along the upward-angled silver spikes as Elurin sucked, using a hint of teeth.

A lance of desire shot straight between Rachel's legs at the slight pressure. It wasn't pain, exactly, but it lit her nerves on fire.

"You have these ticklish little hairs all over your skin," Elurin mumbled, releasing Rachel's nipple. She dragged her tongue up along Rachel's sternum, and its ever-so-slightly rough texture soon had Rachel reeling. "Oh fuck. Maia was right. You taste like candy."

"What?" Rachel had absolutely no idea what Elurin was talking about, and the eager way Elurin latched onto her other nipple didn't help clear her head.

"Salt candy." Elurin tried to explain, while also not letting go of Rachel's nipple for too long. "That thing you do, the saltwater cooling thing. Tastes good."

Sweat. *A little weird, but if she thinks I taste like candy, I guess that means more mouth for me?* Being Elurin's personal popsicle probably wouldn't be a hardship. She hooked one of her knees around Elurin's leg, tilting her pelvis up. "The more of a workout you give me, the more I'll sweat."

Elurin bit down on the side of Rachel's breast, almost too hard, and growled. The flash of pain, combined with the vibrations, made Rachel's hips jerk. She was rewarded with friction against Elurin's bare stomach. Her pants and underwear were still on, but she wanted them off yesterday.

Elurin hooked her fingers into the waistband of Rachel's pants, helping her shimmy out of them. She had to roll off for a moment while Rachel kicked her fatigues onto the floor. Rachel offered a sheepish smile, then Elurin was blazing a trail down her stomach, all sharp teeth and hot mouth.

A shiver raced down Rachel's spine. *What if Elurin's weirded out by what she finds? I know ikthians don't have hair or anyth—*

Elurin tugged her underwear down and ducked beneath her knees, eclipsing Rachel's thoughts.

Rachel waited, unsure whether to watch or stare at the ceiling. After a moment, she decided the ceiling was completely lame. Elurin grinned up at her, both hands rubbing gentle lines on her thighs.

"You have vilodent stripes," she said, sounding very pleased.

"What?"

Elurin ran her fingertips along Rachel's thighs. Age and puberty had left her with a few faded stretch marks. She'd never given them much thought, but she laughed as Elurin dragged her tongue along one of them, apparently fascinated.

"Stretch marks," she explained. "Don't ikthians have—"

She lost all interest in explaining as Elurin started kissing her thighs. Heat swelled within her, and Rachel curled her toes. She didn't want to rush Elurin's exploration, but her clit had its own heartbeat, and she was pretty sure there'd be a puddle on the sheets before Elurin's mouth even reached its destination. But then, Elurin's tongue stopped abruptly.

Rachel couldn't remember how to breathe. *What's she doing?*

Slowly, reverently, Elurin brought her hands up, peeling Rachel's outer lips apart with both thumbs. Her blue eyes widened, and the delight Rachel saw there eased her nerves.

"It's so soft," Elurin whispered, sliding her thumb pads higher to graze Rachel's pubic hair. She'd kept it somewhat trimmed, but she wished she was better prepared. Elurin clearly enjoyed the texture. "What does it feel like for you when I touch it?"

"Nice," Rachel forced out. "Really nice."

"What about this?"

One of Elurin's thumbs moved inward, brushing the tip of her clit. It was a light touch, but Rachel's hips almost levitated off the bed. "Fuck!"

"I'll take it you like that," Elurin laughed.

Rachel hissed as she felt her hood being pulled back.

"Cute! It's just a little nub. I mean, I looked on the extranet, but..."

"Elurin," Rachel rasped, clawing the back of Elurin's crest, "stop talking."

So Elurin sucked, and Rachel saw stars.

The pressure was hot. Firm. Intense. When Elurin's tongue actually wrapped around her and squeezed, Rachel nearly came right then and there.

After that, Elurin dove in without hesitation. She licked and sucked in what had to be a frenzy rather than careful deliberation, but that didn't stop her from hitting all the right spots. She grabbed Elurin's head with her other hand too, biting her bottom lip to keep from screaming. *Aw, fuck it. What do I care?* She screamed, and the sound became Elurin's name.

***

Rachel's flavor filled Elurin's mouth, all warm salt. It left her dizzy, making it almost impossible to concentrate. Luckily, Rachel didn't seem to mind. Each stroke Elurin tried with her tongue caused Rachel to clutch her crest harder, and every spot she focused on earned more moans. Her confidence swelled. She wasn't entirely sure what she was doing, but as long as Rachel enjoyed it, she would gladly count her efforts successful.

Soft, curly hairs tickled Elurin's cheeks and chin as she explored, but she loved how they felt. Loved how Rachel smelled and tasted. Loved when Rachel whimpered her name. Hearing Rachel—strong, beautiful, take-no-shit soldier Rachel—make such a vulnerable sound drove Elurin crazy. It was all because of her. For her.

Eager for more of Rachel's flavor, Elurin released the swollen bud of her clit and slid down toward her entrance. Pressing her tongue forward, Elurin found more delicious heat. She released a muffled groan, pushing as deep as she could.

Rachel jack-knifed off the bed, digging her heels hard into Elurin's back. It didn't hurt, but it took her by surprise. She withdrew, fearing she'd gone too far.

"Don't stop," Rachel pleaded, scratching the back of Elurin's crest. The edges of her claws—*nails,* Elurin reminded herself, another delightful human feature—made her scales itch in the most wonderful way. She gave another thrust of her tongue, and Rachel's plea became a continuous chant. "Don't stop, don't-stop-oh-fuck-don't-stop!"

Elurin thrusted and swirled until her jaw ached, reaching as deep as possible. Rachel's inner walls were silky and smooth, but they had some texture. Soft ridges that swelled the more she rubbed against them.

They twitched when her nose bumped Rachel's clit, so she made sure to do it on purpose.

Above her, Rachel had started panting. "Fuck. 'Lurin. Gonna come..."

If her mouth hadn't been busy, Elurin would have beamed. She'd learned from her reading that humans were capable of orgasm, but the theoretical knowledge wasn't even in the same universe as the reality. The fact that Rachel was coming because of her made it something else entirely.

She doubled her efforts, moving her tongue deep and hard, catching Rachel's clit with her top lip. Rachel went rigid, every limb trembling. After a timeless second, she melted. Her entire body shuddered, and she sobbed something that could have been Elurin's name. Elurin decided it was, because she dearly wanted it to be.

The warm muscles around her tongue contracted, picking up a throbbing rhythm. Elurin held her position and was rewarded for her efforts. Sticky heat flooded her mouth, its taste heavier and more concentrated. If she'd thought Rachel's taste was delicious before, this was even better.

She kept curling and sucking, applying as much pressure as she could, until Rachel's tremors stopped and she flopped onto the bunk, clearly exhausted. Her beautiful brown skin had taken on a gorgeous sheen, and when Rachel gave a weak tap on her forehead, urging her to move to less sensitive areas, Elurin wasted no time licking the sheen, from Rachel's thighs all the way back to her nipples.

"You're gonna kill me," Rachel laughed.

Her gentle pushing became stroking, and Elurin crooned as Rachel's fingers dug into her crest. She really liked the way human nails felt when they grazed her skin. Immensely satisfying. The next time her scales felt dry, she'd have to ask Rachel to ease some of the discomfort.

Wait. That's an awfully intimate thing to ask. What if Rachel isn't in this for the intimacy? She obviously feels some kind of way about me, but what if it's the product of wartime stress? What if it isn't that serious?

Her what-ifs dispersed when Rachel started rubbing the back of her neck, gazing up into her eyes. "That was fantastic. Can I try? That is, if you're up for it."

The hot ball of need in Elurin's lower belly blazed. She did need, desperately. "Please," she moaned, flipping onto her back beside Rachel and spreading her legs. "Do whatever you're comfortable with. Just please do something, because I think I'm going crazy."

Rachel's brown eyes flashed. With curiosity, maybe. Desire, definitely. She rolled on top, and Elurin sighed with happiness. She didn't know if Rachel's build—lush curves and fat sculpted over sheets of strong muscle—was a common human thing, or just a Rachel thing, but she was obsessed with it. She loved how Rachel's body felt against hers and how Rachel's mouth felt as slid down her chest.

Rachel spent a short time playing with her breasts before continuing the descent, but Elurin stole a ragged breath as Rachel nipped her stomach. Her third eyelid threatened to cloud her vision. She blinked, wanting to commit the moment to memory–not just the visual, but every amazing feeling and sensation.

The minute passed in a blur. Rachel ended up between her legs, spreading her open. Elurin felt a wave of empathy. The hints of embarrassment she'd thought she'd seen on Rachel's face made a lot more sense. The heat of Rachel's gaze made Elurin feel incredibly vulnerable, although it wasn't all bad. Something about it was sexy, too. Being exposed. Open for Rachel to see and touch and taste.

"Whoa."

Elurin tried to work some moisture into her dry mouth. "Hm?"

"You're really beautiful."

Elurin couldn't help laughing. "Thanks? I guess I shouldn't have called yours cute?"

Rachel didn't seem upset. She breathed deep and swiped with her tongue, running it over the ridge of Elurin's clit. It felt good. Really good. More blunt pressure than dexterity, but her tongue was warm and smooth. Combined with the sight of Rachel's gorgeous face between her thighs, and the feel of Rachel's curly hair grazing her skin, it was more than enough.

"I'm gonna come in two seconds and embarrass myself," Elurin gasped.

She grabbed Rachel's hair, although she was careful not to pull hard. The texture of Rachel's hair felt just as good rubbing against the webbing between her fingers as it did tickling her thighs.

Rachel made a low noise, almost a growl. "Don't care. Wanna make you come."

Her tongue started moving again, and though Elurin desperately wanted to keep watching, her head lolled to the side. She curled her toes, fisting the sheets in one hand and Rachel's hair in the other. All she could do was hold on for the ride.

***

Elurin looked different.

Though her parts were similarly structured—a set of swollen outer lips, a hoodless clit, and an opening underneath—Rachel noticed the variances. There weren't as many inner folds near her opening. Her scales became larger and smoother as her skin tone transitioned from silver to purple, and they were covered in shimmering wetness.

Rachel had pleasured herself enough to know what her own wetness felt like–thick, smooth, stringy depending on the time of month. Elurin's wetness felt more like oil–warm, thin, and slippery. Two of her fingers slid in effortlessly, and Elurin clenched around them.

"Oh!"

Rachel paused to make sure the sound was a positive one, but when she checked Elurin's face, she saw that the ikthian's eyes had rolled back. "This okay?"

Elurin took several seconds to get her bearings. "How? You're so deep."

Ah. Her fingers didn't have any webbing between them. Obviously, ikthian fingers made for somewhat shallow penetration. *Well, I've gotta have something going for me, since she has that incredible tongue.*

"Keep going," Elurin urged, rocking her pelvis.

Rachel brought the pad of her thumb to Elurin's clit, rubbing in time with the deep, curling thrusts of her third and fourth fingers. More oily slickness spilled out, coating her palm and dripping onto her wrist. She swallowed, remembering how it tasted. Sweeter than expected, but also slightly musky.

She replaced her thumb with her lips, sucking Elurin's clit as she worked her fingers. Her combined efforts soon had Elurin shuddering. She muttered into the pillow, mostly about how good it felt, interspersed with a few words that Rachel's translator couldn't interpret, even with updated naledai software.

"More," Elurin grunted, tugging on Rachel's hair.

Rachel took the hint and sucked harder, curling her fingers until the tendons in her forearm burned. She needed to make Elurin feel as amazing as Elurin had made her feel.

"Fuck!"

A flood of wetness hit Rachel's chin and the heel of her hand. It was more than she expected, but she took it in stride, hooking her fingers hard and applying as much pressure as possible. Elurin made a strangled noise, then went limp, her inner walls throbbing while the rest of her quivered.

Rachel's heart fluttered along. She'd always enjoyed making her partners come. It was fun and made her feel accomplished as a lover. But something about making Elurin come was different. She couldn't describe what, exactly, but some part of her knew it was important.

Elurin moaned. "Rachel, stop. Done."

With some reluctance, Rachel released Elurin's clit. She stilled her fingers, satisfying herself by licking Elurin's wetness off her own lips instead. She grinned, and Elurin returned the gesture with a weak but grateful smile.

"So, I did okay?" Rachel asked.

Elurin rolled her eyes. "You were decent, I guess." Rachel almost choked, and Elurin started laughing. "Come on. You know I'm messing with you. That was fantastic. Your fingers are magic."

"Yeah?" Rachel gave them a curl.

Elurin's head lolled against the pillow as she groaned. "Still sensitive. You'll make me come again."

"So?"

"Just give me a minute. Then we can go again."

"Yes, please." Rachel felt another insistent tug between her legs at the offer, but she ignored it in favor of removing her fingers. Without thinking, she popped them into her mouth, enjoying Elurin's slack-jawed stare. She clambered up the bunk and flopped down next to Elurin's sprawled form. "That wasn't as weird as I thought it would be," she said, only half-realizing she was talking aloud.

Elurin snorted. "That's good, I suppose?"

"No!" Rachel's face burned. She hadn't meant to say it like that. "I guess I was expecting something more...alien?"

"Don't tell Maia," Elurin said. "She'll give you a whole lecture on the Ancients and their genetic seeding project, and start listing all kinds of biological overlap between our species—"

"Elurin?"

"Hm?"

"Forget Maia right now."

"You started it."

Rachel smiled and rested her cheek on Elurin's shoulder. "I would've figured out a way even if you did have a weird shaped clit. You overheard that part of the conversation, didn't you?"

"Yeah," Elurin chuckled.

"I mean, I'm glad I could work with your set-up, but something else wouldn't have been a deal breaker."

"That's sweet," Elurin said. "Weird, but sweet."

Rachel huffed. "You're weird."

"Thanks. You know exactly what a woman wants to hear after sex, Harris."

"You called me weird first!"

That devolved into a tickle fight, which soon turned into more making out. Before Rachel knew it, they were lost in each other's lips again.

Chapter Fourteen

VACCINE. VACCINE. VACCINE. THE subject stuck in Maia's mind all morning and well into the afternoon. After grabbing a quick bite to eat, she spoke to one of the guards on duty about securing a private terminal. Logic dictated that there was a vaccine, and when she considered who might know where, only one name came to mind—Irana.

Odelle had been privy to many Dominion secrets, but not as many as the Dominion's former spymaster. That meant talking to her mother again—a prospect Maia was willing to endure, if there was even the slightest chance of preventing others from succumbing to Corvis' bioweapon.

"Here you are," the naledai guard said, a woman with a roguish smile and equally roguish scars. By naledai standards, she was most certainly attractive. "I had to sweet-talk a few folks to reserve this room, but you won't be bothered. Will it do?"

The room had several monitors and a standing silver terminal, empty of people except for the two of them. Maia suspected this room had once been an office, probably belonging to one of the employees working in the broadcast station. She gave her escort a smile. "This is more than adequate. Thank you...Jethra, correct?"

She was relieved when the soldier returned her smile. "Yep. You're a friend of Elurin's, right?"

"I believe so," Maia said. She'd never had the opportunity to make many friends in the past, although she'd had decent enough relationships with some of her colleagues before her defection.

One of her only close friendships before meeting Taylor had been with a member of the janitorial staff on Akram, the first world she'd visited to begin her postgraduate research. The older naledai had provided one of her first friendly interactions with aliens—sharing part of his lunch when she'd forgotten hers. She'd brought him lunch the next day, and continued to do so, knowing he surely couldn't have much to share in the first place.

Despite the short time they'd known each other, his friendship had left a profound impact on Maia. She had become acutely aware that the DNA she was studying served as the foundation for sentient beings, with their own hopes and dreams.

She couldn't help wondering where he was for a wistful moment. *Pay attention. You have work to do, or more people might end up like the naledai in Odelle's broadcast.*

"Should I leave you to it?" Jethra asked, tilting her head.

"You may." Maia knew she must have made things awkward, staring into space while she reminisced. "I wouldn't want to keep you from your duties. Thank you again."

"You got it, Doc." Jethra threw a casual, arms-across-the-chest salute, then strode off.

Once Maia gathered her courage, she approached the terminal and inputted the familiar codes to contact the base on Jor'al. It took a little explaining, cajoling, and name-dropping, but since she was on the short list of individuals allowed to speak with Irana, it wasn't long before she'd convinced the guards to establish a connection on a secure comm.

"Maia," Irana said, staring at her with piercing blue eyes from the terminal screen. *"I must admit, this is a surprise."*

Maia fidgeted as she eyed her mother's image. Irana sat in the same secure room where Maia had last visited her. It hadn't changed, and neither had Irana's appearance. Not much, anyway. Perhaps she'd gained some weight.

"Why would it be a surprise?" Maia asked.

Irana's faint smile faded. *"The last time we spoke, you made it clear that you were ashamed of me and my choices."*

Her tone was neither sharp, nor accusatory. It was soft. *Regretful?* Maia couldn't be sure, and she was under too much stress to make guesses. Socializing with Odelle, Jethra, and then the guards had drained her limited supply of extroverted energy. *Good. She should feel ashamed.*

"That is not what I called to discuss," she said.

If Irana was surprised, the image didn't show it. *"You need more information."*

That was obvious enough. Information was the primary reason Maia had re-established contact with her mother, aside from the foolishly optimistic hope for emotional closure.

"I do."

"What kind of information?"

"Where we might find more information about this bioweapon. A vaccine, perhaps. Surely your scientists developed one, for self-preservation if nothing else."

"As I told you before, I knew Corvis was developing something at those coordinates, but I never had the chance to become involved before my imprisonment," Irana replied.

"Would you have? Become involved, I mean," Maia blurted, unable to stop herself. A heavy stone had settled in her stomach, burning as though surrounded by fire.

Irana hesitated. "I would have had serious reservations. Such a weapon could easily escape control. Perhaps that is part of the reason Corvis had me locked away. She knew I would object to such risky methods."

"Because it might escape Dominion control," Maia repeated, numbly. Not because of those tiny bodies. Dead. Not because it would kill innocent naledai. Or humans, like Taylor.

Irana shifted on the edge of the bed and Maia caught a glimpse of her expression, sorrowful, without a doubt. "Yes. And because it would very likely kill civilians. That goes without saying."

"Does it?" Maia asked, but she didn't have the energy to muster up more than a brief flare of bitterness. She wouldn't forget which concern her mother had mentioned first.

"Of course." After a moment, Irana seemed to shake off her hurt. "As for where a vaccine might be housed, I hesitate to speculate, but if I were to hazard a guess…"

"Tell me," Maia said, with growing hope. Her heart beat a little faster. "If you truly do care about saving lives, or even about me, now is the time to prove it."

"This is not solid information," Irana warned. Her lips pulled into an uncertain frown. "If I were developing a bioweapon, I would keep the vaccine close at hand."

Maia realized what her mother meant at once. "Korithia," she said, feeling a tingle along her neck ridges. It made chilling sense. If the virus spread far more rapidly than the Dominion intended, or mutated, surely Corvis would want the vaccine close to preserve the homeworld and inner planets. The ikthian test subjects made more sense. Surely the Dominion's scientists would want to know how the virus would affect their own kind—and if it did, lessen that effect.

"This is only a guess," Irana said.

141

Maia braced her hands on the cold surface of the terminal stand. "Continue guessing. If there is a sample of the vaccine on Korithia, or even data on how to recreate it, where would it be?"

A furrow appeared in Irana's brow beneath the blue mottling of her crest. Her milky third eyelids slid across her irises several times. *"Corvis' ship, the Wavestar. The one she uses in states of emergency."*

Maia gasped. Surely human and naledai leaders had something similar–a mobile command center that could remove a leader from danger swiftly. Upon reflection, it was the perfect place to keep a sample of the vaccine. Secure, mobile, close

"How certain are you?" It was an unfair question to ask, but Maia did so anyway. *If I could get my hands on that vaccine, nothing like the images I saw—that I caused—would ever happen again.* She already felt the relief, the release of guilt, such an action would bring. It flooded her heavy limbs with new energy.

"It is a reasonable guess," Irana said. "In your position, I would send a team to investigate."

The risk of sending a team to Korithia, no matter the danger, paled in comparison with the chance of stopping the bioweapon. The lives that might be lost if they guessed wrong—or even guessed right—were far outnumbered by the lives that might be spared.

"I will speak to the leadership." She licked her lips. "Mother?"

Irana met her question with an expectant gaze.

"I do not forgive you, but when we spoke last, you assumed I thought you were a monster. I do not think you are a monster," she said, with all the sincerity she could muster. *Considering you a monster would be easier, but it would remove the burden of guilt for my own complicity. The truth is far more complex and painful.*

Something about Irana's posture relaxed. Her shoulders became softer, as did her eyes. *"Thank you."*

***

"I realize acting on this information could prove dangerous." Maia addressed the same terminal she had used to contact her mother, which now displayed Generals Kross and Oranthis on-screen. "However, I fear we have no other choice."

Sorra and Odelle, who had arranged the call, stood beside her. Though she and Sorra weren't quite on friendly terms, Maia appreciated her presence—and, of course, Odelle was always a steadfast source of support. Though Maia was certain of her own opinion, she didn't know what the generals would think.

The generals held their silence. Oranthis dipped his shaggy head in thought, while Kross adjusted his eyepatch, scratching the scar that bisected his snarled eye socket. Behind them, naledai soldiers and a few ikthians rushed between blinking terminals, twisting to pass each other in the crowded space. Obviously, the generals had considered this call urgent enough to take in the Jor'al command center.

"Dangerous is an understatement," Kross rumbled. "What you're proposing is downright reckless."

Before Maia could respond, Odelle spoke. "The decision is ultimately yours, but in my mind, the risk is necessary. A vaccine sample could prevent loss of life on a tremendous scale."

Sorra folded her arms, nodding. "Kalanis says it would take months to develop our own vaccine, if not longer. Most of our scientists are weapons experts, and most of our doctors are trauma specialists. We just don't have the resources for a project like this."

"I also believe Irana is right about the *Wavestar*," Odelle added. "There must be a sample aboard. I worked with Corvis for years. She would keep the vaccine close in case of emergency."

Oranthis' thin black lips pulled into a grimace. "Why not vaccinate herself and her people preemptively?"

With renewed confidence, Maia answered. "We are discussing an extremely deadly biological weapon. A vaccine, while lifesaving in most cases, could have drastic side effects. I am not a medical doctor, but I would have reservations about vaccinating an unexposed population. Judging from the test subjects Sorra filmed in the Askari lab, ikthians aren't immune."

"It's still a gamble," Oranthis pointed out. "We only suspect the vaccine is aboard the *Wavestar,* after all. Is that suspicion worth launching a retrieval mission for?"

"Yes," Kross said, turning toward him, "but the spread of the bioweapon is a certainty. I think we should strike."

"You would," Oranthis snorted.

Maia thought she detected a hint of amusement. It was obvious the generals had known each other a long time.

"Now is the perfect time," Sorra said. "Most of the Armada is holding the blockade around Earth. No one's expecting an attack on Korithia, and I doubt most of the fleet will be near enough to respond."

A smirk spread across Odelle's face. "I also received word a few hours ago. There are riots on the homeworld. It seems our first broadcast created quite a stir. It's only a few hundred thousand planet-wide at the moment, but I expect those numbers to grow. Corvis must be unhappy."

A surge of joy pulsed through Maia. Odelle hadn't informed her of that news prior to calling the generals, but she was thrilled. It comforted her to know that not everyone on her homeworld was willing to accept the Dominion's rule. For the first time in years, she felt a flicker of pride for Korithia.

"You think Corvis might take the *Wavestar* out for a spin while these pesky little riots are going on?" Oranthis asked with a toothy grin.

"I do," Odelle said. "I was quite familiar with Corvis' safety protocols before my defection. I can even help you recreate blueprints of the ship, since I've been aboard several times. They won't be perfect, but it's better than going in blind."

Kross folded his large arms. "What about the *Monsoon?* While the *Wavestar's* in flight, the *Monsoon* will be right on her tail."

Behind the generals, several heads turned. Multiple pairs of eyes, naledai and ikthian, widened. Maia chewed her lip. In her eagerness to convince the generals, she hadn't thought about the *Monsoon,* the battle cruiser that protected *Wavestar.* Though its specs were a carefully guarded secret, its existence was not. Even people on Korithia knew about the dreaded *Monsoon.*

"The *Monsoon* will be tricky," Sorra admitted, gloved fingertips drumming against the side of her crossed arms, "but we only have to engage her for a few minutes. The *Wavestar* will run away from the skirmish, like it's supposed to. Then, we make our move."

Looks of approval crossed both generals' faces. Oranthis turned to Kross. "How many stealth fighters do you think it would take to occupy the *Monsoon* and breach the *Wavestar?*"

"Maybe twenty?" Kross tapped at the nearest terminal interface to pull up several charts. "That's a good portion of our fleet. What we've got is what we've got."

"But imagine the payoff," Oranthis said, clearly warming to the plan. The shaggy fur around his neck fluffed in excitement. "We'd have the vaccine, possibly take out Corvis, and demoralize the entire Dominion by attacking the homeworld. They're so busy waging war on Earth I doubt they'll have more than a few dreadnoughts in orbit, and those respond slowly. If we hit fast, we might pull it off."

"We'll need our best pilots," Kross said, without looking up from the terminal. "Four to a ship. Pilot, copilot, two soldiers. We'll fly in cloaked, follow all the *Wavestar's* likely evac routes until we spot her, and engage the *Monsoon* first. One or two ships can attach to the *Wavestar* and try to board her."

"I can assist with the planning," Odelle said. "Irana as well, if she wishes to continue being helpful. We have information about the inner workings of Korithia's planetary defense system, as well as the *Wavestar's* security measures."

Maia's breathing sped up. Finally, they had a plan! A way for her to make up for her mistakes and possibly halt the bioweapon before it caused any more destruction. "Sirs, I would like to volunteer. I have completed significant medical training in the past several months, and I am a certified copilot as well."

The generals looked mildly surprised.

"I assumed you'd want to go," Kross said. "I've been keeping an eye on you, Kalanis. That includes your marksmanship scores and your flight sims. I know there's a great deal more to you than your academic background."

Maia tried not to flush with pride. "Thank you."

"There's only one problem," Oranthis said. "What if we fail? If things go wrong, someone needs to warn Earth. The blockade isn't allowing any messages to pass through, so they haven't seen Odelle's broadcast. They have no idea about the bioweapon. Earth is the last holdout against the Dominion. If its population gets infected…"

A heavy moment of silence followed as they all considered what that would mean for the rebellion. Though the Coalition was no longer officially allied with the naledai resistance, thanks to the xenophobic Councilman Bouchard's efforts, Maia knew Earth was throwing everything it had at the Armada, and the Dominion was throwing everything it had back.

The generals exchanged wordless glances. "Sorra, get me Elurin. Harris, too, and Valerius. I know I said we'd need all our best pilots for this mission, but we'll have to spare one. Getting past the Armada and Earth's planetary defenses will be even more difficult than a hit-and-run on the *Wavestar*. There's only one pilot I know who has a chance of making it through alive."

"Sending Harris is the right call," Sorra said. "You'll need at least one human to talk to the other humans. But Akton? You aren't sending him too, are you?"

Kross chuckled. "No. I'm going to direct the attack on the *Monsoon* and the breach of the *Wavestar* personally. I'll need a reliable commander to assist. Any objections?"

He aimed the question at Oranthis, but there were none. Maia beamed. Akton had become a very close friend since he'd helped her escape from San Diego base, and she was pleased by the thought that his skills and efforts would be rewarded. That is, if they managed to survive.

* * *

Rachel paused on the *Riptide's* gangway, taking a moment to admire the view. Elurin's blue flight suit was a bit faded, but it hugged her rear end in all the right ways. Rachel hadn't known "save my homeworld" was on her list of kinks, but part of her wanted to jump Elurin's bones right there in the Jor'al hangar, regardless of the pilots and mechanics preparing other ships for departure.

However, a larger part of her felt oddly tired. Maybe it was thoughts of Earth, the home that had cast her out, whirling through her head, but the usual hum of adrenaline before a high-stakes mission was absent. She felt heavy, lethargic. *Then again, Elurin hasn't let me get much sleep recently.*

"You ready for this, Harris?" Elurin asked, glancing back over her shoulder. Judging from her smirk, she'd felt Rachel's stare.

Rachel rubbed the back of her neck, suppressing a yawn. "I guess? It's complicated."

Elurin nudged her with an elbow. "You guess?"

Rachel forced a weak smile. "Didn't leave Earth on good terms, as you know."

"I'm sure the Coalition will let bygones be bygones once you tell them why we're there," Elurin said.

We. That was another problem. It made perfect sense to team up with Elurin. She was the rebellion's best pilot, and Rachel doubted anyone else could get them to Earth in one piece, but the Coalition would not be happy to see an ikthian. It would take some serious convincing to prove Elurin was an ally. Just the thought of explaining herself to a bunch of soldiers made Rachel itchy.

"They will if they know what's good for them." Rachel passed Elurin on the gangway, walking up and patting the *Riptide's* curved side. "How fast does your baby go, anyway? I've never asked," she said, eager to

146

change the subject. If there was one thing Elurin could talk about for hours, it was her ship.

"I know she's small, but I wouldn't call her an infant," Elurin said, tilting her head in confusion.

That put a real grin on Rachel's face. "No, it's a term of endearment."

Elurin's eyes brightened. "Baby. Right. Um, is it for inanimate objects? Children? Lovers?"

"All three." Rachel could already tell where Elurin was going with this. "Why, baby? You jealous?"

Elurin's head spots flushed a brighter shade of purple. "Of a ship? No."

"Should I be jealous?"

"Maybe." Elurin strode over to the ship, patting it as well. "She used to be a Dominion stealth fighter until we captured and retrofitted her. I customized the thrusters and worked on the cloaking software myself."

"Wait, you can code too?" Rachel's brows rose. "How did I not know that?"

Elurin smirked. "I'm full of surprises. That's why I named her *Riptide*. You don't see her coming 'til it's too late, and she packs more of a punch with the guns than you'd expect."

Rachel laughed. "Fitting."

"Harris!" The sound of a familiar voice caused Rachel to remove her hand from the ship's exterior. She caught sight of Taylor striding across the hangar at a fast clip, arms already open for a hug. She swiveled past Elurin and made her way down the rest of the gangplank to meet her.

"Morgan. Why didn't you catch a ride to Jor'al with us this morning? Too good for me and Elurin now?"

Rachel didn't miss the way Taylor's eyes darted between the two of them. She offered a subtle nod. While she wasn't ready to share details, she figured she should at least give Taylor a heads up, especially since she'd been part of bringing them together. Whatever "together" meant in the middle of a war.

"Didn't know when you two were headed here," Taylor said aloud. "Was hoping I'd catch you and Elurin here before you left, though. So. Earth, huh?"

Those two words said a lot more than it seemed on the surface, and Rachel understood. "Yep. Home sweet home."

Taylor slugged her shoulder. "If anyone tries to throw you in the brig, punch 'em. Real hard."

Rachel laughed. Trust Taylor to put humor in the grimmest of situations. It was probably part of the reason she'd survived Daashu when so few others had. "Oh, I might do more than punch. I'm calling out Bouchard for Roberts' murder first chance I get. Again. I don't think I ever told you, but I told the truth about what happened in my debriefing. Not that anything came of it."

Taylor's grin faded, but she nodded. "You'll make them listen this time."

"I will," Rachel said.

A throat cleared behind her, and Rachel noticed Elurin had come down to join them. "Rachel told me about your former commanding officer," Elurin said to Taylor, in a soft voice. "I promise Rachel and I will do what we can to spread the truth."

"Thanks." Taylor clapped Elurin's shoulder. "Tides be with you. You'll need all the luck you can get to sneak past the Armada."

Elurin clasped Taylor's forearm. "Who needs luck when you've got skills?"

"Skills, you say?" Taylor's eyes slid over to Rachel. "Do tell."

Rachel's face burned. "Get going, Morgan. And don't die, you hear? I didn't break into an ikthian prison, get stranded on an alien planet, chewed on by a vilodent, and shot at by seekers so you could get blown up on Korithia. Got that?" *Well, when I list it all out like that, it's no wonder I feel under the weather.*

"Got it. And don't you die, either. The two of us are gonna have a nice personal conversation after this is all over."

Rachel groaned, but Taylor pulled her in for one last hug. "Who's like us?"

"Damn few, Loo. And they're all dead."

"Damn right."

With a final clap on the back, Taylor departed, leaving Rachel with stinging eyes and a knot in her chest. She took a deep breath to loosen it. *I'll make sure Earth's safe, Taylor. For both of us.*

***

Odelle placed her hands behind her head and stretched, hoping to ease the soreness in her neck and shoulders. She wasn't sure how many cycles she'd been awake, preparing broadcasts, reading reports, and checking whichever Dominion news outlets she could gain access to. She felt like she'd spent a year in this cluttered room full of equipment, at this same standing terminal, typing and editing and playing clips on loop.

The reaction to her first broadcast had been mixed. Though the Dominion's official response had been predictable—claims of fake footage—she was dismayed by a portion of the general populace's response. The extranet overflowed with articles about ikthian test subjects. *Ikthians. Not the dead naledai. Not the threat of genocide toward the humans. Too many of us only care about ourselves.*

While there was definitely an undercurrent of outrage from the more radical sectors, many of the protests and riots had centered on the fear of a government conspiracy. A real one, in this case, but it reminded Odelle of a formative incident from her early adolescence.

Growing up, the only naledai she had encountered on Korithia were those who worked for her family, including a kindly old groundskeeper named Natan who had tended their water gardens. Odelle had listened to Natan tell stories of Nakonum, where he'd grown up.

One day, he failed to come in to work. A new gardener had shown up instead. When Odelle had inquired after Natan, her parents had hugged her and wept. She heard the news from them first, but it was repeated on all the local stations and in everyone's mouths–a terrible accident. Hovercar crash. Two young ikthians her age, from her neighborhood and school, taken from life in a most cruel and abrupt manner. None of the news outlets mentioned the naledai pedestrian who had also been caught in the accident. No one grieved for Natan. No one cared.

That was when Odelle had started asking questions, and upon receiving reprimands from her parents, had done her own research. She'd begun questioning who wrote the news. Who chose the stories. Who was really directing her eyes, ears, and mind.

Convincing her parents to send her to Nakonum for university had been hard, despite its sterling reputation as a beacon of ikthian enlightenment on a savage alien world. She'd been utterly ripe for rebellion on the fateful day she'd met Sorra. Sorra, who had convinced her not just to question but to act.

The sound of the doors opening behind her made Odelle turn around, and she smiled as the object of her thoughts appeared. Sorra strode in with her usual confident gait, smiling. "I know someone who wants to talk to you," she said, in a rare sing-song voice she wasn't normally chipper enough to use.

Odelle was intrigued. "Besides you?"

Sorra ushered Odelle aside and took her place in front of the terminal, establishing a video connection. Moments later, another familiar face appeared, a slender male ikthian with muddy bluish markings. His face lit up when he saw her, and Odelle's heart leapt for joy.

"Why, if it isn't my long-lost husband," Sorra drawled. "How's Korithia, Joran?"

"Terrible," he said, still smiling broadly. "Just awful."

Odelle beamed. Though she and Sorra had become separated from Joran—their friend and ally, who had played the role of Sorra's fake husband on Tarkoht—she'd been relieved when he reached Korithia some weeks back. He had been a valuable source of information for the rebellion ever since.

"There are all kinds of protests and riots against our leaders," Joran continued. "It's been years since we've had such chaos."

"How utterly horrible," Odelle said.

Though the responses to her broadcast were far from perfect, the fact that there had been a response at all was something of a miracle. Homeworld ikthians were conditioned from early childhood to accept their leaders' decisions. To follow those with the longest lineages. For many, pushing back against the Dominion was unthinkable. And yet, it was happening.

"I have more good news," Joran said. "I heard from a contact of a contact that your predictions came true. Sorra told me about Kalanis' plan to go after the vaccine. Several of the riots going on are close to the capitol, and Corvis is directing the response from the *Wavestar*."

"I've already informed the generals," Sorra said, excitement pitching her voice. "Kross was pleased to hear he wasn't hauling himself and a bunch of his best pilots to Korithia for nothing."

Odelle's heart swelled with hope. She, Maia, and Irana had been right. Corvis had retreated to the *Wavestar*. If everything went to plan, her excessive caution would be her undoing. More importantly, it would allow Kross, Akton, and the others to retrieve the vaccine.

"Thank you, Joran. I'm so glad to see you, and grateful for everything you've done. Are you safe?" Odelle couldn't tell much about the room he was in, but it was filled with stacks of crates.

"Safe enough," Joran said. "I might have had a hand in directing one of the riots, and I'm terribly sorry to inform you that your previous place of work has been temporarily shut down, for security reasons."

Odelle's eyes widened. "You directed a group of protesters to target CC?" CC—Central Communications—was where she had performed her role as the Dominion's Executive Media Coordinator. She wouldn't be sorry to see it burned to the ground.

"What can I say? I would do anything for my dear wife's beautiful lover. And I have one more bit of good news for you." Joran ducked out of sight, and Odelle waited eagerly for his return. He reappeared with a small lizard in his arms. Its blue tongue and double tail marked it as a male, as did its prominent neck frill. The lizard blinked sleepily at the camera, as though Joran had disturbed his afternoon nap.

"Tazmar!" If Odelle could have hugged Joran through the terminal, she would have. She'd been forced to leave her beloved pet with her neighbors on Korithia, an elderly couple who had no idea she was a rebel "traitor." To see him not only alive, but with Joran, brought tears to her eyes. "How did you find him?"

"It's a long story," Joran said, "but the next time I go off-world, I'll be sure to bring him. He has plenty of bugs, but I think he misses his mom."

Odelle leaned into Sorra, who wrapped a comforting arm around her shoulders. "Thank you, Joran," she said, for which Odelle was immensely grateful.

"Thank you," Odelle repeated, wiping her eyes. "Hi, Taz!" She crooked her fingers at him and made "shhh" noises, like the sound of the sea. The little lizard's head perked up. He crawled along Joran's arm, leaning toward the monitor as if searching for her. "Is Uncle Joran taking good care of you?"

A loud wail filled their room, and purple lights flashed overhead. Odelle exchanged a frightened glance with Sorra.

"We'll contact you as soon as possible, Joran," Sorra said, cutting off the feed. She checked her wrist comm, which had just started blinking.

Two naledai guards burst into the room, wearing armor and carrying rifles. "We've got three destroyers in orbit around Hakkar, and Ancestors know how many fighters in the atmosphere," one of them informed Sorra, in a rapid-fire manner that bordered on panic.

Destroyers? Here? Odelle's heart pounded. According to her sources, the Dominion's Armada was well-occupied. She and Sorra had been counting on the Dominion's limited resources when they made their plan to steal the comm station.

I suppose Hakkar became a higher priority when we started broadcasting and causing riots. Odelle shook herself, trying to regain her composure. Sorra was already barking orders at the guards, who rushed from the room. Odelle gave her a questioning look, and Sorra explained, "We're evacuating. Now."

"We?" Odelle repeated. Somehow, knowing Sorra, Odelle doubted the "we" included her. At least, not until the rest of the rebels had made their escape. *And she will expect me to go with them.*

Sorra jogged for the door, and Odelle followed, abandoning her equipment. Though she wasn't a trained soldier, she wished she had a weapon, as well as the knowledge to use it. For Sorra's sake, as well as her own.

Chapter Fifteen

"BRIEF ME ON EARTH'S defenses," Elurin said without taking her eyes off the ship's interface. She stared at the grids and blips, processing them all in the back of her mind. She'd been a pilot for so long it was second nature.

"Seriously?" Rachel gave a sigh from the copilot's chair. She sat with her head lolled back, looking oddly tired for someone about to go on a dangerous mission. "We've been over this twice already, and that's just on the trip so far. We talked it through a million times back at Jor'al."

Elurin offered an apologetic smile. Talking through the logistics hadn't done much to settle her roiling stomach. *Maybe it's because the stakes are so high. Or is it because Rachel's here? If I go down, she does, too.* That thought made her stomach do an extra flip.

"Sorry," she said to fill the silence. "I just like being prepared."

"Nervous?" Rachel asked.

Elurin nodded.

"Why?"

Because I don't want anything to happen to you.

Elurin glanced at Rachel. "Shouldn't I be? We're sneaking past the galaxy's most powerful Armada and infiltrating one of the galaxy's best planetary defense systems to warn a species who'd love to see me dead about a bioweapon my people developed."

She meant it as a joke, but Rachel must have taken note of the real fear in her tone. "Well, this human doesn't want you dead." She gave a weak laugh. "Where else am I supposed to get my orgasms?"

"Think you're sharp coral, don't you?" Elurin quipped, forcing a smile. Rachel's comment only served to remind her of a future that might not come to pass. The fact that Rachel seemed interested in that future only increased Elurin's anxiety. "Are you okay? You seem off."

Rachel made a noncommittal noise. "M'fine."

"You don't sound fine. If something's wrong, I need to know before I fly us straight into the enemy."

Rachel lifted her head from the neck rest, blinking a few extra times. "Feel a little logey. That's all."

"Logey?"

"Lethargic. Slow. My neck hurts, too."

Elurin felt a stab of panic. *The virus. What if Rachel's infected? What if her quarantine wasn't long enough, or the dormancy period is longer for humans and we didn't know?* She took a deep breath. *The doctors cleared her. Maybe she's sick, or allergic to something.* But this was the absolute worst time for her copilot and gunner to come down with the sniffles.

"Are you good to go?" she asked. "Tell me the truth."

Rachel cracked a smile. "I'll shake this off. Anyway, I trust you to get us through the Armada."

Elurin snorted. "You make it sound easy."

The plan was to use one of the rebellion's precious Dominion authentication codes—few in number, saved for missions like this—and hope it hadn't been flagged as stolen. She'd try her best to blend in with the fleet once they reached it in the next few minutes.

"Earth won't be bad," Rachel continued. "I doubt they'll fire on us once I make contact."

"Yeah, but what if the range of their plasma cannons is longer than the range of the radio? We know the Armada's blocking communication."

According to Rachel, Earth's plasma cannons used the natural plasma present in the outer layer of the planet's atmosphere to fire on enemy ships. Their deadly accuracy was the primary reason Earth hadn't fallen to the Dominion.

"We'll be between the Armada and Earth by that point." Rachel brought her forearm over her eyes, as if to shield them from a bright light, before leaning back in her seat. "Communications won't be too badly affected. Right?"

"Right," Elurin said, with confidence she didn't feel.

"It'll be fine. I mean, they might arrest us if we get EMP'd, but I have friends and allies back home. I'll get someone to listen."

"I know," Elurin said.

Rachel was as stubborn as she was brave. Surely someone on Earth would give them the benefit of the doubt once they delivered their message. There wasn't much time to dwell on it. When Elurin checked her scanners, she noted several ships. The Armada. It had to be, from the sheer number. She took another deep breath.

"I'll get as close as I can without arousing suspicion," she explained for Rachel's benefit. "I know the Armada's general tactics and flight patterns. Fighters like ours generally move in group orbits, protecting dreadnoughts when they aren't running missions. Our best bet is to join the patrol line."

"What if we're made?" Rachel asked.

"Made?"

Rachel's forehead scrunched, like she was trying and failing to concentrate. "Caught," she explained, after a worryingly long pause. "Sorry. Is it bright in here? Because it feels really bright."

"No," Elurin said, but she dimmed the lights anyway. *It's not the virus,* she told herself, willing herself to believe it. "If we're contacted, we use our code. If they don't buy it, we fly like a storm's chasing us and hope Earth sends out an EMP. We actually want the Coalition to disable and board us."

The sound of urgent beeping from the ship's nav display demanded her attention. The *Riptide* was approaching the range of the dreadnoughts' scanners. Selecting the nearest one, she flew in at a casual speed.

To her relief, no one made radio contact. Elurin held her breath as she joined a line of ships similar to her own, small silver orbs winding patterns around the far-larger dreadnought.

"Are they buying it?" Rachel whispered.

Elurin heard her as if from a distance, focused on the display. Their fighter approached the edge of another patrol ring, and at the perfect moment, she slipped into the next line. She proceeded like that around several dreadnoughts, weaving her way closer to Earth.

As she joined a patrol circling the front two dreadnoughts, the ship's radio crackled to life. *"This is the Stormrider. State identification."*

Elurin's mouth went suddenly dry. "S3-18700. Designation—*Riptide*. Just swapping out."

The silence was deafening as she and Rachel waited for a response. Several other fighters left their patrol of the dreadnought and circled them, a swarm of silver orbs hanging against the blackness of space.

"Fuck," Rachel grunted.

Elurin opened the thrusters, flying straight for Earth. She dipped and weaved to avoid the salvo of shots from the Dominion fighters, ignoring the shrill, warning beeps of her dash. It would be a race to Earth.

***

Taylor sat in the rear of the stealth fighter, wishing Elurin was their pilot. Though she had her own mission to worry about, she couldn't help thinking about Rachel and Elurin. Surely, they were close to Earth by now. Perhaps they were even planetside.

Elurin's the best pilot the rebellion has, and Rachel's one hell of a soldier. Plus, Maia and Akton are doing their part here.

A smile spread across Taylor's face as she glanced at Maia, seated directly ahead of her in the copilot's chair. Their fighter was one of eighteen following the *Wavestar's* potential evac routes. The other soldier onboard was Jethra, a fact Taylor found amusing. Of all the rebels she could've been paired with, she'd ended up with Rachel's "competition."

She peered through the wrap-around viewport, taking in the ocean of clouds surrounding them. White and fluffy, they reminded her of fair-weather clouds back on Earth. Maybe Maia's homeworld wasn't so different after all.

"This is SF-15. We have a sighting."

Taylor went ramrod straight as the fighter's radio squawked. She and Maia were in *SF-7. SF-15* was following a completely different route, part of a three-person wing.

"This is *SF-7*," Akton replied. "Our wing is close to your position. Can we assist?"

Taylor felt the flutter of excitement and fear in her belly. She waited with her heart in her mouth.

"Come join the party."

Akton chuckled. "Guess we're some of the lucky ones."

Taylor swallowed down her mixed feelings. Though she desperately wanted to play her role in this mission, Maia was on the ship. *If something happens to me, something will probably happen to her, too.* But thinking that way was a recipe for disaster. She could handle this, and so could Maia. *Besides, Akton's one of the best, and Jethra looks pretty tough.*

The short stretch of time between the comm conversation and their arrival seemed longer than it was. Taylor tried not to fidget. She waited, trembling with excess adrenaline, until the radio activated again.

"SF-15 to SF-7, 8, 9. Monsoon has been engaged. Wavestar in retreat. SF-13 and 14 are inactive. Do you have an opening?"

Inactive. Taylor's heart rate spiked. They'd been taken down.

"SF-7 has an opening," Akton said, a note of excitement in his growl. "I repeat, we have an opening." He turned to Maia. "Ready, Kalanis?"

"Ready."

"Shoot anything that moves. Morgan? Kertamen? Suit up. We're boarding."

A chill shot down Taylor's spine. Boarding. She numbed herself as she unfastened her harness and stood, pulling her liquid-like armor on over her flight suit and checking the seals on her helmet. This was her role. Who she was. A soldier. The fact that Maia was with her wouldn't change that.

Another voice came over the comm. General Kross. *"Chancellor Corvis, our fighters have your ship in our sights. Stop, or we'll shoot you down."*

Taylor felt their fighter speed faster through the atmosphere, rumbling with soft vibrations. That was the only noise aside from Kross' voice. She sat back down, looking out the viewport again. A spherical shadow emerged from the clouds. It was twenty times as big as their fighter, a giant glittering silver orb.

"They aren't stopping," Maia said, her voice tight. "Do you think they'll even respond?"

"We didn't expect them to," Akton said.

"Chancellor Corvis, this is your final warning," Kross said via the comm. *"We are willing to negotiate to avoid a firefight."*

A painfully silent pause followed.

A voice finally responded. Male, ikthian. *"The Chancellor will listen."*

"Of course she will," Jethra muttered. "Doesn't want to risk getting blown up."

"Stow it, Kertamen," Akton ordered. "We're approaching."

The silver orb grew larger in the viewport as Akton steered the ship underneath, following its giant curve until they were flying below the structure, matching speed.

"We will allow the Wavestar *to proceed unharmed if you provide a sample of the vaccine,"* Kross said.

"The chancellor wants to know what vaccine," the male ikthian said.

"Tell the chancellor she knows exactly what vaccine," Kross said, voice lowering. *"This is your last chance. How long do you think those shields of yours will hold under fire from thirty fighters?"*

Taylor felt a brief flicker of amusement. Thirty fighters? Kross really was something.

"Ready yourselves," Akton said. "We're all boarding once the ship's connected. First priority is a live sample of the vaccine. Second priority is to scan one, or transmit any data offered in exchange for hostages. Understood?"

Taylor nodded along with Jethra. "Understood," they answered.

"Kalanis, extend the gangway once we're attached."

Taylor unfastened her harness, examined her rifle, then checked the stats on her helmet's visor. Armor seemed to be holding. Beside her, Jethra did the same, although she carried a grenade launcher and a blaster.

"Hope you know how to use those," Taylor said, to break the tension.

Jethra gave a single bark of laughter. "Better than you do, I'll bet."

There was a groaning shudder, and the fighter came to a stop—or, at least, it felt like it did. The clouds moved, but the sound of their engine had quieted. They had attached to the *Wavestar* and were being towed along.

"We are secured," Maia said, rising from the copilot's chair. She came to the rear, standing beside Taylor. Taylor put a gloved hand on Maia's arm. It was the only reassurance she could offer in these final moments, and she tried to draw strength from Maia in return. *We'll both make it out alive.*

Akton joined them. "Ancestors guide us," he said, bowing his head. When he lifted it again, his eyes blazed. "Take the gangway and blow down their door. I'm on point. Morgan, cover our rear. Kertamen, get that launcher ready."

Jethra caressed her grenade launcher almost lovingly. "My pleasure."

Taylor took a deep breath. It was time.

***

The hall outside the broadcast room was chaos. Soldiers clomped down the corridor, gathering valuable equipment, shepherding the few rebel noncombatants to the lower floors. Sorra dove into the panic.

"Leave the equipment," she barked, grabbing a nearby soldier whose arms were laden with extension cords. "Don't bother setting up a defensive perimeter, either. Just get everyone to the evac ships as fast as possible."

"What about the destroyers?" Odelle asked in a tremulous voice asked.

Sorra's stomach churned. She wasn't used to Odelle being present for situations like this. Just like on Tarkoht, it chilled her blood. *Come on, Sorra. Focus. You're the highest-ranking person left here.*

"They can't shoot us down if we don't go past them." She activated her comm, setting it to one of the general emergency channels. Ideally, all the rebels fleeing the station would receive the message on their own comms. "Attention. This is Commander Sorra. Evacuate immediately and take shelter on the far side of the planet. Rendezvous coordinates to follow."

"We aren't leaving?" Odelle asked, breathless.

Sorra shook her head. "Our ships would be paper boats for those destroyers. There's a large natural gorge on the other side of the planet. We can take shelter there for a day or more."

Odelle caught on quickly. "If we're lucky, they might think we already snuck past them into open space and send the destroyers away."

It wasn't the best plan, but it was the best Sorra could come up with. She grabbed Odelle's elbow and dragged her to the stairwell, taking the steps two at a time. When they arrived on the ground floor, she was relieved to see several ships already taking off. The last one in line burst into a plume of fire, spiraling down toward the red dust of Hakkar's surface. Her heart lurched. Dominion fighters had already surrounded the station.

Sorra whirled around. She gripped Odelle's shoulders. "Get on the nearest ship. The sooner you're airborne, the better your chances."

Odelle's jaw set at a stubborn angle. "Not without you."

Sorra suppressed a flare of anger. Just the thought of Odelle being shot down, the burnt remnants to become one with Hakkar's dust, formed an empty void inside Sorra that threatened to swallow her. "Don't argue with me this time. Please."

"There is no argument." Odelle gave Sorra a small smile that broke and mended her at the same time. "You're staying, so I'm staying."

It was a smile Sorra couldn't say no to. Blinking back tears of fear, anger, and love, she ran for the nearest door that led outside, brushing past several harried stragglers on her way. Sorra heard Odelle's footsteps and harsh breathing between rounds of weapon fire. *Tides take me. Why wasn't I wearing armor or carrying my rifle? Stupid, stupid, stupid.*

In the bright midday sky above, the battle raged on. Ships swerved around each other. A blast struck the ground several yards away from where Sorra was running. It shook the ground and left a burnt black furrow that smelled of fire and plasma. She changed course, cutting toward her destination, one of the guard towers above the wall.

"You first," she said when she reached the ladder, motioning for Odelle to climb ahead.

To her relief, Odelle obeyed, climbing swiftly. Sorra followed. On the other side of the station, another evac ship went down. It crashed into the laser atop the station's main building. With a horrible groan, it fell, tossing up a cloud of red dust. As it crashed to the ground, a chunk of the wall crumbled beneath its weight.

Sorra climbed with renewed vigor. The Dominion wouldn't be able to make use of the station again without serious repairs. If the pilot had crashed that way deliberately, they'd done their Ancestors—ikthians or naledai—proud.

When she reached the top of the tower, Odelle was already in the open-view bubble, activating the defense terminal in the center. She stepped aside. "You'll be better at this than me."

Then why didn't you leave with the others? Sorra tried not to think about it as she took Odelle's place at the terminal. She pulled up the tower's firing grid and dragged her fingers through the three-dimensional display of light, selecting her target. On the grid, it was a moving purple blip. In reality, it was a Dominion fighter. She fired the cannon.

The blip disappeared, but Sorra didn't check to see if she could spot the ship going down. She selected another target and fired, again and again. The dogfight continued, though purple dots slowly ebbed. The blue dots—her group—disappeared from the edges of the grid, hopefully to hide. Sorra allowed herself a brief smile.

Suddenly, a large circle of purple dots appeared on the outskirts of the grid, converging on her position. Her scales itched. They were making a run on the tower!

"We have to go," she said, heading for the stairs.

Odelle lifted the hatch, allowing Sorra to climb down ahead of her. "And do what?"

"Hope there's still an evac ship somewhere around," Sorra said. She doubted there was, but she clung to the possibility anyway.

"Did we buy the others time, at least?" Odelle asked.

Sorra hopped the rest of the way to the ground. "Yeah. We did."

She scanned what remained of the comm station, hoping to find a way out amidst the wreckage. Small fires burned, and the remains of crashed ships from both sides littered the courtyard. Sorra's eyes locked on one of them—a ship that had landed close to the wall. *She's mostly intact. Maybe she'll fly a short distance?*

Sorra sprinted toward it, arms swinging, heart pounding. Trusting Odelle to follow. Then, the world exploded in a shower of light and choking red dust.

***

The sound of wrenching metal filled Maia's ears, painfully loud despite her helmet. The *Wavestar's* heavy door became a crater of blackened metal as shrapnel rained against the walls and floor. Her footsteps felt unsteady, but she didn't waste time. When Akton and Jethra climbed through the hole, Maia made sure she was close behind, aware of Taylor's solid presence behind her.

At first, there was nothing to see except a richly carpeted hallway, but the peace didn't last long. A complement of guards in shiny black armor rounded a corner at the opposite end of the hall and opened fire.

Akton flattened himself against the wall on one side, while Jethra took the other. They returned fire, and Maia tried to assist. Her nerves got the better of her, and her first several shots went wide. *Remember what Akton taught you.*

The guards erected their telltale blue barrier, but Maia's shot caught one of them on the shoulder. He staggered, and Taylor, who had joined them, followed up with a headshot. He fell.

That was the opening Jethra needed to advance. She fired another grenade. It blasted through the blue barriers, taking out several guards as well. Akton finished off the rest with his rifle, and the hallway was clear again.

"They have to know we're here now," he said. "Kalanis, direct us."

Maia brought up the reconstructed blueprints Irana had helped the rebels design in one corner of her visor. "Forward and left. A lift."

"Stairs?"

"Right beside it."

"Stairs," Akton said. "Move."

They moved swiftly over the wreckage their grenades and rifles had left. Though her stomach lurched at the dead bodies, a shiver of excitement raced through Maia's body, as it often did on missions. She wasn't a born soldier like Taylor, but her instincts knew something. Hunting as part of a pod. Her pod just happened to contain two naledai and her human lover.

They encountered more resistance on the short stairway, between the *Wavestar's* first and second levels. This time, Akton heard them coming and threw down a barrier of their own before the guards arrived. Maia hit all her targets dead-on. *Four dead below us. Three dead here. How many guards does the Wavestar have?*

They proceeded to the second level, where Maia checked the blueprints again. "The bridge is on this level," she said. "There is a high likelihood that Corvis has gone there to command the pilots. Forward."

They continued, bypassing several closed doors. The hallway broadened, branching with two possible directions. "Either way," Maia said. "It forms a diamond pattern."

Akton paused. He cocked his head as though listening carefully. "Right."

They headed right, but after only a few yards, a bright flash bounced off the shiny metal wall near Maia's head.

"Hostiles!" Taylor shouted, firing before Maia could even turn. They were face to face with three more guards taking cover in one of the hall's open doorways. A body lay sprawled on the ground, one who hadn't been fast enough to avoid Taylor's rifle.

"Fall back," Jethra barked. "This launcher does corners."

Maia hurried down the hall with Akton. She heard another distant explosion, mingled with screams. Risking a glance back, Jethra had remained in place and aimed the grenade at a difficult right angle. The doorway had been blown off its hinges, and whoever had taken shelter inside didn't seem likely to come after them.

They hurried down the hallway. The floor became a metal grill, and the walls turned to silver paneling. At the end of the hallway, a set of double doors appeared before them. Once more, Jethra raised her launcher.

"Damn it, Kertamen, you're having all the fun," Taylor grumbled. "I want to use the launcher."

A little of Maia's fear turned into amusement. To her surprise, Jethra handed the launcher over and swapped it for Taylor's rifle.

"Be my guest," Jethra said. "Just press the big button."

Taylor grinned. "Fuck yeah." She aimed and fired.

The doors blew out much like the first one had. Though they didn't collapse, the launcher had made a sizeable hole in the warped metal. They raced through, Akton first, then Jethra, Maia, and Taylor.

Maia stopped short. They'd run straight into ten armed guards, standing in front of two terrified-looking pilots and a shorter, robed figure. Maia caught a brief glimpse of the robed figure before she disappeared behind a wall of protection. She knew that face, those markings.

Chancellor Corvis.

Chapter Sixteen

RACHEL'S HEAD SPUN AS white bands of starlight and laser fire streaked past the viewport. The ship shuddered as an enemy shot struck the *Riptide's* shields. Sweat soaked her skin beneath her armor, and she felt like she was about to lose her lunch.

I'm sicker than I thought. She tried to warn Elurin, but her voice failed. All she could do was moan and clutch the armrests as space whirled around her.

"We're approaching Earth's atmosphere. Why aren't you firing?" Elurin's voice sounded distant, and Rachel could barely focus on it.

*The guns. I should be firing. Enemies are chasing us...*She tried to take the controls, but her hands weighed a thousand pounds. It took several precious moments to summon the strength to reach out.

Another shot struck their ship, forcing Elurin to course correct. The jerking motion sent Rachel reeling. She tried again to speak, let Elurin know something was seriously wrong, but all that came out was a nauseated groan.

Her sweat turned cold, and she started shivering. A moment later, a low noise vibrated around her, and the ship's lights flickered. Elurin's navigation system winked out, and the weapons system in front of Rachel dimmed.

Finally, she managed to say something. "EMP."

Even in her dazed state, she knew what had happened. Earth had knocked out all their electronic systems, as well as the systems of the fighters pursuing them. That meant a Coalition boarding party was sure to follow...or worse, a plasma cannon blast.

But Elurin wasn't listening. She shouted into the ship's radio, using English words Rachel had taught her just in case she encountered hostile humans in the field. "Hold fire! Hold fire!"

Nothing happened. Elurin turned toward her, wearing a panicked look that wove and warped before Rachel's eyes. "Rachel, are you ready? A Coalition ship's approaching. They're about to board. Rachel? What's wrong?"

"Sorry." Rachel squeezed her eyes shut, trying to focus, but she couldn't. She wrapped her arms around herself. *Fuck. What's wrong with me? I can't have the virus, can I? The doctors cleared me.*

The ship rocked as something attached to its side. A moment later, the doors blew open. The smell of smoke-filled Rachel's nose. She blinked rapidly as a line of shiny black boots marched in. Coalition soldiers. She'd worn the same boots enough times to recognize them.

She tried to reach for the rifle, but her fingers scrabbled weakly without grasping it. She could barely summon enough energy to be scared as half a dozen rifles pointed at her.

"Hold fire. Harris, is that you?" One soldier stepped forward from the rest. Male, tall, broad-shouldered. He cleared the tinted visor of his helmet, allowing her to see his face. It took her a few moments, but she'd seen that face, those brown eyes, many times before. She'd even kissed those lips.

"Andy?" A wave of relief washed through her. Andrew was a good guy.

"Rachel!" He lowered his weapon, kneeling beside her chair. "What's wrong?"

Rachel tried to answer, but her mouth felt fuzzy, filled with cotton. There were two Andrews in front of her, and she wasn't sure which one to focus on. She trembled with fear and exhaustion. Fuck. It had to be the virus. "Get back. Sick." She placed her gloved hand on his shoulder, trying to shove him away.

"Sick?" Andrew raised his gun again, pointing it at Elurin. "What did you do to her, fishface?"

"Nothing. I'm with Rachel and the naledai..." Elurin still sounded far away.

Rachel could feel herself fading. Blackness closed in with alarming speed. Elurin and Andrew became smeared blotches of color, black armor and silver scales. Her shivering gave way to exhaustion, a weighted blanket over her chest and shoulders.

"Andy," she said, forcing the word past her lips. "Listen to Elurin. Help her. Please. Listen."

The last of her strength gave out. She surrendered to the darkness. *He'll listen,* she thought before her mind shut down.

***

164

"Stand up, hands behind your head," a soldier warned.

Elurin obeyed, her eyes darting to Rachel. She should be paying attention to the man pointing a gun at her, but all her instincts screamed for her to do something. Rachel had passed out, slumped at an odd angle, head lolling.

Keep calm. Your goal is to keep the humans from shooting you and get Rachel help. She's depending on you. The thought lent Elurin fresh determination. "Rachel said your name was Andy, right?" *Use his name. Establish rapport.*

"Andrew," he said, with cold hesitation.

"I'm Elurin. I'm not your enemy. I came here with Rachel to warn Earth."

"Warn us?" Andrew said. He looked at Rachel, frowning. "What's wrong with her?"

"She's sick," Elurin said. "Not completely sure what with, but I can guess. She needs medical attention immediately, and to be quarantined."

"Quarantined?" His eyes widened. "She's contagious?"

She flipped her weapon around, handle at the soldiers instead of barrel. "I'll explain everything once you get us out of here. I'll let you take me into custody. Just get Rachel to a hospital and send someone in to debrief me. Someone who has the authority to make things happen. Your planet is in danger."

Andrew stared at her for a long moment.

Elurin willed him to trust her. If he didn't, she and Rachel were both as good as dead, and so was Earth. "Rachel trusted me. Listen to me, for her sake."

"You aren't seriously buying this, are you?" one of the other soldiers said, speaking up from the line behind Andrew.

Andrew answered in a harsh, commanding voice. "Shove it, Jenkins. We've got a soldier down and a prisoner willing to surrender and offer information. I'm in charge here, and if that's what's for sale, I'll buy it." He motioned the other soldiers forward. "As long as she cooperates, no excessive use of force. She has valuable intel."

Elurin could barely contain her relief. She made no move to resist as two Coalition soldiers took her weapon and removed her from the pilot's chair, nor when they cuffed her arms behind her.

"Take care of her," she pleaded, casting one last look at Andrew. "I'll tell the Coalition everything as long as you help her."

The human's brown eyes, not so different from Rachel's, softened. He offered Elurin a tentative smile. "I will. For her sake. The two of us go back."

Elurin nodded. She allowed the soldiers to escort her off the *Riptide,* mentally rehearsing a simplified explanation about the bioweapon. She'd undoubtedly have to speak to several people while climbing the Coalition chain of command, and if any of them failed to believe her...

She didn't want to think about it.

***

Tides take me to a place of peaceful repose. A place with neither sorrow nor suffering.

Odelle didn't know why the ancient prayer was stuck in her head. The thought sounded muffled, whispering beneath the painful ringing that threatened to split through the sides of her crest. She tasted blood.

A place where I may join the ocean of stars with those who came before, and those who will follow after.

She opened her eyes. The world around her was a wasteland of red dust and wreckage. Something wet streamed down her cheek, and as she raised a weak hand to touch, it came away dark purple. Her cheek didn't hurt, but the agonizing ringing grew louder. *Sorra. Where's Sorra?*

She tried to pick herself up. One of her arms hung limp at her side, as though her shoulder had popped from its socket. Useless. Her legs shook as she clambered into a semi-standing position. Sorra's body was sprawled a few yards ahead, her arms were outstretched, reaching toward Odelle.

Odelle stumbled toward her love. "Sorra," she coughed, but the dust clogged her throat. She had to swallow and try again. "Sorra!"

She wept with relief when Sorra shifted, as though seeking the sound of her name. She was moving, albeit barely. *The Tides will not take us yet.* Fueled by sheer determination, Odelle stumbled toward Sorra's dirt-covered form.

"Odelle." Sorra clambered upright, swaying dangerously before finding her footing. Bleeding in several places, her shirt was torn on one side.

Odelle didn't care. She launched herself into Sorra's arms and clung, nearly breaking down. They held each other for a desperate moment they didn't have, until Sorra said, "Ship..."

She pointed at a ship some distance away. It was ikthian in design, a silver sphere that might have marked it as an enemy vessel, but it wasn't crumpled or on fire, as far as Odelle could tell. Good enough.

The sound of fighters zooming overhead snapped her back to reality. She shook off her terrified haze and headed for the ship. They staggered together, supporting each other.

None of the ship's passengers were alive. Several bodies lay just beyond the doors, mere feet away from a means of escape. The pilot was strapped in, but a piece of shrapnel had pierced in his chest. Miraculously, there was no damage to the dash, although the seats had several tears.

Odelle and Sorra unstrapped the pilot and laid him on the ground with the others. Sorra took his seat, heedless of the blood smeared there, while Odelle strapped into the copilot's chair. Sorra tried to fire up the engines, and by some miracle, they worked. Odelle nearly laughed in relief. Escaping the fighters surrounding the base was far from a guarantee, but at least they had a chance.

***

"Maia Kalanis, I believe," Corvis said in a calm voice, looking between her wall of guards. "It has been some time."

A storm of anger brewed in Maia's belly. She had seen Corvis on a semi-regular basis growing up. Her mother had always ordered her to remain silent in Corvis' presence. The older she grew, the less often she'd seen the chancellor, likely because Irana found her interest in xenogenetics embarrassing.

Corvis looked much the same now as she had then–thin, medium height, but sharp-eyed and intense. On the older side of middle-aged. The shine of her scales looked purchased rather than natural. Surely, she used expensive oils. She wore a luxurious purple robe, which flowed from shoulder to ankle.

There were a frightening number of weapons pointed at Maia and the boarding party. She couldn't afford to lose her concentration or nerve. She looked to Akton for orders, but the naledai commander shook his head. Maia got the message, and he spoke instead.

"Looks like we're in a stand-off, Chancellor. Your guards can shoot us, but one of us will shoot you at the same time."

The guards closed ranks even further around Corvis. Maia hated that she could no longer see Corvis' face. She heard Corvis' voice, however, confident and insistent. It made her want to grind her teeth.

"A strategy that does not guarantee success. Maia, surrender is your only option. Surely you see that."

Once more, Maia looked at Akton. She was angry on his behalf—that Corvis would not deign to speak with him, even though he was in charge. This time, Akton nodded. Maia took a moment to come up with a response.

"We will not surrender," she said, with all the courage she could muster. Her hands shook on her rifle, but she kept aim at one of the two guards directly in front of Corvis.

Corvis did not rush her words. "Then tell me, why are you here?"

"For the vaccine," Maia said.

"I have no idea what you are talking about."

Maia's fury swelled. It burned hot in her veins, and her trigger finger itched to fire. "We know all about the bioweapon. Do your guards?"

The guards barely reacted, but Maia saw one of them shift his feet. The subtle movement of uncertainty gave her an idea, but in a situation like this, they had very few options.

"My guards have only two duties—to protect me and eliminate threats," Corvis said. "They never fail at either."

"Really?" Akton said. "We didn't have any trouble getting here."

Maia thought she heard a sharp intake of breath, as though Corvis were offended, but her mind raced, putting together the pieces of her plan.

"You may have entered my bridge," Corvis said, with the same fervent emphasis she always used when speaking—the kind of emphasis that grabbed attention and made people listen. "But I assure you, none of you will leave alive."

"Correct," Maia blurted. "None of us will leave alive. That includes you."

"Brave words," Corvis said. "Tell me, how do you expect to get this supposed 'vaccine' once my guards shoot you?"

It was now or never. Maia remembered that Taylor was beside her, stalwart as ever. She even risked a split-second glance. Taylor held the grenade launcher at the ready. Maia readied herself as well.

"You will hand over the vaccine because we have infected ourselves," she said.

A beat. "What?" Corvis replied.

"We are carriers," Maia lied. "The air in here is recycled, correct?" She knew from its filtered scent, and from Corvis' failure to answer, that it was. "And we are standing awfully close to you."

One of the guards lowered his rifle. Not enough to lose aim, but it fueled Maia's confidence. "The negotiations with the stealth fighters were merely a distraction, allowing us to board your ship. Give us a sample of the vaccine, and we will make sure you receive a dose as well."

"What's to stop me from ordering my guards to shoot you where you stand?" Corvis asked. "If you are infected and I am in possession of this vaccine, as you so clearly believe, I can dose myself once you are eliminated. The virus has a lengthy dormancy period."

Maia's heart leapt. Was it her imagination, or did she finally hear a trace of doubt in the chancellor's smooth river of a voice?

"This huge fucking grenade launcher." Taylor's statement rang clear. "I'll blow you and your guards to pieces. Maybe they shoot us, too. Maybe we go down with you. But the rest of the stealth fighters waiting out there will board the *Wavestar* and tear it apart until they find the vaccine. Even if you manage to hide in a nice little escape pod before they get here, you'll be infected."

Maia dared to chuckle. "So the question is, how do you want to die?"

Chapter Seventeen

ELURIN, WHERE ARE YOU?

Murmurs, like the lapping of waves against sand. The gentle hiss reminded Rachel of Elurin's voice, but she couldn't be sure. When Rachel looked around, she saw varying shades of grey that shifted like light on water. It was much better than the blinding whiteness that had burned through her before.

The noise of the waves grew louder, sharpening into something familiar. "We've stabilized her, but her condition is still fragile. We haven't been able to isolate the cause of her symptoms."

Not Elurin. English.

"Understood. Can you estimate when she'll regain consciousness?"

"There's no way to be sure."

I'm here! Rachel tried to shout, but her body was one with the waves.

"Lieutenant Valdez, what's the other prisoner's status?"

"Elurin's in interrogation now, ma'am."

Elurin? The name tugged at Rachel like an undertow. The lights grew brighter, her awareness of her body returning. With it came the creeping sensation of dull, body-wide pain.

"And is she talking?"

A snort. "She won't shut up, ma'am. Keeps saying she's with the naledai rebellion and came here with Harris to warn us about a bioweapon."

Rachel smiled. Or, at least, she thought a smile. *That's my girl.*

"Do you believe her information is accurate?"

"Not my area of expertise, ma'am. But yes, I do."

Rachel felt weight press into her. The force of someone's eyes. She was being observed. Her lashes fluttered, and the shifting lights solidified into the white walls of a room.

"Admiral Moore, she's waking up."

Rachel blinked, then tried to move. Her skin screamed. So did she. A bulky shape hovered over her, someone wearing a hazmat suit. After a couple of seconds, blissful coolness coursed through her veins. Pain meds.

Rachel was able to piece her fragmented thoughts back together. An echo of the pain was still there, but manageable. She could think. *Maybe I can talk?* She opened her mouth, and after a few tries, she managed a single word. "Elurin…"

"Don't try to talk."

The voice wasn't coming from the doctor in the bunny suit, but from one of the walls. A window. Two figures stood on the other side. One was Admiral Ines Moore, perhaps the least frustrating member of the Coalition brass. The other was Andrew Valdez, her old friend and former lover.

Oh shit, Andrew. I've got so much to tell you.

"Ensign Harris, can you understand me?"

Rachel tried to nod, but her head was too heavy. "Yes."

"Your ikthian companion has informed us that the Dominion has engineered a deadly airborne bioweapon. Is this accurate?"

"Yes."

"Is there reason to believe you have been infected?"

Rachel tried to answer, but her voice failed her. The pain relievers the doctor had given her were taking hold, and the whiteness faded to grey. Terror filled her as she remembered the dead bodies she and Akton had stumbled upon. She had barely interacted with them, but…*am I going to die like that, too?*

Death made her remember Roberts, shot in the chest as his life bled from between his fingers. Soldiers rarely died peaceful deaths. Still, she hadn't thought it would end like this. She'd hoped for more time. Time with her friends and Elurin. But there was time enough to keep one particular promise.

"Taylor…"

"Are you saying ex-Lieutenant Taylor Morgan infected you?" Moore asked.

"No. About Roberts. Bouchard killed him. When Taylor escaped." She cast a pleading look at Andrew, praying he would understand.

"That slimy bastard. Doesn't surprise me one fucking bit," Andrew blurted, then glanced sheepishly at Admiral Moore. "Sorry for the language, ma'am."

Admiral Moore's eyes remained fixed on Rachel through the window. "Are you saying Councilman Bouchard shot Captain Roberts in cold blood, without acting in self-defense?"

"Yes," Rachel croaked.

Admiral Moore's face hardened. "Understood. Thank you, Ensign."

Rachel's worries faded. She trusted Admiral Moore and Andrew would do what they could, at least in the short term. Her eyelids drooped, but she fought off unconsciousness for a few moments longer.

"Andrew?"

Andrew pressed one of his gloved hands against the glass. "I'm here, Rach."

"Elurin. Use her. She's the best."

"At what?"

"*Top Gun.*"

Admiral Moore turned to Andrew. "The best at *Top Gun*? Is that some kind of program?"

Andrew laughed, and the sound soothed a little of Rachel's pain. "I think she means the movie, Admiral. It's an old one about fighter planes. They restored it on holo a few years back. Rachel's saying Elurin's a skilled pilot, and we should use her."

Rachel nodded. She couldn't fight for Elurin right now, but there were others on her side.

* * *

Elurin had long since stopped tracking the barrage of questions. Sometimes, they came from a set of speakers in the ceiling. Grey and nondescript, lacking any furniture, the only interesting feature of the room they'd locked her in was its square shape. Most ikthian architecture was spherical.

Other times, humans entered to speak with her. They wore masks and white, puffy uniforms, probably the Coalition version of biohazard suits, and never showed their faces. They asked the same questions in increasingly harsh tones, and Elurin always answered the same as well.

"Who are you?"

"Elurin. Rebel pilot."

"Why are you here?"

"To warn Earth."

"What's the Dominion planning?"

"A bioweapon. I told the last guy. You're talking to each other out there, right?"

"What's the Armada's next move?"

"No idea. I'm fighting against the Armada."

She told the same story to anyone who would listen, until her mouth was dry and her eyes started to film over. Her fear had worn off, simply because her body couldn't sustain that amount of panicked energy. She was horribly thirsty, her scales were itched thanks to the lack of humidity, and she desperately wanted to curl up for a nap.

It became harder to push away thoughts of Rachel. Part of Elurin didn't want to. *Is she okay? Is she getting medical attention? Does she really have the virus, or is she just sick?* Somewhere deep in her bones, Elurin knew the truth. Rachel had been infected, probably from the first time she'd encountered the bioweapon. The doctors had made a mistake in clearing her. Perhaps the dormancy period lasted longer in humans than naledai?

What if I have it, too? Will I start showing symptoms? Will it hurt?

The sound of the doors opening interrupted Elurin's thoughts. She sat up, rolling her neck. While the straight walls were useful for leaning against, they hadn't done her shoulders any favors. Neither had the electromagnetic cuffs around her wrists.

More soldiers came into the room. For a second time, Elurin found herself surrounded by eight heavily armed Coalition soldiers, staring down the barrel of their plasma rifles. She slouched back down on instinct

"Down on the ground!" a booming voice shouted.

Since Elurin was already on the ground, she settled for holding still.

"This is a mistake," she said, fighting to keep her voice calm. "I'm in custody. I'm unarmed. I'm cooperating. Where's Andrew?"

"You see?" said a high-pitched, nasal voice coming from somewhere behind the wall of soldiers. Though the speaker used the same language as Rachel, the words sounded like the harsh clang of bells to Elurin's ears. "Ikthians cannot be trusted. Always with the lies and manipulation. Pretending to be harmless. Invoking a human soldier's name as though they're allies."

The soldiers formed a small gap, allowing Elurin to see the speaker, an older human with thinning grey hair atop his head, an angular face, and drooping folds of skin beneath his chin. The skin hung there like loose reptilian flesh.

Elurin's mind raced. This man was clearly an enemy. She swallowed, trying to get the sour taste of fear out of her mouth. "I'm not lying. I came here with Rachel Harris to warn the Coalition about a Dominion bioweapon. I'm trying to help—"

"Ensign Harris?" The man sneered, fixing his cold blue gaze upon her. "I'm well aware of the 'help' she's offered the Coalition. By falling under the sway of an ikthian, she's proven as traitorous as her former superior officer, ex-Lieutenant Morgan."

But the mention of Rachel's name caused one of the guards to speak up, a red-haired female with brown spots on her face. "Sir? I knew Harris. Are you saying she's with Morgan and the Dominion now? She never struck me as the type to turn traitor."

Traitor? Elurin's anger flared, feeding off her fear until it became a fire. She didn't know who this leathery man was, but she'd had enough. *Rachel's dying. I'll probably die here, too. If someone doesn't listen, the humans are as good as dead.*

"I'll tell you something, *piscfut,*" she said. "Taylor's headed to Korithia right now to get a vaccine sample, so Earth's population won't get wiped out. And Rachel? She snuck through the entire armada parked outside your planet on the slim chance someone here might listen. Tides! I thought Dominion leaders were horrible, but if you're what humanity has to offer, your species won't survive this war."

She panted, lungs burning, trying to catch her breath in the unbearably dry air.

The man stared at her in silent shock. His eyes grew wild. "How dare you? Soldiers, execute the prisoner immediately!"

Elurin curled in on herself, even though that wouldn't do anything against eight rounds of plasma, but none of the guards moved to obey. At last, one of them spoke, a very dark-skinned male without any hair atop his head.

"Councilman Bouchard? With all due respect, sir, you don't have the authority to order the execution of this prisoner. The admirals have to—"

"The admirals? I sign the admirals' paychecks! I sign their defense budget into law! The admirals are nothing without us."

But Elurin was hardly listening. His name, Bouchard, triggered a memory of speaking with Rachel while stranded in the wilderness. She felt as though she'd dived straight into freezing water. "You're the one Rachel warned me about. You murdered her old commanding officer and banished her to cover it up."

***

Sorra gripped the controls, hands shaking, trying to pull herself together. Muscle memory took over. She went through the same pre-flight motions she'd done hundreds of times before. In a matter of moments, they were off, speeding over the wall and across Hakkar's rusty red landscape.

"Sorra?"

The sound of Odelle's frightened voice was like a splash of cold water. "What?"

"We're being followed."

Sorra checked the flight grid. Three blue dots were tailing them at a fast pace, approaching from either side to try and outflank her. *Time to channel my inner Elurin.*

"Take over the guns," Sorra told Odelle. "Just point and shoot."

Odelle stared warily at the copilot's gunner controls, but took hold of them anyway, making use of her own grid. While she familiarized herself with the display, Sorra pulled into a steep climb, juking left to bring them over one of the pursuing ships.

"Fire!" Sorra yelled.

Odelle fired. The shots missed but forced the enemy ship to change course. Sorra sped ahead, weaving around one of the many towering rock formations. Behind her, a different enemy ship cut the turn too close. It collided with the stone, going down in smoke as a loud boom rippled through the air.

There were still two fighters in pursuit, one behind, one to her right. She and Odelle would have a better chance of shooting them down if she flew higher, but it would be a risk. She'd lose the cover of the rapidly changing red landscape.

In the end, the landscape made the decision for her. A wide canyon appeared in front of them, and Sorra plunged, flying as close to the wall as possible.

One of the remaining fighters sped overhead and fired on her. It was all Sorra could do to weave away from the blasts while also avoiding the canyon walls. The other fighter wasn't so lucky. When the gorge banked right, the pilot didn't correct quickly enough. They exploded in a shower of sparks and metal.

That left the last fighter. Try as she might, Sorra couldn't tempt them down into the gorge. She considered ducking into a crevice in the hopes the pilot might lose her, but any delay could mean a direct hit. *But if I go on the offensive, can Odelle make the shot? She isn't trained...but what if she doesn't have to hit a moving target?*

"Odelle."

"What?"

"See those rocks ahead of us that form a ledge?" Sorra nodded her head forward, gesturing out the viewport. There was indeed a ledge, almost like a naturally formed stone bridge stretching over the gorge, only its other half had long since crumbled away. "When I say, shoot it. Dead on."

"Okay."

Sorra poured all the power she could into the engines and flew low, skimming mere feet above the canyon's bottom. A series of rapid shots came from above, but Sorra veered. She stayed low, hoping the enemy pilot would follow.

The pilot took the bait. When the fighter came into position behind her, Sorra sped under the ledge and shouted, "Now!"

Odelle fired. Twin blasts of light shot from the front of their fighter, hitting the rocky outcropping. There was a rumble, then a loud roar, and the atmosphere around their ship vibrated as the ledge collapsed behind them, bringing a hail of rubble down on top of the enemy.

Both she and Odelle cheered as Sorra sped away from the landslide, finally free and clear of the Dominion fighters. She looked over at Odelle, her chest bursting with happy disbelief. They'd made it.

***

Taylor waited, barely breathing, for a response from Corvis. She didn't know what to expect. Disbelief. Derision. An order to shoot. She kept the grenade launcher ready just in case, prepared to fire at the slightest movement from anyone. They remained still as statues, until Corvis finally said, "Very well."

"You will give us the vaccine?" Maia asked.

"It's on the third level. I will radio for one of the crewmembers to bring the sample here. Acceptable?"

Taylor, Maia, and Jethra looked to Akton.

"Acceptable," he said. "But one wrong move, and Morgan here is using the launcher. We're prepared to die if it means taking you down with us."

Corvis ignored him. Taylor couldn't see what she was doing behind the wall of armed guards, but a few moments later, she heard Corvis' voice. *"This is Chancellor Corvis speaking. Please bring the sample from the storage unit to the bridge immediately. Thank you."*

Please. Thank you. Apparently, evil and politeness weren't mutually exclusive.

"Kertamen, watch the hall," Akton said.

Jethra turned away from the guards to face the warped hole in the bridge's rear doors. Taylor swallowed. That was one less weapon trained on Corvis and her guards. It had to be even worse for Jethra, her back to the enemy.

The next two minutes passed in tense silence. Taylor stared down the guards, and they stared back. Some showed minor traces of fear on their faces—darting eyes, dry breaths. It was the same fear Taylor felt thundering in her chest, but none lowered their weapons.

Finally, Jethra spoke, her words fast and clipped. "Lone ikthian approaching. No armor. Appears unarmed."

Taylor wanted to turn, but she held her position until she heard the sound of footsteps behind her. There was a frightened gasp, then a female ikthian arrived wearing a purple uniform. She carried what looked like an oversized silver thermos.

"The samples," Corvis said, addressing Maia again.

Taylor caught a glimpse of the chancellor's face from between two of the guards' shoulders, but she couldn't read anything in it.

"Remove one and leave it here," Corvis said. "Retreat from the bridge with the others. You will not be followed."

Warning sirens went off in Taylor's brain. It sounded too simple. Surely Corvis wasn't about to let them go? *Then again, she's a self-preservationist. Maybe she doesn't want to gamble with her own life.*

She looked to Akton, who gave Maia a decisive nod. Maia put her rifle on her back and took the silver container from the trembling crewmember, who obviously hadn't expected to walk into an armed stand-off. Jethra trained Taylor's rifle on the crewmember, while Taylor kept the grenade launcher aimed at the guards and Corvis.

"Fire!" Corvis yelled.

After the briefest moment of surprise, the guards opened fire. Several rounds of plasma collided with Taylor's chest plate, knocking her back with painful force until she smashed into what remained of the door. The small icon in her visor representing her armor's shields went out.

She fired the grenade launcher.

BOOM.

The bridge rocked. Lights flashed. Sparks flew as the scream of tearing metal filled the space. Taylor curled in on herself, but not soon enough. Several pieces of shrapnel struck her back and arms as she threw them up to protect her head. Smoke filled the air, the scent of plasma so strong it passed through Taylor's air filters. Damaged, like the rest of her armor.

Her vision swam, but she saw several bodies on the floor. Or pieces of bodies. Most of Corvis' guards. Both pilots. Jethra and Akton had been knocked down as well, unmoving. Only Maia remained standing, one arm braced on the wall, her face twisted with horror.

Taylor glimpsed movement amidst the wreckage. She thought it was a guard and prepared to fire again despite the risk. Then she saw the singed purple robe. Corvis. The chancellor had taken refuge behind her guards and one of the pilot's chairs. She grabbed one of the many discarded weapons on the floor and took aim at Akton's prone form.

"No!" Taylor shouted.

Taylor dropped the grenade launcher and threw herself between Akton and Corvis, hoping her armor could take one more shot. Fire struck. White-hot pain consumed her. Everything went black.

Rae D. Magdon & Michelle Magly

Chapter Eighteen

ELURIN'S STATEMENT HAD AN immediate effect on the soldiers. They turned to Bouchard. The human's leathery face, which had been crimson with anger, became paler.

"The ikthian is lying," he declared, speaking far too fast.

"Seriously?" Elurin scrunched her nose. The more nervous Bouchard came, the more her confidence grew. "Dominion politicians lie a whole lot better than human ones."

Several of the soldiers exchanged glances. "Rachel Harris told you that Councilman Bouchard shot Captain Roberts?" the same red-haired, spotty-faced female asked Elurin.

Elurin nodded. "Yeah. She witnessed it herself and told me the whole story. She reported Bouchard for shooting her CO, but he covered it up. Then your admirals sent her on a suicide mission to find Lieutenant Morgan."

The red-haired female shook her head. "Holy fucking shit. Most of you knew Harris, right? Do you think she'd lie about something like that? I don't."

The hairless soldier with dark skin nodded. "I knew Roberts, too. Best damn captain I ever served under."

His brown eyes hardened as he glared at Bouchard. He and the red-haired soldier trained their rifles on Bouchard. Within moments, the majority of the guards had followed suit.

"You cannot be serious!" Bouchard sputtered. "I order you to lower your weapons immediately! This is treason!"

"Murdering a Coalition captain is treason," the redhead growled.

Elurin felt an odd surge of euphoria. At least one of Rachel's most hated enemies was finally getting his comeuppance. *I really wish she could see this.*

The door to the interrogation room opened again. More guards filed in, directed by a silver-haired human with a narrow, severe face. Her eyes widened as she took in the scene.

"You," she barked at the dark-skinned soldier. "Explain what's going on."

The soldier put his rifle away and saluted. "Admiral Moore, ma'am! The ikthian prisoner just informed us that Councilman Bouchard is responsible for shooting Captain Roberts, ma'am. He also ordered us to execute the prisoner."

Elurin's mind latched onto the first word. *Admiral. He said Admiral Moore.* Apparently, her message had been going up the chain of command after all.

The admiral gave Bouchard a look that Elurin could only interpret as disgust. "At ease," she said, gesturing to the group who had turned on the councilor. "I've heard the same report. Ensign Harris regained consciousness in the medical ward, and she had some interesting things to say."

Medical ward? Rachel's conscious?

Elurin forgot all about Bouchard. She forgot about the danger Earth was in. Her entire body nearly melted with relief. Thank the Tides Rachel was awake and talking and receiving medical treatment. Elurin felt like she'd finally broken the water's surface to take a gulp of air.

"Is Rachel okay?" she blurted out.

To Elurin's surprise, the admiral smiled. "I'm not sure, but she had some interesting things to say about you, too, Elurin." The fact that the admiral knew her name was even more surprising, but she didn't get a chance to respond. "Soldiers? Remove the councilor from this room. All of you, out. I'll deal with him later."

Bouchard blanched. "How dare you? The council will hear about this! I'll tell them all about this slander, this…"

"Bouchard, for once in your life, do me the courtesy of shutting up." She nodded at the soldiers, who seemed all too happy to march Bouchard out of the room. A moment later, he was gone.

"I've wanted to do something about him for years," Admiral Moore said, in the most nonthreatening tone Elurin had heard since her imprisonment. "I never approved of the council's decision to withdraw support from the naledai rebellion, and now the truth about Roberts has come to light." She shook her head. "He was a good man."

"The Dominion has a deadly bioweapon that infects humans," Elurin said, "as well as other species. Kross and Oranthis are trying to retrieve a sample of the vaccine, but in the meantime, you need to make sure the Armada doesn't distribute the virus on Earth."

Admiral Moore nodded. "I believe you. We've already got fighters in position behind the plasma cannons and EMP defense grid. If any ikthian ships get through, we'll know." A comm unit around her wrist buzzed. Admiral Moore turned away, walking out of the room.

Elurin's relief turned to anxiety as she waited, counting the seconds. *What's going on? Did she get a message about the Armada? About the virus? About Rachel?* There was nothing she could do in her present position. She tried to get her wild thoughts under control.

At long last, the admiral re-entered the room. Her comm was off, her expression, serious. "Speaking of ikthian ships," she said, as though their conversation hadn't been interrupted, "how much do you know about taking out Dominion stealth fighters?"

"Everything," Elurin answered.

"Everything, eh?" Admiral Moore's mouth spread into a thin, determined smile. "Well then, Top Gun, let me work some of my magic. See if I can get that nice, shiny ship of yours out of custody."

"You're putting me back in the *Riptide*?" Elurin said, barely able to contain her excitement. "What's Top Gun mean?"

"Suffice to say, Ensign Harris thinks highly of your piloting skills. Are you ready to prove her right?"

"Absolutely," Elurin said. "Anything for her."

A few hours later, Elurin waited beside the *Riptide* in the San Diego Base docking bay, watching the flurry of activity around her with wide eyes. It was both like and unlike other docking bays she'd been in during her time as a pilot. The smell was smokier, acrid. The ships surrounding the *Riptide* were clunky boxes rather than spheres. The human fleet was not impressive, despite the Coalition's top of the line planetary defense system.

The air of manic urgency all around felt familiar, as did the overconfident jokes from groups of human pilots nearby. Apparently, humans weren't so different from ikthians and naledai, after all.

"How we feeling?" Andrew asked.

Admiral Moore had handed Elurin off to him, and he hadn't left her side since. Elurin didn't mind. If Rachel trusted him, she would, too. It was far better than being alone among aliens on a strange planet.

She shot him a smile. "Good. Ready. How about you?"

"Same." Andrew returned her smile. "If Rachel says you're the best, I believe it."

"Funny. I was just thinking that." The first things she'd asked Andrew upon seeing him again were all about Rachel. How was she?

Awake? Comfortable? Safe? Unfortunately, Andrew hadn't been able to tell her much, other than that the doctors were taking care of her and she'd been able to speak to a certain extent.

"Gotta admit, I wasn't expecting her to come back home with an ikthian in tow," Andrew said. "When we were stationed together, she..."

Elurin realized what he was trying to say. "Hated my species and wanted to kill us all? Yeah, she's past that. Who do you think changed her mind?"

"I asked around after Taylor escaped with that ikthian prisoner and Rachel got sent away," he told her in a low voice, as though confessing a secret. "Taylor's smart. She wouldn't have helped an ikthian without good reason. So I talked to some human soldiers who'd worked with the naledai rebellion. I had no idea what an open secret it was that ikthian defectors were part of their organization. Believe me, the regular Coalition foot soldiers weren't told. The council laid on the anti-ikthian propaganda pretty thick. I didn't know how much I didn't know until they both disappeared, and I started digging."

"Well, we've established that your council's pretty dumb, but I can't criticize," Elurin said. "My species' leaders are genocidal fascists, and it took me longer than I'd like to admit to see through their lies."

Andrew gave her a nod. "Yeah, I—" Whatever he was about to say was interrupted by a wailing siren. Red lights flashed overhead, flickering throughout the docking bay. The human soldiers nearby hurried to their ships, and Andrew turned to the *Riptide.* "You ready for this?" he asked, walking toward it.

Elurin took a deep breath. "Bet your life."

"I am," Andrew said. "I'm getting in a ship with you, aren't I?"

"You're getting in the fastest, safest ship here," Elurin said. She hurried after him, opening the doors to the fighter and climbing inside. "The *Riptide* can fly rings around any of these Coalition clunkers. No offense."

Andrew snorted as he strapped himself into the copilot's seat. "None taken. Guess ikthians are just as cocky as humans."

"Sometimes." Elurin activated the navigation display and fired up the plasma engines. The ship hummed and in spite of the dire circumstances, she felt a shudder of delight. This was what she'd been born to do, and she had someone special to do it for.

She had to stifle a laugh. *If saving Rachel's homeworld doesn't show her how I feel, nothing will.*

***

Maia watched Taylor fall. She seemed far away. Divorced from reality. More like a holo or a memory than something she was currently experiencing. Swaying to the ringing in her ears, she felt as though she were someone else...or perhaps no one at all.

The feeling did not last long. She dropped the container and rushed to Taylor's side, but a shot rang out. Akton had found his rifle and fired. Corvis fell, missing part of her head. A purple pool formed around what remained.

Maia hardly noticed. "Taylor," she sobbed, staring at her lover's prone form. Taylor lay sprawled on the floor, sucking in wet, rattling breaths as blood spilled from a burnt hole that took up most of her left side. She still had a torso, at least, but her side was a mass of shiny red and crusty black.

"Come on." Jethra crouched beside her. The naledai held the silver container Maia had dropped. "We gotta move!"

Maia shook her head. She wouldn't leave Taylor. Never again.

"I'll carry her." Akton had managed to clamber to his feet. His voice was commanding and reassuring, and Maia listened. She helped him lift Taylor's limp body, allowing him to do most of the work, but unable to let go.

Maia couldn't be sure how they made it back to the lower level of the *Wavestar*. Warning sirens blared, and red lights flashed in the stairwell. She saw the rise and fall of Taylor's chest, just barely. Her love was alive, but for how long, Maia had no idea.

They ran back down the fancy carpeted hall; toward the first set of doors they'd blown open. Maia almost tripped on an errant limb, and Akton had to steady her in addition to bearing Taylor's weight.

"Almost there," he panted. "Keep going."

Keep going. She repeated those words in her head with every step, until they arrived at the gangway. Relief flooded Maia's body. Their stealth fighter was within reach, Tides be.

Jethra went first and called back, "All clear!"

Maia and Akton followed into the fighter. Behind them, the warning sirens and flashing lights faded. Akton helped her lean back one of the rear seats, placing Taylor in it before rushing to the pilot's chair. "Kertamen, you're my new copilot. Kalanis, do what you can."

Jethra took the copilot's chair, while Maia hurried to remove Taylor's armor. The breastplate came off first, and blood came with it. A lot of blood. It had soaked through most of Taylor's shirt, and Maia nearly broke down. Helping in the med bay and taking first aid courses did nothing to prepare her for caring for an injured lover.

She chained her feelings down. *Taylor is depending on you. Get to work!*

Leaving Taylor for a few moments, Maia went for the first aid kit in the rear of the ship. She removed more of Taylor's armor to expose her hip and administered the injections. One to slow blood loss and another for pain. Taylor groaned.

Next, Maia removed Taylor's shirt. On second look, the wound wasn't as bad as she'd feared. Taylor's left side was torn open, with charred flesh around the edges, but the flow of blood was sluggish. Maia applied gauze and pressure, heedless of the blood that stained her hands.

Once she was confident, she had the bleeding under control, she removed the gauze and rummaged for a tube of ion-based sealant. It would help close and heal the opening in Taylor's side. Taylor moaned again as Maia smeared it over the blackened, bloody hole.

Maia blinked back tears. *She'll be all right. She has to be.*

Distantly, she heard Akton speaking, talking into the comm. "This is *SF-7* leaving Korithian airspace. We have a live sample. I repeat, we have a live sample. Pull back your ships."

Hope flickered in Maia's chest. The vaccine. She'd barely spared it a thought since Taylor was injured, but they had it. They'd succeeded. As long as Akton steered them safely back to Nakonum, there was a chance the scientists could stop the spread of the Dominion's bioweapon.

She had done what was necessary to atone for her part in its creation, and she could only pray that Taylor wouldn't pay the ultimate price for her mistakes.

***

Elurin scanned the *Riptide's* main grid. So far, she hadn't spotted any hostiles. All she could see out the viewport was the gleaming blue surface of Earth's ocean. Her shoulders lifted with mounting tension, and she ground the points of her teeth. *Fuck. Where are they? Those fighters have to be somewhere.*

The *Riptide's* dash made an urgent beeping noise. Six purple blips appeared on the three-dimensional blue grid, and Elurin's stomach did a somersault. Six. The humans had dispatched all the pilots they could spare, but most were scouting the rest of the coast, which was about 14,500 kilometers long. There were only four other Coalition ships anywhere nearby, all a fair distance behind.

Elurin steeled herself. *Come on, soldier. Time to add some more numbers to your rebel kill score.* "We've got company," she told Andrew. "You okay with her weapons system?"

Andrew nodded. "Practically point and shoot."

"It is." Elurin forced a grin. She kept close watch on the purple blips. They approached at a fast clip, no doubt heading straight for her. "All right. Here we go."

The first three Dominion fighters streaked toward her in a V formation. Elurin spun the controls, dipping into a controlled dive. When they plunged after, she juked right, aiming the guns at one of the two ships in the rear. "Fire!"

Andrew's first shots went wide, but he kept shooting until Elurin adjusted. The ship went up in a satisfying plume of orange-white fire. "Nice!" he crowed.

Elurin didn't share his elation for long. The other two ships had banked, and more approached from above. She barely breathed, watching the empty spaces in front of the enemy fighters. That was key, predicting where they would go. Doing that with ten ships threatened to make her head spin.

She swerved for several precious seconds. The *Riptide* shuddered, struck by enemy fire. Elurin's dash pulsed with purple warning lights. In the corner, she saw what remained of the ship's shields–74%. One hit had taken out almost a fourth of their power.

"They're packing serious firepower," she told Andrew, guiding the *Riptide* into a steep climb. Bright beams of light flashed outside the viewport as the enemy fighters shot at her. "They sent their best."

"But you can take them, right?"

She didn't miss the fear in Andrew's voice. Elurin tried to bring the *Riptide* into position above the remaining four fighters, but the choice left her vulnerable. Two of the ships opened fire, and another two hits rocked her shields.

58%.

39%.

Andrew managed to shoot down one of the fighters, but they'd sacrificed precious protection.

Ignore the shields. Find your opening.

Elurin banked to avoid a horizontal blast from one of the remaining three ships. As soon as she did, she swiveled the thrusters and dodged another incoming line of fire from above. The Dominion fighters converged, blocking escape. The *Riptide's* cockpit remained eerily silent, aside from the thud of a volley glancing off the shields.

19%.

One of the ships closed in from behind.

"On our six!" Elurin shouted.

Andrew fired, blowing the fighter away. "Two to go!"

Elurin was too focused to answer. The ships seemed to dance away from her, no matter what she tried. As much as she despised the Dominion, she had to acknowledge skill when she saw it. Whoever was flying them was good. One of the ships fired from above. She swerved, but the shot grazed the *Riptide's* right side.

11%.

How many more hits could she take? Although Elurin couldn't tear her eyes from the dash, Rachel's face flashed into her mind. Dark, curly hair. Brown skin. Her blunt teeth, and the soft dashes of hair above her burning black eyes. The *Riptide* rocked with another blast, throwing Elurin into her harness and forcing the air from her lungs. The grid gave another warning pulse of purple light, brighter than the previous ones.

5%.

Elurin struggled to bring the ship back under control. Andrew fired. By some miracle, he hit the ship that had just shot them. It spiraled toward the ocean in a grey-black trail of smoke.

One ship left.

It dove and darted, avoiding everything she and Andrew aimed at it, but Elurin didn't give up. She went on the offensive, feeding all the power she could into the thrusters and speeding straight toward her target.

They fired at the same time. The final ship exploded in a billow of fire, and the *Riptide* shuddered, giving an awful screech. Sirens blared throughout the cockpit, and the ship plummeted into an uncontrolled dive. Streaks of blue and white whipped past the viewport, and beside her, Andrew screamed.

Despite harsh rattling of the ship and the churning of her stomach, Elurin's eyes remained locked on her readouts–Shields 0%, Thrusters 13%. *Time to take another dive.*

.

Chapter Nineteen

"HOLD ON!" ELURIN'S FINGERS flew over the interface, following well-remembered patterns. She diverted power from everything she could and fed it into the remaining thrusters. Only three out of eight worked, and two of those were only at partial capacity.

She steered the *Riptide* into a dive, doing everything she could to lengthen the angle. Beside her, Andrew screamed. If he was shouting actual words, Elurin didn't understand.

What if I die and Rachel lives?

Elurin pushed the thought aside. The ocean approached at a terrifying pace, swamping the viewport. She could make out the white peaks of giant waves.

What if I live and Rachel dies?

She gritted her teeth, holding her breath.

I'm glad we had what we had.

The *Riptide* hit the water with enough force to send Elurin forward into her harness as her ship skipped across the ocean's surface. Her safety harness kept her mostly in place, but she felt a rib crack. The impact dazed her, and all she saw was blue. White noise roared, but it sounded strangely distant. *Is it the ocean or my heartbeat?* The ship came to a rocking rest on the surface of the water. Gradually, Elurin's world returned to normal volume.

Andrew's delighted shouting came through first, slamming his hands on the dash and pointing to the ocean surrounding them out the viewport. "We're alive! Elurin, you fucking did it!"

Elurin laughed. She was alive. Her heart hammered far faster than usual, but it was beating. The *Riptide* didn't appear to be sinking. She bobbed up and down like a boat at sea, seemingly content to drift.

"This is *D3-Black* to *Riptide*. Do you read us? Over."

The radio still worked, too.

"We read you," she answered, in English. One of the phrases Rachel had taught her. Then, in her own language, relying on her translator, "Thrusters are out. Can we get a pickup? Over."

"Copy that."

When she caught sight of several fighters overhead, dipping toward her position, she sagged into her seat. With a groan, she unbuckled her harness and let her head loll back. "Fuck."

Beside her, Andrew laughed. "Fuck is right."

Elurin joined in, a few tears leaking from her eyes. Terror turned relief. Beside her, Andrew had started saying something, but she couldn't bring herself to listen. Her thoughts were back at San Diego base, with Rachel fighting off the bioweapon coursing through her bloodstream. *Rachel, I'm coming back. Keep fighting until I get there. If I won, you can, too.*

***

"Taylor?"

White lights danced above her, cold and distant.

"Your vitals are better."

The lights grew brighter. Clearer. They blossomed outward, shining like stars...odd, evenly spaced stars.

"So, when you are ready, wake up."

A purple shadow passed over the stars, forming a silhouette. Cold, soothing pressure folded around her hand.

"I should tell you to let go, if that is what you need to do, but I am too selfish. I need you."

That was Maia's voice. *Maia needs me.*

Though it took several attempts, Taylor opened her eyes. Her lids felt unbearably heavy. The light above her wasn't stars—they were the lights of a medical ward, and she was lying in a hospital bed while someone held her hand. With tremendous effort, she shifted her gaze down. Webbed, silver fingers interlaced with hers.

"Mm," she said.

The hand holding hers tightened. "Do not try and speak yet," Maia said.

Taylor tried to say something anyway, but her throat protested. Burned. She winced.

"I told you not to try," Maia said. "You had another incident shortly after we arrived. The medics intubated you to assist with your breathing."

How long was I out? Taylor's heart thudded, and a chorus of frantic beeps started beside her. At least Maia seemed okay, judging by her calm voice. *Shit. What about Akton? What about Jethra and the others? Rachel and Elurin on Earth?*

Maia's cool hand moved to Taylor's forehead, brushing her hair back. "Rest, Taylor. You have done enough. The vaccine is safe on Jor'al, and the generals are attempting to contact Earth to inform them." She gave Taylor a soft, pointy-toothed smile, still blurred thanks to the lights and Taylor's watery eyes. "I have no doubt Rachel and Elurin will break the blockade."

Taylor blinked so her vision became clear. Despite Maia's earlier warnings not to speak, she tried to summon her voice. "Akton..." Just the one word made her throat feel like it was coated in boiling lava.

Maia withdrew her hand, caressing Taylor's cheek. "He's alive, thanks to you." She bent down, pressing their foreheads together.

Despite the lingering taste of blood in Taylor's mouth, she smelled Maia's warm scent, and its familiarity comforted her. She closed her eyes, and when she opened them again, she felt stronger. "Luhoo."

Maia drew back, a furrow forming in her brow. "What was that? My translator could not—"

"Love you," Taylor said, struggling to make the words clear.

Tears glistened in Maia's eyes. "I love you, too. For as long as stars do shine."

"Longer." Taylor managed to make herself understood without quite so much pain.

Maia kissed her again. "Yes. Longer."

***

Odelle gave her shoulder a cautious roll, testing its range. Though there was some lingering soreness, the sharp, stabbing pain that had previously clouded her mind every time she moved was gone.

"There you are," the naledai medic said, adjusting the ion patch pasted onto the area. "How does it feel?"

She sighed. "Much better, though it hurt a lot when you popped it back in."

"Sorry about that. And your head?"

She smiled. Though her head wound had seemed to bleed significantly at first, the medic had declared it mostly superficial. Some gel and a temporary bandage had been all the treatment needed. "That's better, too."

"Now, for those ears." The medic shone a pen light in the crevices on either side of Odelle's crest. After a few contemplative noises, she turned the light off. "No visible damage. With all those explosions you said were going on around you during your escape, I'm surprised."

"I'll take it," Odelle said. "And thank you again."

With a few friendly parting words about staying hydrated, the young medic moved on to her next patient, leaving Odelle to look around the ship. It was a large transport vessel, one of the few with a proper-sized med bay to have escaped the Hakkar comm station. Tucked away in the massive gorge, they were safe enough. Though for how long, Odelle couldn't say.

The med bay was overcrowded with patients, but Odelle was relieved to see most of the injuries appeared superficial. *I suppose those who were badly injured in the attack weren't able to make it to safety.*

She looked to the cot beside hers, where Sorra was arguing with a different naledai medic.

"It's fine," Sorra growled, batting his claws away as he tried to offer her another injection. Her shirt was off, and the shrapnel wound in her side had been cleaned, sealed, and bandaged. "I don't need more pain meds."

The medic gave her a look. "You could develop an infection. There's lots of foreign material that could worm its way inside you, if you're not careful. Your people didn't terraform Hakkar, remember?"

Sorra looked like she was about to continue arguing, but Odelle scooted over and kicked lightly at her boot. "Do what he says. What good will you be to anyone if you get sick?"

Begrudgingly, Sorra allowed the naledai to give the injection, though she didn't watch the needle go in. "Hate injections," she muttered to Odelle, pulling a face.

"I know. And medical treatment in general." She had often been the one providing such treatment for less serious injuries during their wild university years.

"I'll let you be," the naledai said, seemingly relieved to be done. "But if you feel feverish, tell someone immediately."

"Thank you," she said on Sorra's behalf. "We will."

Sorra made a vague noise of agreement, which seemed to satisfy the medic since he moved on to the next patient.

Odelle went to sit beside Sorra. "How are you, really?"

"Fine," Sorra said. Her expression had softened, and she managed a smile. "Glad we got out of there."

"Well, we aren't in safe harbors yet. Those destroyers are still in orbit around Hakkar, aren't they?" She linked hands with her love.

Sorra gave a somber nod. "I'm just grateful they haven't found us here."

Odelle wasn't sure how long they sat together on the cot, holding hands while the rest of the world bustled on without them. Rather than dwell on her fears, she tried to be grateful. She and Sorra were alive. That had to be enough for the moment. She squeezed Sorra's hand tighter, and Sorra squeezed back.

Her comm buzzed. She released Sorra and activated it, pleased to see an image of Oranthis on the screen. He gave her a toothy grin, and for once, Odelle didn't find the unnatural naledai smile off-putting. It probably meant good news.

"General Oranthis. I see we've re-established secure lines of communication." Normally, that sort of thing would have been part of Odelle's job, but due to her injuries, she'd left it to the capable group of technicians who'd also escaped the station.

"Better than that," Oranthis said. "We have the vaccine, and Corvis is dead."

Sorra gasped. "Dead? When? How?"

"Shot," Oranthis said. "By our Akton Valerius, no less."

Odelle's heart soared. Though she'd never been a soldier, nor the gun-slinging rebel Sorra was, this was one particular death she couldn't find it in herself to mourn. "Good!"

Oranthis rumbled with laughter. "That was my reaction. The destroyers around Hakkar have been recalled to Korithia. My troops and I are already on our way to your position. We'll arrive in a few hours to escort you back to Jor'al."

Odelle beamed at Sorra, then threw both arms around her, pulling her into a tight hug.

"Ow! Easy. My side, remember?" Sorra murmured.

"Odelle, why am I staring at a wall?" Oranthis said.

Odelle gentled her embrace but didn't let go. She couldn't bring herself to. She held on until Sorra carefully disentangled herself and unfastened the comm from Odelle's wrist. She took charge of it, saying, "Sorry. Will you send me a copy of the mission report?"

"Already on its way," Oranthis said. "You should find it entertaining. It reads like an action holo."

Sorra grinned. "If Valerius wrote it, I'm not surprised."

"Kertamen, actually," Oranthis drawled, showing a hint of amusement in his beady eyes. "She's even worse."

Sorra snorted. "Anything else?"

"Just sit tight. We're coming for you."

Once Oranthis had disconnected, Odelle rested her chin on Sorra's shoulder, closing her eyes and breathing easily for the first time since their panicked flight from the station.

"They did it," she whispered. "They actually did it."

Sorra wrapped an arm around her, placing a kiss on top of her head. A rare public gesture of affection. "Yes. We did it."

Chapter Twenty

AS MAIA WALKED DOWN the hall toward her mother's cell, she felt better than she had in months. Lighter, like she was afloat in a calm ocean. The weight she always carried on her shoulders—guilt for what had happened to Taylor and how her research had been used—had stopped trying to drown her.

Taylor was recovering swiftly, more swiftly than after her liberation from Daashu. Apparently, battle wounds were easier to heal than long-term malnourishment. Scientists were well on their way to replicating the vaccine on a mass scale. If the Dominion managed to launch another attack, the rebellion would be ready.

The riots on Korithia had continued. There were daily casualty reports from the front lines, where the rebellion fought to reclaim naledai territory, colony by colony.

But Corvis was dead. The Dominion had been dealt a staggering blow, facing resistance from without and within. Earth was no longer in immediate danger. In fact, the Coalition was helping the naledai reclaim Nakonum, in a long-overdue show of solidarity.

But if there was one thing she'd learned during the course of the war; it was that some wounds never fully healed. After all that happened, she felt compelled to flush this one before it had the chance to fester.

When she arrived at the familiar hallway, the naledai guards nodded and stood aside. One even flashed her a smile. *And Taylor says my teeth are sharp.* Still, Maia returned it.

"Kurda. How is your leg?" Though Maia didn't visit her mother without some larger purpose, she had familiarized herself with some of the guards on rotation.

Kurda snorted through her lightly silvered muzzle. "Hurts," she growled, though not unkindly.

"Give it time," Maia said.

"S'what the medics keep saying, but I want to be out there, fighting to free the homeworld."

195

Mia nodded. "Of course, but you do have that fine scar on your neck from the same battle. I doubt anyone will say you failed to do your part."

That seemed to placate Kurda. She scratched at the aforementioned scar with a claw. Kurda and the other guard stepped aside, allowing her to pass into Irana's room.

It had been outfitted with slightly more furniture since Maia's last visit. A privacy screen had been erected around the shower and toilet, which Maia was pleased to see, for her mother's sake. An adjustable humidifier had been installed. A desk sat in one corner, and on it, a terminal. Irana stood before it, though she powered off the display and turned when the doors opened.

"Maia." A hesitant smile spread across her face, and she took a step forward.

Maia grinned reflexively. A very small part of her was glad to see her mother. "Hello." She licked her lips. "I have news for you."

"Oh?"

"Corvis is dead."

Though Maia searched Irana's face, it showed little to no emotion. "How did it happen?"

"We infiltrated the *Wavestar*. Corvis was shot during our efforts to acquire the vaccine. The bioweapon is no longer nearly as dangerous a threat."

"Are you sure?" Irana asked. "Vaccines are only effective if enough of the population is inoculated."

"We are working on that. Earth and Nakonum have already started programs," Maia replied.

"We," Irana repeated. She gazed at Maia for a long time. "I have never seen you so integrated into a group before, nor so committed to a cause."

Maia tried not to show her surprise. It certainly wasn't the reaction she'd expected, nor the subject she'd come prepared to discuss. "I suppose I have changed a great deal recently."

"An understatement," Irana said. "This is part of what I wanted for you. To command the respect of your peers and have an impact on the wider galaxy. You have not achieved this in the manner I expected, but you have achieved it nonetheless."

A few years ago, Maia would have given anything to hear those words. She had craved her mother's approval ever since she could conceive of it, and Irana had rarely expressed it. And yet, the sentiment didn't have nearly as much power as Maia expected. *She is proud of me. In her own way, at least. Why don't I care?*

The answer came to her.

Because I am proud of myself, and that is all I need. Besides, Taylor and my friends were already proud of me, and I respect their opinions far more.

Maia stood a little taller. "The rebellion appreciates your help and the information you have provided."

"And you?" Irana took a cautious step forward.

Maia was shocked by the realization that their life-long positions had reversed. Now, it was her mother looking to her for approval. For reassurance. Acceptance. And Maia wasn't entirely sure she deserved it.

Without her we might have failed. And though she has done despicable things, she has always tried to provide me with the best opportunities. Perhaps that was the only way she knew how to show me she loved me.

"Yes," she said, and she meant it. "I, personally, appreciate the help you provided."

Irana's face softened. "What will you do next?"

For the third time in as many minutes, Maia found herself floundering. Her mother had rarely asked her what she wanted to do with her future, especially without inserting her own commentary and not-so-subtle demands.

Somehow, Maia managed to maintain an outer facade of calm. "Go with Taylor to Earth. She is being reinstated by her people's military. After that? We will go to Korithia. Help rebuild."

Irana nodded. "Good."

Just the one word. *Good.* In her mother's answer, Maia saw a small island of common ground, upon which she could take refuge from the vast sea of differences between them. They both wanted Korithia to continue, better than before. Perhaps she was reading too much into it, but Maia wondered if Irana had admitted to herself that Maia might know more about what their people needed than she did.

"I will keep you informed," Maia said.

"Thank you."

After a beat of silence, Maia asked, "And what are you doing? I see you have a new terminal."

Irana looked at the terminal. "With very limited access and communication capabilities, but yes. And I am grateful for it. This certainly isn't Daashu."

Maia suppressed a shudder. She hated to think of Daashu, and everything Taylor had endured there. Her mother, too. "No."

"I have been cataloguing my knowledge and experiences," Irana continued, "in the hopes Odelle Lastra might find it useful in the future. Though I must admit, it is also rather self-indulgent."

"You have the time for self-indulgence as a prisoner," Maia pointed out.

Irana laughed softly. "I suppose I do."

"Have you communicated with Odelle?"

"Indeed. She and—" Irana's face pulled ever so slightly. "—Sorra have plans to return to Korithia as well. I have some hope that Odelle may eventually be able to establish peace, though how it will look, I cannot claim to know."

"It won't be easy," Maia said.

There were countless factors—the remnants of Corvis's regime, which would surely vie for power with the rebels currently on and headed for the homeworld; the hearts of those who saw nothing wrong with the old government. There would doubtless be more bloodshed. And yet, Maia held out hope. *If Irana can change, even a little bit, perhaps success will come sooner than I think.*

"Certainly not. But I thought I would die in Daashu, and here I am. Still alive, in spite of the odds." Irana replied. "Unexpected things happen, and not always for the worse."

Maia smiled. "No. Not always for the worse."

***

The first thing Rachel became aware of was how badly she needed to pee. She shifted in her bunk, only to realize it wasn't a bunk. She recognized the sharp smell right away. Clinical and sterile. She opened her eyes, blinking back the fuzziness, and realized she was on a hospital bed. She groaned and sat up, grateful to see that she wasn't hooked up to any machines. That was a good sign, although the lack of other beds in the room wasn't.

"Hey, you. Take it easy there."

Her heart leapt. She knew that voice! She looked in the other direction, noticing a chair beside her bed, and Elurin in it. "'Lurin?"

Elurin's gloved hand touched her shoulder. Even behind a white filtration mask, her beautiful face looked even better than usual. "Guess who got to be the first human to use the vaccine to jumpstart their amazing immune system?"

Rachel let out a dry laugh. Even though she desperately needed to pee, she was also parched. "They got it?"

"Yep. Taylor, Maia, and Akton did it. Akton shot Corvis, too."

Rachel suddenly felt more awake. "Akton what?"

"Shot her dead," Elurin repeated, her eyes bright. "There's plenty of other power-hungry dictators back home ready to take her place, but I think the galaxy is a hundred times better off without her."

"And Earth?" she asked, hardly daring to hope. "No outbreaks?"

"Nope. We mopped up the fighters that snuck past the cannons to distribute the virus. I helped." Elurin's eyes sparkled.

Rachel laughed. "I bet you did. Damn it, I missed all the fun. Now I know how Taylor felt."

"It wasn't fun. But I felt you there with me the whole time. Making sure I came back."

Butterflies fluttered in Rachel's stomach despite her exhaustion. Surprised, she took stock of her body and how it felt. *No fever or chills. Tired and sore, like I ran a marathon. Otherwise, I feel kind of good?* She lifted her hand and squeezed Elurin's to test her strength and range of movement.

Elurin leaned into the touch, resting her cheek on Rachel's hand. "I haven't left your side in two days, you know. Admiral Moore likes me. She let me stay."

The softness in Elurin's blue eyes swallowed Rachel whole, but before she could say anything, another voice sounded from the doorway.

"Rachel? You're awake!"

She looked past Elurin to see Andrew hurrying in. He was wearing a mask as well, but not a full hazmat suit, which she decided to interpret as a good sign. *Oh, shit. I have to tell him.*

"Hey, Andy," she said, giving him her warmest smile. "Elurin, this is awkward, but can we have a minute alone?"

Andrew held up his hand. "It's okay, Rach. Are you gonna tell me you and Elurin are a thing now?" His tone, though a little wistful, wasn't upset. She stared at him in surprise.

"How'd you know? I don't talk in my sleep, do I?"

"Elurin gave it away. You should hear her talk about you. Even with a translator, I could tell."

Rachel opened her arms. "C'mere. I mean, if you're allowed to. The doctors haven't told me—"

"Eh, I'll have to go through decon anyway on my way out of the room." Andrew came in for a hug. His arms were strong and familiar, and Rachel smiled into his neck. "Also, I come bearing news. Guess who was impeached from the council a few hours ago?"

"Our favorite douchebag?" Rachel asked, her excitement rising.

"Yep."

"What?" Elurin asked, looking adorably confused. "My translator definitely doesn't have whatever that word is."

"I'll explain that one later," Rachel said, patting Elurin's knee. "So, they're investigating him?"

"Hell yeah. From the scuttlebutt I heard, I doubt it'll take long. Lots of suits will want to talk to you now you're awake."

"Ugh. Great." The prospect of being interviewed about Roberts's murder wasn't quite so exciting, but Rachel still felt relieved. Hopefully, Bouchard would finally pay for his crimes.

"It's not so bad," Andrew said. "The rebels are making progress on Nakonum. They've taken over half the planet back now. And I have more good news."

"More? Here I was, thinking I'd already hit my good news quota," Rachel joked.

Andrew gave her a light punch on the shoulder. "The final member of our Terrible Trio is headed to Earth. We're getting the band back together."

That filled Rachel with another bolt of happy energy. "Taylor's coming?"

"Yep. She took a hit on Korithia, but according to Akton, she's doing better. Getting the vaccine earned her a lot of popularity points, even with the people who threw her to the wolves when she went AWOL."

"When does she get here?" Rachel asked.

"Sometime tomorrow, I think? I'm sure she'll visit you as soon as she gets in."

Before she could question him further, Rachel noticed two masked doctors, one with a datapad and the other with a cart of testing equipment, standing a few yards away.

"Sorry to interrupt, folks, but we need a minute with Junior Lieutenant Harris," one of them said.

"Junior lieutenant?" Rachel parroted, grinning. "Did they seriously promote me while I was unconscious?"

"Oh, did we forget to mention that?" Elurin asked, without looking the slightest bit sorry. "Congratulations, Junior Lieutenant Harris." With a brief caress of Rachel's arm, she left the bed, and Andrew followed, making room for the doctors.

"We'll be outside," Andrew said. "Have fun getting probed!"

"Seriously?" Rachel's smile faded.

Elurin laughed, bumping her shoulder against Andrew's as they headed for the door. "You and I are going to get along really well."

***

Taylor inhaled, taking her first breath of fresh Earth air. Well, it wasn't exactly fresh, and it wasn't exactly outside, but it was still special. Her heart leapt at the familiar sights, sounds, and smells of the San Francisco docking bay. Finally, after what felt like a lifetime, she had come home.

Taylor turned, offering Maia a smile. "Better than last time, huh?"

Maia responded with a snort.

Akton, who was currently ambling along the gangway a few steps behind, offered his own opinion. "Smart move, Morgan. Remind Maia about the time she was a prisoner, and the three of us almost got shot smuggling her offworld."

"It's all right, Akton," Maia said, with a gentle laugh. "I can take a joke. This *is* better than last time."

Akton gave Taylor a soft tap with his claw, which was forceful enough to rock Taylor. She took a step forward to stabilize herself and grabbed Maia's arm for support. "Easy there, big guy. I took a shot for you, remember? Still kind of wobbly."

He made an aggrieved rumbling noise. "And you haven't let me forget it since."

"Just keeping you humble, buddy," Taylor quipped. "Since you're the hero of the century now."

Akton had already been awarded more medals, titles, and honors than Taylor could count. His face was on every naledai news broadcast within streaming distance of Nakonum, and he was rapidly on his way to becoming a household name among the civilian population.

"Please, don't remind me." Akton seemed mildly embarrassed by his newfound fame, but that wasn't going to stop her from teasing him about it. "Wish I'd saved you instead. I'd get bragging rights and a sexy new scar, and your stupid face could be everywhere."

Taylor shook her head. "No tradesies. You're stuck with the glory. Sorry."

"Loo!"

Rachel's voice caused Taylor to turn. A broad smile broke across her face as she spotted two figures hurrying across the docking bay to greet her. Rachel and Elurin jostled each other to be the first to greet her. Part way there, Rachel stopped, bending slightly and resting a hand on her knee. Elurin came to an abrupt halt beside her, placing a hand on her back.

Taylor went to meet them. "You okay, Harris?" she asked, brow furrowing.

Rachel straightened, though Taylor didn't miss the visible line of sweat on her brow. "Fine. Just got a little too excited. Still recovering." She pulled a face.

Taylor laughed before pulling her into a gentle hug. "Oh, I've been there. Twice."

Rachel gave her an extra squeeze before letting her go. "Yeah. Heard you took a hit for that fleabag over there. How are you, Mister Hero?" She grinned at Akton.

"Come on," he rumbled. "Not you, too. Taylor's already taken it upon herself to remind me every five minutes she saved my life." After a playful ruffle of Rachel's curls with his giant claws, he gave Elurin a hug as well. "Speaking of real heroes, I hear you took out six Dominion fighters with the virus on them all by yourself. That true?"

Elurin wriggled out of the hug and gave Akton a playful shove. "It was twelve, thank you. And I took them out while half the *Riptide's* thrusters weren't working."

While they laughed, Maia took her turn hugging Rachel. Taylor couldn't help feeling a brief flash of pride at the sight. Her lover and best friend, finally getting along. It wasn't so long ago that Rachel would have tried to shoot Maia. Actually, hugging an ikthian, and, apparently, dating one, would have been out of the question.

"How are you feeling, really?" Maia asked Rachel.

"Like all the energy got sucked out of me," Rachel confessed. "I feel tired and weak all the time. But otherwise? Pretty okay. Elurin sprung me from the medical ward so I could welcome Taylor home. I'm not contagious anymore—for real, this time—but I'm not technically supposed to be doing anything strenuous, either."

"Think you can use that excuse to get out of the ceremony?" Elurin asked.

Taylor's eyes widened. "What ceremony?"

"Silver Star," Rachel said, sounding smug. "Guess what? You're getting one too."

Taylor blinked. The Silver Star was the Coalition's highest military honor. She'd never imagined she would be a recipient. "I knew they were reinstating me, but…holy shit. Just, holy shit."

Maia wrapped an arm around Taylor's waist, resting a cheek against her shoulder. "Why are you so surprised? You deserve this."

Though she could already feel wings of elation sprouting in her chest, Taylor was still too overwhelmed to move as Akton elbowed her free side. "Ha! Now you have to be a famous hero, too. See how you like it."

She brushed him off, grinning at Rachel instead. "They're giving you a Silver Star for being sick? Standards for the award must've gone down, Harris."

"That's Junior Lieutenant Harris now, ma'am."

"You won't let me forget that, will you?"

"Nope…captain."

Taylor shook her head. Captain. A Silver Star. Maia and all her friends, safe and well on Earth. Short weeks ago, she'd been a prisoner, with hardly any hope left in her broken body. Now everything was almost perfect.

Not perfect, she reminded herself. The newly freed Nakonum needed to be rebuilt and defended. Korithia was still in shambles, although hopefully it would be ruled by better ikthians who didn't believe it was their destiny to conquer the galaxy. There would always be work to do. But as she looked at her friends, she knew there were plenty of heroes around to make it happen.

***

Koritha's capitol, Rho, both was and wasn't as Sorra remembered it. She gazed through the ship's viewport, watching the sea of silvery bubbles grow larger. The buildings formed a series of glittering half-rings, like pearls strung in a necklace, nestled directly against the green Parnassian sea.

For the first time in a long time, Sorra felt a tendril of wistfulness curl in her chest. *Korithia is as much mine as any ikthian's. I won't surrender it to another tyrant like Corvis.*

"Sorra?" Odelle said.

She turned to Odelle, who sat in the passenger's seat beside her. Their shuttle was a larger transport, and Sorra enjoyed being a passenger. Despite her swirling thoughts, she'd nodded off several times during the trip. "Hmm?"

"Just wondering if you needed something to tide you over." Odelle pulled a nutrobar from the small bag beneath her seat.

"Thanks." Sorra took it, suddenly realizing how ravenous she was. She unwrapped it and took a large bite, chewing the tart oats. It had been almost a day since she'd last eaten a proper meal. She'd been travelling and preparing for their arrival on Korithia.

There was already plenty of work waiting for them. Joran had established a base in the remains of the Central Communications building, and the addition of ikthian defectors from Nakonum's rebel force would be a huge benefit.

As Sorra chewed, she stared through the viewport. She recognized the giant bubble of Central Communications, with its shiny circular walkways winding along its sides like the rings of a planet.

Odelle peered past her, looking out the viewport as well. "I never thought I'd be happy to see this place again," she said, sounding tired but pleased. "Smart of Joran to choose it. CC has everything we need to continue sending our message to the populace."

"Lots won't listen," Sorra said, more out of habit than anything.

"Yes. But enough will."

In the past, Sorra might have pushed back against Odelle's statement. She wasn't a natural optimist, just like most ikthians weren't natural rebels. There were many staunch traditionalists, and their society had been totalitarian for so long that most had no idea what change looked like. But a voice spoke in Sorra's head, one that sounded like Odelle's. *Well, we'll just have to show them, won't we?*

She could be, and always had been, something of an idealist. "Enough will."

She munched on the nutrient bar and downed a bottle of water Odelle offered afterward. The transport descended, and to Sorra's relief, there was no interference from enemy ships. Joran had succeeded in keeping the immediate airspace above Central Communications clear.

They touched down behind the building in the parking lot where personal vehicles typically landed. Through the viewport, Sorra saw a squad of armed ikthians march toward them. A few Dominion uniforms scattered among them, some had personal armor sets, but others weren't properly outfitted. *That's one of the first things I'll need to take care of.*

"We'll need to get the standard on their equipment," Odelle said, obviously thinking along the same exact lines.

Sorra nodded. The stylized ship on waves would be easy enough to distribute. Hopefully, it would soon become ubiquitous.

They exited the ship alongside several other ikthian rebels and a few naledai, proceeding along the gangway together. Half-way down, Sorra spotted Joran waiting for them among the welcome party. She sped up, offering him her outstretched palms. He pressed their hands together.

"Glad you made it," he said. "And thank the Ancients, too. Being in command without you is the worst."

Sorra laughed. "Don't worry, dear. Your beloved wife is here to get everything ship-shape. You can go back to being a trophy husband."

Something crawled from the flowing sleeve of Joran's robe, running along her arm to perch on her shoulder.

"Tazmar!" she cried, pulling the small lizard's body against her face.

Tazmar did not protest. She scratched the frill under his chin, and he flicked his tongue at her, clearly pleased to be back in his proper position on her shoulder.

"I told you he missed you," Joran said.

"I missed him!" Odelle cooed and petted Tazmar.

Sorra looked at the waiting soldiers; several watched with interest. They were an odd mixture—some young, some old; some experienced from the way they held their weapons, and others far less so. But they had come, and that was what mattered.

She took a breath and summoned her most authoritative voice. "Attention!"

The soldiers who hadn't been watching snapped their gazes onto her.

"Many of you already know me, and those of you who don't soon will. I'm your new commander." Sorra paused, and only when she decided her audience was suitably riveted did she continue. "The path we've chosen, the path of resistance, is dangerous. But it's the path most consistent with our character and courage. We believe in freedom. We believe every life has inherent value, including our own. But we are prepared to lay down our lives in the fight for a better future. A future I believe we can earn. The future we all deserve."

It was a short rallying speech, but effective. The newly minted rebels, and even the jaded older ones, seemed to hang on her words. In their eyes, Sorra saw something of her past—her burning desire for change. She also saw something of the future. A *better* future.

Joran stood beside her along with Odelle. He gestured to the assembled troops. "Well? Are you with us ?"

A loud cry of affirmation followed.

Sorra smiled. "In that case, we have work to do."

Epilogue

"IT'S SMALLER THAN I remember," Maia said, examining Taylor's old captain's quarters at the San Diego base. Her former prison. The walls, the furniture—none of it had changed. It even smelled the same, like cleaning supplies and recycled air. Nevertheless, it felt different. Smaller. Less threatening.

Perhaps I'm the one who is different.

Taylor nodded. "I guess the universe shrinks to fit whatever space you're in."

"Not all my memories of this place are bad," she said, attempting to lighten the mood. Her stint in captivity had been terrifying, but also transformative. She'd found resources within herself she hadn't known she possessed. *And I fell in love.*

She tried to catch Taylor's eye, but her lover looked away. "I know it worked out, but I still feel guilty," Taylor said.

"For?"

"I was your guard. Even when you consented, I had no way of knowing whether that consent was coerced—"

"Stop." Maia reached out a hesitant hand to stroke her face. She waited for Taylor to lean in before making contact. "Sometimes, things that are terrible in the abstract have unique exceptions. Maybe that's what we are."

Taylor cracked a grin. "An exception?"

"A miracle."

"Really? I didn't think scientists believed in miracles."

"Not in the traditional sense. But if you think about it, the two of us have faced a hundred perilous situations and made a hundred risky choices." Maia ran her thumb along Taylor's high cheekbone. Her face had filled out considerably over the past several weeks, and with her hair cut short, she looked almost like her old self. "Considering all those variables, isn't it miraculous that we ended up with this specific result?"

Taylor grasped Maia's hand on her cheek and kissed it, causing Maia to shudder at the warm brush of her lips. "It sounds downright romantic."

They crossed the living room, passing the empty fridge and couch in order to enter the bedroom. The sheets had been stripped, making the room seem barren. Nevertheless, Taylor sat on the edge of the mattress.

"Are you tired?" Maia asked. "Do you need water? Food?"

"I'm fine." Taylor patted the spot beside her. "Sit with me."

When Maia sat, Taylor rested a hand on her thigh, but looked toward the bathroom door almost wistfully.

"What is it?" Maia asked.

"Just remembering..." Taylor's grin returned. "You walked through that door completely naked in a cloud of steam, and I'd never seen anyone or anything so beautiful in all my life."

Maia buried her face in her hands. "I had no idea you were there," she moaned, hiding the mottling at the top of her crest with her fingertips. Surely it had grown darker with embarrassment.

Taylor's palm moved to the middle of her back. "Hey, it's okay. I just said you were beautiful. Why are you embarrassed?"

With a huff, Maia let her hands fall away. "That memory may be *slightly* embarrassing."

"But not bad?" Taylor asked with a hopeful tone.

"No. Not bad." Maia rested her cheek on Taylor's shoulder. "I remember other things, too. How giving you were when we made love."

Taylor stared at the ceiling and heaved a contented sigh. "We had our moments here, didn't we?"

"Indeed."

Maia remained snuggled against Taylor's side for several moments then forced herself to move. She didn't want to postpone their plans any longer, now that they weren't staring down death.

"May we go now?" she asked.

"You really don't know the meaning of the word patience, do you?" Taylor laughed.

"Not when it comes to this." Maia rolled onto her knees, staring at Taylor with unbridled eagerness. "Please? I want to see it."

Taylor raised an eyebrow. "I thought you wanted to see this room? Relive old memories? Banish old ghosts?"

Maia chewed the inside of her cheek. That had been her intention, but now that she'd seen this room again, she realized the things she wanted to see were out there on Taylor's homeworld. Things like the place they were supposed to go.

"Taylor."

"Fine, fine." With a grunt, Taylor hopped off the bed and grabbed the bag she'd packed earlier, slinging it over her shoulder.

Maia hurried to join her. "Let me."

"I can get it." Taylor offered her a reassuring smile. "I was in combat a few weeks ago, so I think I can handle one bag."

"Stop reminding me." Maia stared at her.

Taylor adopted a pleading look. "C'mon, babe. I haven't been able to lift or carry anything. I'll have to give up my butch card."

Maia shook her head and smiled. She still didn't fully understand the complex relationship many humans had with gender, but she knew Taylor's fell somewhere outside the norm—from Taylor's comments more than others' reactions. "Human culture is strange. Are your males and gender-nonconforming females truly expected to carry everything?"

"Hey, where do you get off calling my culture weird? Ikthians have a gender binary, too." She started toward the door. "Dumb Ancients. I blame them."

Maia smirked, following. "My female ancestors led pod hunts."

"Oh, women and nonbinary humans did plenty of important shit in the past. Men just liked to pretend we didn't."

As they stepped into the hallway, Maia felt a weight lift from her shoulders. Her excitement grew as they approached the elevator and made their way to the land-based shuttle parked beside the building.

There were few soldiers outside, much to Maia's relief. The base was running on a skeleton crew, since most of the Coalition's forces were "mopping up"—as Taylor put it—the remainder of the Dominion blockade. Their efforts were going well, and there had been no outbreaks of the bioweapon, either. Thank the Tides.

"How far to the ocean?" she asked. She could smell the tinge of salt on the breeze, and it made her scales tingle.

Taylor chuckled as she put the bag in the back seat. "Two minutes." She started to hop in on the driver's side, but upon receiving a look, slouched over to the passenger's side.

Maia took the pilot's chair, familiarizing herself with the controls—a steering wheel as opposed to an interface—but it seemed intuitive enough.

Starting the engine, Maia felt the pleasant rumble vibrate beneath her legs. "Directions, please."

"So bossy." Taylor tsked. "Head due west."

Maia did. The drive was brief. Before Maia knew it, their shuttle was whipping along a shallow coastline of jagged red rock, dotted with clinging palm trees. She delighted in both the similarities and differences to her home.

"There," Taylor said, pointing to a specific spot further down the shore. "It's a small inlet. Private."

Maia spared her a glance. "Oh?"

Taylor winked. "I might have made arrangements."

Spotting a clear piece of sand, Maia parked the shuttle, powering off the engines. It was a rusty golden color, and when she opened the door, the scent of salt caressed her face on a cool breeze. She smiled so hard her cheeks hurt.

"I can hear it," she said, walking toward the glittering sapphire expanse of the ocean without bothering to close the shuttle door. She was wrapped up in the whispering roar of the waves, broken only by the high-pitched cries of seabirds wheeling above.

"Why are you crying?"

Maia hadn't realized she was until Taylor came to stand beside her, wiping a wet streak from one of her cheeks. She closed her eyes and tilted her face toward the sun. "This is the first time I have ever been to an ocean with you, and it is your ocean. An Earth ocean." She opened her eyes again. "Do you know the saline content?"

Taylor grinned sheepishly. "Uh... we don't exactly memorize that kind of stuff about our oceans."

"I suppose you would have no need to," Maia replied.

After leaning over to steal a quick kiss, Maia bent down to remove her boots. Taylor left her to it, ducking back into the shuttle to retrieve their bag. Maia shoved her webbed toes deep into the sand and wiggled them, pleased by the silty texture.

"Here." A piece of cloth came flying at her, and Maia barely raised her hands in time to catch it. "It's a swimsuit," Taylor elaborated.

Maia looked up and down the beach. There was no one else in sight, just as Taylor had promised. "If you did, as you say, made arrangements for privacy, are swimsuits really necessary? Swimming naked is much more freeing. Ikthians never wear anything in the water."

Taylor, who had returned to the shuttle for an umbrella and beach chairs, stumbled a little on the uneven sand. "I guess we don't need them."

With her assistance, Taylor carried their supplies closer to the waterline. Once the umbrella, chairs, and blankets had been set up, Taylor sank into one of the chairs. "Ahh. This is more like it." She pulled a pair of dark glasses from out of the bag and perched them on her nose. "Never thought I'd get to spend a relaxing day at the beach again."

Those words made Maia swell with joy. *I would be a fool to waste the opportunity.*

Without her boots, it was easy to remove the rest of her clothes. She tossed them in a pile on the blanket, shooting Taylor a wide grin. "I'm going swimming. Will you come with me?"

Taylor tipped the tinted glasses down, peering over the lenses. "In a few minutes? I hope so."

Maia's spots flushed. She offered Taylor her hand. "In that case, let me help you with your clothes."

***

Taylor peeled off her shirt, enjoying the sun's warmth on her skin. She grabbed a tube of sunscreen from their bags, waggling it in Maia's direction. "Mind slapping some of this sunscreen on me? Protects my skin from ultraviolet rays."

Maia's eyes widened. "A chance to rub lotion all over your naked body. Say no more." She took the tube and sat behind Taylor, pouring a generous dob of sunscreen on her palms and massaging it into Taylor's shoulders.

Taylor sighed with pleasure. It was a relaxing massage more than anything. With Maia's hands stroking soft patterns over her skin, she couldn't think of anywhere else she'd rather be. Before long, she was stretched on her stomach while Maia lotioned her legs, taking plenty of time to coat her thighs.

"Not too high with that stuff," Taylor warned, even as she spread her legs to offer more access. "No clue what it'll do on my sensitive bits."

"I will be careful," Maia said.

Taylor closed her eyes. She shuddered as Maia's hands squeezed her backside. Maia's touch—combined with the warm sun, cool breeze, and the hiss of the surf—almost caused her to drift off.

Almost.

When something wet and warm dragged along her back, Taylor's eyes popped open. "Oh!" She grasped the blanket as Maia's tongue followed her spine. The pointed tips of Maia's teeth nipped at her neck.

"Have I ever told you I love the way your flesh tastes?" Maia whispered.

Taylor snorted. "That'd be a creepy thing to say in any other situation."

"I'm serious," Maia murmured against the side of her throat. "It reminds me of Korithia's seas." She began to suck, and tingling heat blossomed in Taylor's belly.

"I think that's enough sunscreen on my back," she said.

Maia laughed. "Well then, shall I move onto your front?"

Taylor flipped over, grinning as Maia straddled her stomach. Her eyes darted between her lover's legs, and the sight took her breath away. Maia's silver lips were already swollen, showing the purple inner folds. They gleamed, and Taylor ran her tongue over her lips. "Why not scoot up a little higher?"

"Soon, perhaps," Maia purred. "But first, I have a surprise." She twisted, reaching into the bag nearby and withdrawing something.

Taylor's eyes widened. "Holy shit. Is that—"

Maia clutched the same double-sided, flesh-colored strap-on she'd purchased a few years ago. The one they'd used during her time as Maia's guard, and the same one she'd left behind when they'd escaped Earth. Fighting for her life, she hadn't had much opportunity to think about it. But now, she couldn't help laughing.

"How did you even find it? Or is it a replacement?" she asked.

"It's the same one," Maia replied. "I filed a request to have your old things returned. They were in a box in one of the base's storage facilities."

"Kind of awkward, since that means someone took it from the room in the first place and some other soldier had to catalogue it, but I'm glad you found it! That's awesome."

"I cannot deny a certain amount of selfish motivation." Maia dragged the tip of the toy down Taylor's stomach. "I was hoping you would wear it for me… if you would like."

"I'd like," Taylor blurted. "I'd like a lot."

"Then allow me."

The first brush of Maia's mouth was soft, so tender and sweet that Taylor had trouble processing it. She wrapped her arms around Maia's waist, drawing her close. The strap-on remained nestled between their stomachs, but Taylor was distracted by Maia's tongue as it brushed her lips.

Soon, they were exploring each other's mouths, slowly and deeply. Maia cupped Taylor's hip, and Taylor twined their fingers together, guiding Maia's hand between her legs.

The first touch of Maia's fingers had her arching off the blanket. They found her clit, circling until it stiffened. Maia's other hand slid over the muscles of her stomach then up along the outline of her ribs. Goosebumps erupted over Taylor's skin despite the sun's warmth and Maia's body stretched atop hers.

"Tease," Taylor moaned, nipping Maia's bottom lip.

"Patience." Maia's fingers slid lower, pressing in on either side of Taylor's swollen lips. "I need to make sure you're ready."

Taylor took the toy, bringing it between her legs. "Trust me," she said, pressing it into Maia's hand. "I'm ready."

"That is for me to decide." Maia accepted it. Rather than searching out Taylor's entrance, she dragged the blunt tip up and down. As it probed, spreading her wetness, warmth bloomed in the cradle of Taylor's hips. She tried to rock forward, only to find herself disappointed.

Maia chuckled. "There's no rush."

More tension left Taylor's body, the weight of a lifetime, and she remained utterly limp as Maia finally positioned the toy at her entrance. It slid inside, although her breath hitched at the new stretch. Soon, the shorter end had found a home within her, the sensation transmitter lined up with her clit.

"It's working, yes?" Maia's hand gave the shaft a testing squeeze.

Taylor's sigh became a loud groan. "Fuck. Yes, it's working."

"Excellent."

Maia let go, causing Taylor to make an embarrassing noise of disappointment.

"What are you—" She released another moan as Maia stretched back over her, sucking briefly at her neck before beginning a thorough exploration with hands and mouth.

She made no more complaints as Maia poured out more sunscreen and worked on her front, starting at her shoulders and descending at a crawl. She cupped Taylor's breasts, and as she did, Taylor's lashes fluttered.

After a few brief passes over Taylor's stomach to make sure it was covered in sunscreen, Maia abandoned the bottle and tended to Taylor with her tongue. One of Taylor's hands shot to Maia's crest, grasping in search of an anchor, especially when Maia's pointed teeth tugged one of her nipples.

"S'good," Taylor sighed as Maia let go and nuzzled her sternum, kissing across to the opposite side.

Maia sucked a good portion of Taylor's breast into her mouth, pulling greedily before releasing and licking her lips. "I should hope so. I had an excellent teacher, and I am, as you know, an excellent student."

She moved closer still, bringing their bodies into a long line of soft, warm contact. Taylor wrapped both arms around her, surging up to claim Maia's lips. She barely noticed the faint taste of sunscreen on them.

Maia's skin felt so good against hers, and with the beautiful ikthian cradled in her lap, Taylor was content to kiss her for as long as her lungs would hold out. The toy's shaft—*my cock,* she thought, with a surge of old confidence—rubbed against Maia's stomach, and Taylor repeated the motion, beginning a slow grind. Her clit jumped beneath the transmitter, and the shaft gave an answering twitch in turn.

"Fuck," she mumbled. "Wanna be inside you."

Maia straddled Taylor's hips.

Taylor kissed her, releasing a low groan as warmth and wetness brushed the underside of the shaft. She grasped Maia's rear, squeezing and supporting as their hips found each other.

"Taylor," Maia gasped into the corner of Taylor's mouth. She gave an exploratory push of her pelvis, and Taylor went rigid as Maia's slickness brushed her head.

"Tell me if it's too much," she murmured as she pulled Maia down. She needn't have worried. Adopting a look of adorable determination, Maia slid the rest of the way in one fluid motion, taking the entire length with a choked whine.

Taylor's limbs locked up. She desperately wanted to move, to thrust, but wasn't sure whether she should until Maia braced both hands on her shoulders and said, "Please?"

The look in her eyes was pure love, and Taylor gladly rocked her hips, bringing their bodies as close as possible.

Soon, Taylor's hands were splayed across Maia's back, while Maia's arms remained braced on either side of her. She felt Maia's breaths and smelled her scent, sweet and warm. Felt the clenching of her inner muscles. Each sharp tug sent an answering pulse along Taylor's shaft, and she throbbed. *No. Not yet.*

But Maia seemed to have no intention of slowing down. She rocked then added some lift, allowing a few inches of Taylor's cock to slide out before sinking back to the base.

Taylor busied herself leaving a trail of bites along Maia's throat, where she knew the ridges were sensitive. Whenever her teeth sank in, Maia rippled around her. It became a game, seeing how much urgency she could inspire. Taylor scratched her nails lightly across Maia's crest and down her back before arriving at her waist.

Maia grabbed Taylor's head and kissed her fiercely, the rest of her body going utterly still. Then she broke away from Taylor's lips, threw her head back, and cried out.

Taylor stared in awe. In all the galaxy, she'd never see a more beautiful sight. Maia's chest heaved, silvery skin shining. The image drove Taylor wild. She sat up and wrapped Maia in her arms, reversing their positions without withdrawing. Maia was warm and slick. Perfect.

Maia legs eagerly wrapped around Taylor's torso, clinging like her life depended on it. Taylor set a shallow but steady rhythm, one that rocked through both their bodies with the insistence of a strong tide. It curled through her core, and Taylor gritted her teeth.

She didn't want to come. Didn't want this to be over too soon. She wanted to move in and out of Maia forever to the sound of the surf behind them, to ride the waves and feel them build without a crest.

But then Maia's sharp teeth nipped the shell of Taylor's ear, and she murmured a request that shattered Taylor's defenses. "Taylor, fill me."

Her thrusts became longer, deeper. When Maia's fingers dug into her back, Taylor's body locked, bracing against a powerful series of shudders.

She whispered Maia's name and buried her face in Maia's neck. Nuzzling, not biting, simply existing in the warm, dark space of comfort. She lived there as she throbbed within Maia's heat, completely overwhelmed.

"Maia..." Taylor whispered.

Maia's heels dug into her ass. "Stay," she begged, even though Taylor had no intention of leaving. Hazy though she was, some part of her could tell Maia wasn't just talking about the connection between their bodies.

"Not going anywhere," Taylor said. "Not without you."

She meant it, too. Deep down, part of her knew they couldn't remain on Earth forever. Maia's sense of duty would likely draw her back to Dominion territory, but that was all right, because as long as the two of them were together, they could find moments like this. Make them. Fight for them, even.

For the first time in a long time, Taylor believed things would be okay. Good, even. She had Maia, and that was more than enough.

"Taylor? Where did you go?"

Taylor noted the soft furrow in Maia's brow and hurried to kiss it away. "Nowhere you can't follow."

"You had me worried. I feared I might have overexerted you."

"God, no. I feel better than I have in... ever, really."

Maia's sweet smile returned. "They say the sea has that effect."

"It's not the sea. It's you. I love you."

"I know."

Taylor gasped in mock offense then slid her fingers under Maia's arms to tickle her exposed sides. Maia wriggled beneath her, only weakly trying to defend herself, before stifling her laughter by biting Taylor's bicep.

White-hot pain forked through Taylor's arm, but she laughed. "Ow! Watch the teeth."

Maia looked only mildly repentant. "You should know better than to start things you cannot finish." She placed an apologetic kiss on the mark.

"Oh, I finish things." Taylor gave her hips a teasing push, delighting in Maia's breathy gasp. "And I'm not finished with you, either."

Maia's arms wound around her neck, and Taylor kissed the curve of her jaw, starting a slow rhythm. She intended to remain on this beach with Maia until the sun set and the stars came out. They had time.

About the Authors

Michelle Magly

Michelle Magly is a queer writer and academic scholar. She lives for writing about far-off lands in the distant future and fantasy landscapes.

Michelle co-authored her first novel *All the Pretty Things* with Rae D. Magdon. They followed with *Dark Horizons*, and its sequel, *Starless Nights*, won a Rainbow Award.

Michelle's first solo work, *Chronicles of Osota – Warrior*, debuted in July 2014. She is now working on the second book of the series.

When not writing, Michelle hikes, goes rock climbing, skis, and plays a lot of video games.

Connect with Michelle Online

Facebook: Michelle Magly

Twitter: Michelle Magly

E-mail: michellemagly@gmail.com

Rae D. Magdon

Rae D. Magdon is a writer of queer and lesbian fiction. She believes everyone deserves to see themselves fall in love and become a hero: especially lesbians, bisexual women, trans women, and women of color. She has published over ten novels through Desert Palm Press, spanning a wide variety of genres, from Fantasy/Sci-Fi to Mysteries and Thrillers. She is the recipient of a 2016 Rainbow Award (Fantasy/Sci-Fi) and a twice-nominated GCLA finalist (Fantasy/Sci-Fi). When she isn't working on original projects, she spends her time writing fanfiction for Mass Effect, Legend of Korra, The 100, and Wynonna Earp.

Connect with Rae online

Facebook: Rae D. Magdon

Tumblr: https://raedmagdon.tumblr.com/

Twitter: Rae D. Magdon

Email: raedmagdon@gmail.com

Cover Design By : Rachel George
www.rachelgeorgeillustration.com

Note to Readers:

Thank you for reading a book from Desert Palm Press. We appreciate you as a reader and want to ensure you enjoy the reading process. We would like you to consider posting a review on your preferred media sites and/or your blog or website.

For more information on upcoming releases, author interviews, contest, giveaways and more, please sign up for our newsletter and visit us as at Desert Palm Press: www.desertpalmpress.com and "Like" us on Facebook: Desert Palm Press.

Bright Blessings

Made in the USA
Columbia, SC
18 January 2021